At 7.30am on Wednesday 21st Nov
Leeds CID arrived at author Mick I
him and his wife. The house was se
preparing for school, and 14 items
Bridewell, the suspects were photog........., ...g.......... and
DNA extracted before being released on bail. Neither had a police
record, not so much as a parking ticket.

They were arrested under 'suspicion of making malicious phone
calls' using a SIM card that Mrs McCann had given away four to
five years earlier. This was the third time they had been questioned
by the police regarding this SIM card.

In the West Yorkshire area (a population of approximately 2.5
million people) during 2005, four people were proceeded against
and convicted under the Communications Act 2003, Section 127.
In 2006, nine people were proceeded against and seven were
convicted.

Given these convictions are likely to have been connected to more
serious crimes, and that threatening and malicious phone calls
among such a large population must run to thousands a month,
why was this family targeted in such a way and why were more
resources than are given to policing Leeds City Centre on a
Saturday night used in the arrest?

In this novel, Mick McCann gives an account of the real events
and then weaves them through a fiction that is *Nailed - Digital
Stalking In Leeds, Yorkshire, England*.

Nailed

Mick McCann

**Digital Stalking
In Leeds, Yorkshire, England**

Published by Armley Press 2008

Copy Editor: John Lake

Layout: Ian Dobson

Cover Design: John Wheelhouse & Mick McCann

Contact: <armleypress@hotmail.co.uk>

Armley Press, Hollywell House, Hollywell Lane,
Armley, Leeds, LS12 3HP
ISBN 0-9554699-2-9

Background And Context

I'm an author, me. I've written a book and that. Not this one. A different one. But this fact, tumbled up with a whole load of other mental, circumstantial bollocks, has thrown a big, steaming pile of laundered chaos into the McCann family world. Let's hope it all came out in the wash but I really wish we could've left it in the dryer. Who knows? We could get hung out to dry. Fuck, I've spent too long punning on internet forums; sorry, I won't do it again – I wouldn't want to shrink your patience.

I'm writing it, y'know, this whole book, not some unseen voice that hangs in unreality and tells you what's going on. But part of the writer's craft is to slip from first person into third person and into the experiences and expressions of other characters – I should look into that writer's craft stuff really, shunt'a? Y'never know, it could come in useful.

All of the characters are real. I may or may not have met them and I may have embellished their characteristics: that's for you to decide but every last one exists. Even the people off the internet forums are real, although the etiquette of that online community is that we all have assumed names, nicknames. Everybody does it – every other fucker but me, that is. I use my real name. :roll eyes:

The police are real people, although I'll probably have to change their names. Everyone tells me I should, but I don't think they'd want to shut me up or prosecute me and bring further attention to their behaviour and the possible involvement of one of the top three most powerful officers in the West Yorkshire Police Force. TOP COP GAGS AUTHOR would be the headline in the press, and could lead to him losing his job. Us British love to blow a minor misdemeanour into a sackable offence, we love to berate our public figures and hound them from office, we'd call for their heads should they use the wrong phone. We revel in a story of a high-ranking public servant being incompetent, never mind a bit dodgy. I think he'd probably rather ignore my naming and shaming, and hope the book flops and slips unnoticed onto dusty bookshelves, and don't worry, I'll send him a copy.

The one person I'd rather not name is the local TV celebrity: I have no way of knowing for sure if she's simply a victim or whether she leant on her boyfriend, so I'd rather she weren't involved, but by chance she is. It's almost pointless not naming her as her identity becomes obvious, but, dear reader, I'd like to make it clear from the beginning that she is most likely benign and is as much a victim as the other three women and me and my family. But the police – fuck it – I'll use their real names . . . or should I?

Since the initial events, we've had further meetings with the police, and in questioning, they denied knowledge of some of the facts. We are absolutely certain that we gave them the facts, and for us the only possible discrepancy could be *when* we gave them. It is unlikely but possible that some details were discussed at a different time from those stated in the book. Even if they were, the facts were certainly passed on within a couple of days, and these couple of days make absolutely no difference to the overall situation, although the fact that the police deny knowledge of them until a much later date does. This book is written almost entirely from our perspective.

Up to a point, this is a completely true story. The happenings are real, but what is truth and what is reality? At some juncture in the novel, I fly off into pure fiction born out of reality, and weave the reality in, and the one reason I may alter the real names of the police officers is that from this moment I have to fictionalise their speech and actions. The most ridiculous coincidences and chance happenings are actually based on facts, facts so far-fetched that they are almost Shakespearean. Some people cut that Shakespeare fella some slack, because he's not a bad writer, but I promise that the places that you'll want to deny me the slack are the places and occurrences that are factual; really, believe me, you couldn't make it up.

And what sits at the heart of this mystery? What was the catalyst? Where did the real chain of events start? With a piece of plastic, two centimetres squared, thinner than an After Eight mint, a piece of technology that we take for granted as a bit of disposable, almost invisible, tat. Something that within a few years will come out of a quality Christmas cracker along with the memory sticks, tiny MP3 players and miniature digital cameras.

A SIM card.

Have you ever cancelled a SIM card that hasn't been stolen? No, not many people have.

But I think that perhaps you should.

1

Act I, Scene I. The McCann family kitchen

'Could I ask who's calling? . . . Oh, OK, I'll just take you to her, won't be a minute. I was just going to lay into you for cold-calling. . . . Yeh, here she is. Lesley.'

'Who is it?' Mouthed rather than spoken.

'The police,' whispered Mick, with the palm of his hand half covering the mouth bit of the phone – the bit formally called a mouthpiece but now just part of the homogenous object that is a phone.

'Hello. . . Yes, it is Miss Jackson. . . SIM card? Oh wait a minute, I had my phone stolen out of the kitchen about four or five years ago. . . Yes, along with my handbag. . . I don't know but it will be. . . Erm, no, not that I can think of. . . I will. . . just wait a minute I'll get a pen. . . Yes. . . That's OK, yeh. Bye.' She hung up. 'How strange.'

'What?'

'Looks like my phone's surfaced.'

'Didn't know you'd lost it.'

'My old one that was stolen with mi handbag – remember? From the kitchen? Someone left the door wide open?'

It sounded accusational.

'It wasn't me, was it?'

'I don't know; looks like it's turned up in London and is being used for no good.'

'So why the' phoning you?'

'Don't know. I suppose it's procedural. As it used to be mine, they probably need to phone me.'

'Yeh, s'pose, but you'd've thought they'd've just traced it. I mean, what are you likely to be able to tell them?'

'Yeh, you'd have thought. And if the phone's being used in London, I obviously haven't got it anymore.'

'Yeh, probably just ticking a box.'

'Hm, yeh. Probably.'

Neither were sure how the London mob had got the house phone number, but if you're CID, they supposed, most things will be possible. The call came and went, a very minor occurrence in busy lives that was quickly forgotten. Lesley was working too hard and planning holidays, and Mick, in between childcare and part-time work, was all wrapped up in promoting his now published book.

Ah the book, we mustn't forget the book.

Years before, Lesley's friend Sarah had been the catalyst, sat in the kitchen drinking wine.

'Are you still writing, Mick?'

'What? Oh, yeh, I can't stop miself.'

'What are you writing at the moment?'

'Oh, shit-loads of stuff.'

'Yeh-e-eh – what?'

'Erm, a sort of political thriller. A play about love and deceit – domestic, small-scale thriller. Thing about mi youth; being a Bowie fan and situations around it. Y'know the stuff – girly clothes, make-up, trying not to get pulled by forty-year-old blokes on the bus, that kinda thing. Loads of comedy stuff, y'know, sketches, stand-up routines.'

'Can I read some of it?'

'Fuck, yeh-e-eh, course y'can. It's all at different points, there's lots of some and not so much of others. What d'y fancy?'

'That Bowie youth thing.'

'Don't think there's that much of that, and it's very notey, but I'll print it off for you.'

'Now, please.'

'What?'

'Can you set it off printing now, please?'

Mick laughed – 'Course I can, Sair' – and left the room.

That was the end of it until eighteen months later.

'Mick, have you written anymore of that Bowie thing?'

'What?'

'That thing about growing up that you printed out for me ages ago.'

'Yeh, probably. Not recently but I'm sure there'll be more.'

'Can you print it off for me?'

'Yeh, course I can. Did you read that other stuff?'

'Oh, yeh.'

'What did you think of it?'

'I luuurved it. It reeeeeally made me laugh.'

'How many pages did you have?'

'Don't know. About ten.'

'I'll go and have a look.' Mick went away then re-entered the room. 'Yeh, there's twenty-three pages now. I've set it printing but I'm printing it all cos it'll be all higgledy-piggledy, so you'll've already read some of it.'

'Yeh, that's fine.'

Sarah kept feeding back extremely positive comments and asking for more, so Mick felt a compulsion to write it. Before he'd thought about it he'd written 40,000 words. *Fuck, that must be most of a book.* His idea right from the beginning had been to make it episodic and cross-sectional, not linear – chunks of life and incidents, not character development but lots of real characters in real situations. His hope was to write something that could be opened and briefly read at any point, put down and picked up six months later, opened on a different page, read for ten minutes and still make sense and give a pay-off to the reader. He printed it off for other interested friends and was given a lot of positive feedback, friends reacting with genuine warmth – friends that would be brutally honest.

They egged him on, telling him that his book was brilliant. He couldn't tell. He was fired by the tales and stories, the characters, memories and stand-offs, the prejudices, and by the attempt to capture that completely cocksure, fearless kid. Although he struggled admitting it to himself, he was trying to work out a time in his life that he felt in some way important, albeit that it was so long ago that he wasn't speaking about himself but someone else – someone he knew inside and out.

The publishing of the book was decided that summer with a bunch of mates in the front garden. The small sound system on the lawn could be any volume; the privacy of the garden, coupled with the distance from the nearest neighbour, meant that they could be as giddy and noisy as they liked. Paul griping endlessly about the music – like he always did – John deciding that the next track that was shit would usher the end of the compilation CD. He flicked through the CDs in anticipation, pulled out a couple of things – Barry White, Cockney Rebel – and returned to the group waiting for the dead track. The problem was that consensus on such things was impossible within a group of twelve people, and Mick was such a fucking gobby salesman. The compilation was interrupted a couple of times and replaced, but they never quite got through a couple of replacement tracks, partly because John couldn't be arsed flicking through tracks and partly because some people missed the compilations jumping genres with startling regularity. The music settled back to the compilations with Paul still whingeing.

Mick had recently finished reading John's draft of a novel called *Hot Knife*. What a fucking book! Like so many great writers before him, John Lake had a stream of rejections, but he had them via his London-based agent.

'They must be fucking mad.'

On this drunken evening with a group of his best mates, Mick had decided that if John's breathless and grounded novel was getting ignored by the London-based publishers – especially with the aid of a London agent – there had to be a reason. The script was so good that there could only be one reason: the precise and authentic use of a rough-arsed Leeds/Yorkshire accent.

'John if your book had a Dublin accent or Edinburgh, or Liverpool, or any of probably ten accents, it'd be published and in your hands by now,' he'd declared. 'There's a prejudice against the Leeds accent. It's so fucking ugly to those who don't know it, so blunt, and, to those Southern cunts, so stupid. . . as in unintelligent.'

'You could be right Mick. *Hot Knife* is brilliant.' John let out one of his infectious laughs.

'No, it is John, it really is fanfuckingtastic, and the only reason I can see for it not to get published is a prejudice against the Leeds accent.'

'So when you going to start sending it out, Mick?' asked Dosher, replenished with a beer from the freezer and re-joining the group.

'What?'

'Y'book. You are going to start sending it out places, ar't y'?'

'What fo'? To spend two fuckin' years creating leads and sending it out to knobheads just to get a pile of fuckin' rejection letters? If *Hot Knife* hasn't found a publisher, I haven't got a chance.'

'What's *Hot Knife*?'

'John's book. It's fantastic, and even with a London agent, he's struggling getting it published.'

'Wouldn't mind reading that. Could I get a copy John?'

'Yeh, sure.'

Mick jumped in. 'I'll lend y'my copy.'

'So, what, Mick, you just not bothering with yours? That'd be a pity; it's really good, really funny, really. . . '

'No, I am going to do summat with mine. I'll publish it misen.'

Dosher spat out his beer, 'A' y'?'

'Yeh.'

'How?'

'I don't know, but I'll suss it out and do it miself. I tell you what, though, I'll have a copy of mi book in mi hands and available by August. . . No, wait a minute, where are we now? By November – I'll have a fucking book in mi hands by November.'

There was a hint of disbelief among the group blended with a nagging, 'You never know, he might just do it.'

Lesley threw him a look. 'And how are you going to pay for that?'

'Don't worry, I won't do it if there's even a chance of losing money.'

'Never mind losing – if there's a chance of spending money.'

Pat jumped in.

'How much will it cost? I've got some tax money just sitting around that I could lend you.'

'Thanks very much, Pat, but I've got no idea how much it'll cost. We've all drank too much beer so let's talk about it with a clear head.'

And so an idea was born, a statement of fact made, or so it appeared. Mick had been lightly researching 'print on demand' online, and although all he'd found so far were con people or over-complicated procedures, he was confident – looking at the scams – that there was a way to publish economically. Maybe he should look for a book about publishing. The evening continued on through babble and laughs, a joyous collection of Mick's best mates talking deep, talking light, but definitely fucking talking. Mick loved this lot. He'd drunk too much beer and had been less than careful with the endless spliffs. He really loved this lot.

2

When he got chance, Mick spent the following couple of months scouring the internet, and like many things on the internet, nothing was quite as it seemed. Occasionally the sites were quite straightforward in that they were middle men charging extortionate amounts for work, most of which would be done by the supplier, and the rest was simple, cheap and quick to do. At least there was an element of honesty, but these places weren't for him; he was a tight get anyway, but there was *the* one overriding consideration: he couldn't lose money. A couple of promising ones in the US, but no UK offices meant that any money saved would be eaten up in shipping and delivery that would take six weeks – also not good for amazon.co.uk. At last he found a site that appeared to be offering what he was looking for, a simple equation buried on page four of an over-complex site. He'd had to search and read a lot of bollocks to get to it but he'd got to it in the end. *Better check page five and make sure there's no extra charges. . .* No, it had moved on to further complex industry wittering. Was this it? The prices seemed to stack up against those in the US if anything ever so slightly cheaper – maybe it was the exchange rate – but the formulation of the equation looked very familiar, very close to those in the US. He fired off a quick email and, after a quiet day, another:

From: mick mccann
To: enquiries@authorsworld.co.uk
Sent: Friday, July 07, 2006 1:56 PM
Subject: Book

Hi,

I've emailed you once with no response.

I am trying to understand your pricing. The web site says:

'As a rough guide for one-off books it is just over £00.01 per page for black-and-white text or illustrations and photographs, £00.15 for colour photographs and illustrations, and a four-colour soft-back book cover is approximately £1.00.'

Are there extra costs involved, or can I use these to fully estimate the cost?

Thanks,

M. McCann

The response this time was swift:

Donald Cook <donaldcook@authorsworld.co.uk> wrote:

Dear Mick,

Many thanks for your message.

Yes you can use those prices as an indicator. Of course if you buy bulk copies from the printer we may get you a better price.

If you have any further questions please do not hesitate to phone me.

Kind regards,

Donald Cook
Managing Director
Authors World Limited

Phone: 08** 2410543
Mobile: 079** ***460
E-mail: donaldcook@authorsworld.co.uk
www.authorsworld.co.uk

Time to move to a phone call.

'Yeh, Hi, its Mick McCann. We've exchanged a couple of emails.'

'Ah yes, I've received the emails. Is one ready to publish one's book?'

Well, no, I think it's a while off, I'm just planning ahead.'

Yes well, I find that. . . '

Off he went. Mick quickly understood why the website was so text-heavy. Too much detail, and all the time over-complicating and presenting as tricky and skilled things that Mick imagined or knew to be simple. Dismissing it as someone being used to explaining the process and industry to stupid or elderly people, Mick cut him some slack but cut across the babble.

'Yeh, so I can use that formula to calculate the full cost of publishing mi book?'

'Well, as I said, the process—'

Please, no more words, or one more if it's yes or no. Mick cut right across him again.

'Yeh, so I can use that formula to calculate the full cost of publishing mi book? There are no other costs?'

'Have you read the Publish section as I suggested? It's all there. Publishing is a complex business—'

'Yeh, sorry, there's at least twelve pages and it's text-rich, full of hyperlinks that go off all over the place. I'm just after the basic pricing at the moment.'

'Well, as I was saying, publishing is a complex business—'

Mick cut across him again. 'I don't really need to know all that now, I'm just looking for a ball-park figure. Can I use the equation I sent you to fully work out the cost of printing the books?'

'Yes, but you do need to understand that—'

As the man babbled without clearly addressing his question, Mick couldn't work out if he was a confused older gentleman or hiding something, but his prejudice kicked in: too nicely spoken, too 'lovey', to be a con-man.

'It's all there.'

The words awoke a nagging doubt in Mick's brain. His email was very specific and the response seemed clear, but as the bloke blathered, Mick went on through the pages to see if there was information he'd missed. No, the pricing started on page four of the publishing section. The still-talking phone, coupled with flicking through the text-rich pages, were making Mick's head hot. The site had moved onto other babble after the pricing section so it was looking right, but he'd better keep flicking. Another page of six or seven hundred words explaining how untrustworthy other print-on-demand companies were, with complex formulas and links to go off to other places on the site. Mick was just starting to smell the bullshit of another middle man when he opened page six or seven. *Ah, what the fuck is this? No it can't be.* Mick cut across the hum in the background. 'So many publishers find that—'

'What's this £1,598? Is it an optional cost for an enhanced service?'

'No, that's the standard setting-up fee.'

'So it's an extra cost on top of the equation?'

'Yes. You don't really think that we could publish a book by the cost of that equation?'

'I asked you if there were any extra costs involved.'

'I'm sorry, Mr McCann, the link that I emailed you is quite clear.' Fuck that was quite concise; for the first time, a lack of the endless, Shakespearean babble.

'And you answered "No".'

'Well, obviously there's—'

'No, there's nothing at all obvious about the pricing on the website. That's why I emailed and phoned you.'

'And I've answered your questions and—'

'No. I had one question that you conspicuously haven't quite answered – although you've implied the answer was no. I clearly asked you over and over again if there were any extra costs involved other than the equation I copied from your website and you—'

'I'm sorry, Mr McCann, the link that I emailed you is quite clear.'

'But we've spent how long on the phone? At my cost. Spent time exchanging emails. Why didn't you just answer my simple question and save us both the time and energy instead of hiding extra costs?'

'May I say that that is a scandalous accusation. The pricing is quite clear.'

'Yeh, part on page four of the publishing section, surrounded by complex formulas about how complicated the print-on-demand industry is and how you cut through all the bullshit with honest treatment of your customers, while the "standard charge" – an extra cost – is another few thousand words forward on page six or seven.'

'Look, Mr McCann—'

'Sorry, this is a complete waste of my time, and yours. I haven't got another two hours to spend listening to you trying to justify your inability to communicate or post clear pricing. Goodbye.'

With that, Mick put down the phone, tingling with frustration – not just at all the drawn-out bullshit designed to mask the cost of the service but with the apparent solution to his long-standing problem going pear-shaped.

'Fuck it, I'm buying a book.'

He retired to the kitchen to calm down with a fag, a coffee and a few minutes to babble to himself about all the convoluted bollocks that he'd just had to endure. A quick clean around the kitchen, some washing put out on radiators, more dried and folded, and back to his connection to the outside world to search for a book that explains the process simply and hopefully points him directly to a print-on-demand company.

To the computer with a new task – *Let's find a book* – with a reflex check of his email. There was a new email from Donald. He entered a pointless email debate with what he saw as the old-school tosser playing in the modern world, assuming the graces of the literati, speaking in tongues of prosaic and mock-industry bullshit like he was some literary great or publishing expert rather than someone confusing and taking advantage of trusting people with his guff. Mick justified a further waste of time with the fact that his emails were brief and he was keeping a bad 'un off the streets.

Donald Cook <*donaldcook@authorsworld.co.uk*> wrote:

Dear Mr McCann,

May I repeat what I said to you on the phone before you put it down because you did not want to hear what you wanted to hear. Our Publish section is as clear as it could possibly be. There are prices to publish a book and estimated prices to print copies of a book and I repeat I know of no person who has ever got the two issues confused before or complained that our website does not make that crystal clear.

With respect, for you to believe that we can provide all the services we provide at our various book publishing services plus provide 100 copies for about £300.00 is interesting as is your way of dividing the publishing cost by 100 books to get a price. What people pay us for is producing a book for worldwide availability. Having written that, I doubt whether any local printer could do all the work to produce a book and provide 100 copies for the ball-park figure you quoted, albeit you would not get the services and distribution we provide.

With all due respect, I see no point in you getting frustrated with me because you did not take the time to read our Publish section properly.

Kind regards,

Donald Cook
Managing Director
Authors World Limited

Phone: 08** 2410543
Mobile: 079** ***460
E-mail: donaldcook@authorsworld.co.uk
www.authorsworld.co.uk

Mick stared at his computer in disbelief. 'That's the whole point of print-on-demand, you dozy cunt, to provide smaller amounts of books at a lower cost than traditional printers.'

From: mick mccann

To: donaldcook@authorsworld.co.uk
Sent: Friday, July 07, 2006 3:02 PM
Subject: Book

Donald,

You may ramble all you like, here is a simple question:

Are there extra costs involved, or can I use these to **fully** estimate the cost?'

A question that you obviously avoided answering.

I did say: I am trying to understand your pricing.

I suggest that in your pricing section you start it with:

There is a standard charge of £1598.00, and not hide the real cost on page 6 or 7.

Mick

Donald Cook <donaldcook@authorsworld.co.uk> wrote:

Dear Mr McCann,

I see no point in replying to the points you make in so much in the few hours since you contacted me you have accused me of being a liar, put the phone down on me then insult me by accusing me of rambling and hiding our costs. I also find the tone of your e-mail offensive.

I have spent many years building our Publish section to make it as simple as fair as possible and on each an every occasion an author came up with an valid suggestion I have had the publish section changed and whether you like it or not no other author " has ever " interpretated the publish section as you have, in fact I am complimented very single day by authors who find the publish section straightforward and simple to understand.

I therefore feel it best you look elsewhere for a publisher as I have the right and privilege of deciding which authors we publish books for.

Kind regards,

Donald Cook
Managing Director
Authors World Limited

Phone: 08** 2410543
Mobile: 079** ***460
E-mail: donaldcook@authorsworld.co.uk
www. authorsworld.co.uk

Mick giggled along with the sarcastic thespian opening to his next email.

From: mick mccann
To: donaldcook@authorsworld.co.uk
Sent: Friday, July 07, 2006 3:17 PM
Subject: Book

Donald,

Methinks he doth protest too much.

I'm not surprised that you don't reply to my points as they are clearly valid.

As for looking for a different publisher, do you really think that I would develop a professional relationship with someone who has such problems understanding simple English? I repeated your formula of 0.01 pence per page and approx £1 per cover and then asked,

Are there extra costs involved?

Which is not a complex, ambiguous question.

Please do not accuse me of calling you a 'liar' as I have not called you a liar, I have implied that you are confused but not necessarily dishonest.

Mick

Donald Cook <donaldcook@authorsworld.co.uk> wrote:

Dear McCann,

With the utmost respect I have better things to do with my time than spend " bat and ball semantics" with you.

As I have declined to publish your book and there is plenty of competion would you please try your theories and frustrations on our competition.

I stand by 100% what I have written to you.

Kind regards,

Donald Cook
Managing Director
Authors World Limited
Phone: 08** 2410543
Mobile: 079** ***460
E-mail: donaldcook@authorsworld.co.uk
www. authorsworld.co.uk

For some reason Mick thought it important to have the last word.

From: mick mccann
To: donaldcook@authorsworld.co.uk

21

Sent: Friday, July 07, 2006 3:23 PM
Subject: Book

Donald,

I suggest you stop now, you are getting more confused.

I have not shared any theories with you and my only frustration was that, when it was requested, you were unable to provide clear pricing.

I did and would not offer my book to you, to be published, so please don't flatter yourself. The first thing I would look for would be clear communication, a service you appear unable to provide.

Please don't email me back, just accept we disagree, it sometimes happens in life.

Mick

Mick searched online and bought a book, *Print-On-Demand Book Publishing*, Morris Rosenthal, Foner Books, www.fonerbooks.com, although he bought it off amazon.co.uk. Perfect; clearly explaining everything he wanted to know. The book regularly mentioned lightningsource.com, so he found and contacted the UK office. Having worked in the electronic publisher industry for a number of years, Mick could smell that they were honest, professional people. Now he'd found his printer, Mick got on with the production process, true to his drunken garden words, and with the help of friends with the cover design, layout and proofing, the book was in their hands by November.

The costs (including VAT) broke down like this:

£94.00 for a batch of ten ISBNs;

£69.05 for the digital set up of the cover/text files, barcode generation and placement on the cover;

£746.83 for 300 copies of the book;

Total £909.88.

Had he gone with the old-timer, the cost would have been at least £942.00 for 300 books plus the £1,598.00 'standard charge', which offered lots of things that happened automatically when publishing a book using Lightning Source and no doubt other print-on-demand printers. Other than a single template page on the company's dull website and the sending of 5 copies of the book to the British Library (not making clear who pays for the five copies), this 'standard charge' did not appear to include anything other than receiving the files and passing them on to a printer.

All the 'world-wide distribution' bollocks simply meant that the book was available via book distributors such as Gardner's or Bertram's and, in the US, Ingram's or Baker & Taylor, which happened automatically through Lightning Source. No layout, cover design, copy editing or proof reading was included in the 'standard charge', which could be done of course – at extra cost. Mick also noted that the majority of the titles, although listed and featured on amazon.co.uk, were marked as unavailable. This could only mean that the annual seven pounds paid to the actual printer to maintain the digital files and keep them available for production and distribution had not been paid. If someone had laboured over a book the way that these authors obviously had, would they have their book unavailable on amazon and every book shop in the UK – as well as many throughout the world – to save seven pounds a year? Obviously not – it could only be that these authors didn't understand the process, that the middle man actually didn't give a fuck once he made his killing, or that there had been a serious disagreement between the two parties. As the cost of print-on-demand through Lightning Source came down significantly, the 'standard charge' at the middle man site rose to £1,998.

Digital stalking in Leeds, Yorkshire, England

3

He'd seen it coming for a week or so, the blunt monosyllabic responses, the distance, the body language throwing out the clear 'don't come near me' signals. Communication had been fully closed down and now coming fast from the horizon was the meaningless, screaming train, hurtling along chaos tracks, destructive and pointless. They'd got a couple of weeks past the cessation of the ritual, phatic pecks on leaving or arriving, and a grunt was the most he could expect to his habitual 'Hello' or 'Hi'. He made her chuckle a bit last night, trying to remind her who he was, but she soon closed him down. The confrontation was inevitable and if he didn't start it now every hour of delay would increase the casualties. He tickled young Billy out of the kitchen, with its mist and smoke.

'His laugh is so infectious.'

'Mm.' She looked away, face tight with frustration and anger.

'We're not off today, y'know, only tickets I could've got were thirty quid each. Sixty quid? I'm just not paying that.'

Fuck! He squirmed inside. I've just brought up money. Bollocks. Whatever ground this battle took place on, its cause was money, and its mention so early in the skirmish left his flank exposed and vulnerable. Well at least it might be a short war with few grieving wives and mothers, fathers, husbands and children. Wars had a habit of dragging on longer and being bloodier than anyone would predict. Money. Surely she wouldn't go nuclear to start off with, they have to go through all the raging battles, all the vicious hand-to-hand combat, all the basest emotions, and start a mutual recognition of the futility and madness of the war before she'd hit the button. Time for the opening volley.

'What's up?'

'Nothing.' She gazed at the window with a determined toke on her fag, fuming. *Stupid bastard, how can he not see? He knows exactly what's going on, lazy shit.*

'Come on, something's up.' No answer. 'So if nothings up how come you scowl at me whenever I look at you? How come you come home with a growl? How come you aren't speaking to me?'

'That's rich coming from you. It's never the right time is it, Mick? Never the right time, you're always watching telly or too busy.'

'What? No, we've talked about this a million times. I do have a busy time when you come—'

'It's all the time, you, you, you. You tell me shut up. . . '

'I don't, I. . .'

'. . . whenever I open my mouth. . . '

'I don't, it's. . .'

'Always watching fucking football. . . '

'No, the last—'

'Always you who decides what we watch. . . '

'WHAT? Like I really wanted to watch a. . .'

'Yes you do, typical man, don't let me near. . . '

'. . . a full weekend of *Most* fucking *Haunted Live*?'

'. . . the buttons. I want to separate. I just don't care anymore.'

Which words? What words? Some words. He needed words but it'd be useful for them to be relevant and in a coherent order.

'Eh? Where has this come from?'

She had so many words, so many complaints, that it was hard to prioritise and order them.

'I'm not happy, haven't been for years. I'm sick of living in fucking chaos, I want to separate.'

'What y'talking about, chaos?'

'Living in this fucking filth. This place is a hovel.'

They moved through quick attacks and rearguard actions, through the state of the fridge, the fronts of electrical appliances, glass bottles and jars piled up in the lobby. Some points fair, some outlandish, but none discussed.

'I'm just not happy, I want to separate.'

'You may not be happy but I don't think we're the cause, we may add to it but we're not the root. But we've been through this a million times and I'm not going to try to convince you that I'm a good human being who cares for and about you. Half of the time you don't allow me to.'

'You don't care about me, you don't give a shit.'

'Of course I do, I show it all the time.'

'No you don't.'

The volume up, the venom flowing, hurtful words scarring brains. . . .He wished he'd got into fishing as a kid, looks so peaceful. She wished she had a shotgun and an alibi. A domestic pantomime played out up and down the country with varying intensity, from a knife in the chest to a calmly delivered sarcastic one-liner, sharp and compact, suddenly took on a whole new significance. He could see a couple of people approaching the house, looked like they'd be flogging religion, *fucking Jehovah's Witnesses at nine on a Sunday morning, they're taking the piss.* He stood up, going to the door with tension in his stride, opening the door. They weren't exporting God, too world-weary, too unhappy.

'Yes?' Not friendly enough to be selling.

'We're Holbeck CID. We've come to ask a few questions. Is Mrs Jackson in?'

'It's Miss Jackson. Lesley, it's the police.'

If he could hear the 'For fuck's sake, just what I need first thing on a Sunday bloody morning. You're going to have to deal with it, I'm not even fucking dressed', so could they, loud and clear. He was shocked; she was the master of turning off a rage as soon as someone else appeared. He could never get his head around the control, she could go from spitting fury to mundane pleasantries in a second, leaving him projectile vomiting all the inappropriate anger, whether someone else was there or not. He couldn't just turn it off, he'd still be spinning the twenty attacks and criticisms in his head, answers spewing out in a seemingly random mess. He was the one who made the visitors uncomfortable, he was clearly the oppressor. She could cut into a seething row with 'I've had enough of this, I'm off to sleep', roll over and go to sleep. He envied her that.

He led them into the kitchen, two women, one man.

'You want a coffee?'

They entered the kitchen. The man did that male big sniff of abandon, marking the boundaries, but it was clearly a bluff and held no menace. One of the women, tall and powerful, made the moves round here.

'No thanks. We've come to ask you about a SIM card registered in your name.'

'I don't believe this,' said Lesley. 'On a Sunday morning? It's bloody ridiculous. I've already told the police all about this. Why didn't you just call us like the others?'

Mick steps in. 'Les, just calm down a bit and let's sort this,'

She sighed deep and long. 'Sorry, you've caught us at a bad time.'

The severe CID woman, all judgemental and condemnatory, delivers a dead-pan rabbit-punch to the back of the neck. 'Yes, I can see that.' She leaves a threatening and confrontational pause, focussed by her eye contact. 'How many SIM cards have you got registered in your name?'

'What?'

'SIM cards. . . '

'Yeh, yeh, I've got one – one phone, one SIM card.'

'How long have you had it?'

'Erm, don't know. Maybe. . . oh, wait a minute, about three or four years. Look I've already answered these questions to CID in London. Can't you contact them?'

'What's the number?'

'Pardon?'

'What's the number of your current phone?' The inquisitor wrote it down. 'What about old SIM cards?'

'Like I told them, I had a phone stolen from the kitchen about five years ago.'

'Do you know the number?'

'No, but I could probably find it – if you gave me half a day.' Lesley was starting to get slightly agitated.

'Have you had any others?'

Mick doesn't like this. Feels like bullying. 'I really can't believe you've come round and bothered us with this. It's 2007, f'God's sake, if you're looking for a SIM card, track it, trace it, see when and where it was last used, find out who's got it and go see them. Or perhaps communicate. She's already told your colleagues about this and they've probably already traced it.'

'That is not the SIM card.'

'What?'

'The SIM card that was stolen is not the card we are looking for. Mrs Jackson—'

28

'It's Miss Jackson.'

'Oh, sorry, I thought you were married.'

'We are.'

'Other SIM cards – how many have you had?'

'I don't know. Oh, wait a minute, there was another SIM card that I gave to someone at work.'

'Who did you give it to?'

'I'm not sure, I gave it someone on the message-board at work years ago. He was asking if anyone had a spare Orange SIM card and I had so I sent it to him.'

'How did you get it to him?'

'I sent it through the internal mail.'

'And you've just remembered this?'

'YES – I don't spend my life thinking about old SIM cards.'

The detective looked her in the eye, uneasy with the sarcasm and animation. 'Pity.'

Mick could see this getting nasty. 'Look, if this is to do with a SIM card being used for dodgy purposes, record our voices and compare them to whoever's got the phone. I really can't believe you're here. Surely there's loads of ways to track this SIM. Why don't you lot stop bothering us and bog off 'n' do your job? It can't be that hard.'

Lesley shook her head, tired and emotional, and sighed. 'Yeh, and I can check my computer at work for the emails if you don't believe me.'

The detectives looked at each other – 'Thanks for your time' – and moved towards the door. 'If you think of anything else, be sure to let us know.'

'Will do.'

A couple of days after the visit from the police Lesley did call the number and passed on a couple of bits of information that she thought may be useful.

Digital stalking in Leeds, Yorkshire, England

4

The book promotion had started on One Mick Jones before it was even out. He'd thought through the whole thing in terms of internet sales. It'd take him two years to get a distribution deal, if he ever did; anyway, might as well try to get a publisher as a distribution deal, it'll all be sewn up by the majors. Also, he just couldn't be arsed, it wasn't that important, he didn't have time, was too impatient and didn't want to produce and supply loads of stock that could be returned; his was a proper 21st-century, 'just in time' model. The important thing was that it was available to order through any shop in the country, so if it started selling, demand would pull it through the system and stock would be likely to follow. It was an internet book, that's what it was. The title, *Coming Out As A Bowie Fan In Leeds, Yorkshire, England*, although he liked it, was littered with search terms. Enter a search for Bowie and Leeds on any search engine and he'd be there, probably come out top, definitely top three. It was an internet book; that's why he was doing a recce on online/forum etiquette; that's what brought him to One Mick Jones:

James,

How y'doing?

Mick McCann from back in the day. (John Lake's mate from Hang The Dance) I've got a book coming out in a few weeks, Coming Out As A Bowie Fan In Leeds, Yorkshire, England, and just wanted to contact you to check what the etiquette was with me coming onto your site, basically to flog. I don't want to just go on and do it without checking first.

Ta,
Mick Mc

The reply was swift:

Just join and promote it, we all promote our stuff. In fact I'll start the thread for you.

James's thread, *Mick McCann's Bowie Book,* contained a brief description of the book and bit of Mick's personal history playing in Hang the Dance, the area of Leeds he came from, etc., to act as pointers. Mick wasn't experienced on forums and watched the thread go unanswered and slip down under a couple of other threads. Next time he looked at it there'd been a quick flurry of activity, Between Clarke And Hilaire saying that Mick had been a well-respected East Leeds character and confirming that he did go around in girly clothes and make-up in dangerous environments, recounting a tale of Mick chinning some handy lad outside The Staging Post in Whinmoor. Cutsyke concurring with BCAH and added that Mick was a decent five-a-side footballer as well.

This had taken Mick by surprise – who were these people? They obviously knew him but he didn't remember the fight outside The Staging Post, although this didn't mean it hadn't happened. His memory was shit, and the second he read it he'd had a memory of the wall by a parade of shops next to The Staging Post and looking at it whilst in a fury and taking a level of pity on some tosser who'd pushed it too far, but it could just as easily have been a dream or a younger memory. The immediate acceptance and respect shown by these two got Mick a bit emotional and he made his first post on OMJ saying thanks, he felt touched and close to tears. Other posts followed. Glamorous Hooligan stating that he had every Bowie book published and that he'd send his lad to get a copy as soon as it was available; also, as it was independent, he'd persuade him to buy it rather than steal it. Follow Follow saying that she'd had a thing about Bowie as a kid and would like to review it; ononon saying that Mick was indeed a good lad and that he'd followed Mick across Armley Moor. Fuck, that's a bit worrying, thought Mick, a complete stranger who obviously knows where he lives. Dead Bloke saying that he rarely read books and that, when he saw it for 10p in a charity shop, was it really worth a punt? Mick replied that he should save his money for a proper book and not waste it on his shite tome.

32

This was how he started his internet life using his real name; he'd registered in his own name so that when James got the PM, he'd recognise it and read the message; after all it was only a recce. Before he knew it, the thread was up and he was responding, and by this time, he'd decided that there was no problem using his real name, may even sell more books. He also registered on some Bowie boards using his real name.

It was strange, Mick was entering a world he knew little about but he quickly moved away from just posting on the thread about his book. Twotone, Fulmine, Lord Robson, Clacker, these people were so funny, and it was most of them. He regularly found himself laughing at little comments while getting dragged into intense and intelligent debates on other threads. He gradually got attached to many of the people on there, the strange nicknames giving way to the character of the people behind them. After a month or so, he felt like he knew them and thought of many of them as friends. It was bizarre, obviously he'd never met any of them in the real world – although he gradually realised that he did know some of them in the real world – but they were real mates, people he had a lot of time for, and were they to get kicked out by their partner he'd put them up. There was an incredible sense of community, of camaraderie, of fun, of shared, mainly male, experience. Although they would debate furiously, and bitch and contradict, he was amongst like-minded people.

He loved the fact that there were also honest, candid threads in which people discussed openly personal problems or crises, Mick going through, on one, the process of grieving that his first son Ez had travelled with the death of his mother. On the *Depression* thread k0rsika had posted about the awful situation of at some point having to mentor his young son in relation to the inevitable death of the boy's mother through cancer. There was often an awkward silence after such posts as people took in the gravity of them, and unless they had something more than 'Fuck, sorry mate, I feel for you' they'd keep away, only adding their condolences later after someone had said something practical, as men try to do. After his post about the effect on Ez of his mum's death, Mick read through it with a slight sinking feeling. He worried that it may contain much that k0rsika would already know and other stuff that wasn't really relevant. He steadied himself with the thought that sometimes it just needed someone to post. Earlier in that thread, all manner of extremely personal and brave things had been discussed. The thread was a group counselling session.

He'd also found a home at BowieZone, although it was different to OMJ. He first became aware of it when he was contacted through Amazon market place by someone from admin buying a couple of copies of his book. BowieZone was a more conservative place, it wasn't littered with good honest swearing and close-to-the-bone material like OMJ, and he decided to stay pretty much within the board etiquette. He wouldn't want to offend anyone; he liked the individuals too much. The primary concentration on BowieZone was a love of David Bowie, and the main site administrator, Madman, had a great, in-depth knowledge of Bowie and his work as well as a fantastic online catalogue of Bowie rarities, which could be downloaded and played. The site, although certainly a community, was a disparate group of people, more cosmopolitan than OMJ. Although many people on OMJ were scattered around the world, they tended to share roots. On BowieZone they literally came from around the world.

Before being contacted by Kookie from BowieZone he'd checked out some of the other Bowie sites but found teenagewildlife.com a bit too vicious for his liking; he just couldn't be arsed with a three-month rearguard action until they'd accept that he was likely to hang around and wasn't just flogging – his initial reason for joining. After over a year on forums he'd probably view it with new eyes but had fallen into his habitual clicking and stayed with them. He'd sometimes pop onto Bowiewonderworld.com, but just to lurk, and rarely posted there; the people were friendly enough but he was simply out of the habit of posting there.

He saw the irony of his attachment to OMJ – the worldwide web and yet he chose to hang around with people with strong links to his home city; well, and the Bradford, London and Welsh mobs. But the humour, honesty and outlooks felt so comfortable that he could be himself amongst these people and it was often very quick-fire, giving the posting a live, thinking-on-your-feet feel. He loved the excitement of it. He took endless ribbing about his book-flogging but that was OK, the book and the flogging of it had become part of his online persona and this particular online community had been very supportive in their purchasing of his book, as well as the external flogging of it.

Pre-publication, Mick was quietly positive that they couldn't ignore the book, they being the London-based media. It had so many elements that ticked so many boxes: it could be used to explain print on demand and the way it will revolutionise the publishing industry, it was independent, northern/Leeds-based, would be seen as working class. It covered the seventies and youth culture, made bold claims about the accepted musical history of the time being inaccurate and southern-biased and was based around an obsession with David Bowie, who was just coming up to his sixtieth birthday. The list of boxes ticked went on, and Mick had persuaded himself that the national media wouldn't ignore it. Guess what? Other than a piece by Andrew Collins in *The Word* magazine, they ignored it. Mick gradually decided that unless you are part of that back-scratching circle you will get ignored. Yes, they may cover major northern shows or exhibitions or things that included a 'name', but outside that, no matter what, you will get ignored. He became more and more sceptical and frustrated with the apparent cliquiness of the publishing-related London media, the parochial cunts. Rudi from OMJ provided a telling insight. Mick and Russ had become mates – mates in the real world – and during a telephone conversation discussing the nature of the media whores, Russ had told Mick that he knew a Radio 4 producer not in a position to feature his book but in a position to pass it on. Russ'd had a recce conversation with her in which she confirmed Mick's fears. Her considered opinions of how to get a book featured on Radio 4 were:

1) go to the same school/university as a producer/well-regarded researcher, or get to know them professionally/socially;
2) phone them a number of weeks before the release to do an initial flog;
3) send some kind of gift, a good bottle of wine being the preferred option, a couple of weeks before launch;
4) take them out for lunch the week before you want the plug and do your flogging.

The fucking BBC! If they were so corrupt, what chance did Mick have with any other London-based media outlets? The conversation with Russ had moved onto the BBC as Mick described the difficulty in getting even a contact for a producer on *Front Row.* Yes, you could email a standard email address, but even Mick realised that it was pointless battling against other listeners looking for the title of a book or album or complaining because someone nearly said *fuck* before 9 pm. In the past, Mick had emailed these addresses to complain at a lack of realistic swearing that had sterilised a promising drama.

He'd emailed the standard addresses about his book nonetheless, but it had taken him a number of weeks of frustration to get a direct contact for just one producer, and obviously he'd need to contact them all to have even the slightest chance of getting a feature. The hurdles set up to deny access to the common people came into sharp focus as Mick imagined the tosser flogging Faber & Faber's latest tale of hardship and abuse sitting with his/her address book full of contacts of friends s/he would lunch with, who would cover the book no matter how predictable and dull it may be and tell us all how fantastic and fresh it was. Mick felt slightly silly – he'd thought that this may be the case with much of the media, but not the BBC. He'd had a naïve belief that the BBC would work within some kind of meritocracy, some urge to provide the audience with diversity and fresh, interesting material – that the playing field would be even. He was sure that the Radio 4 audience would find his book and its background fascinating but no, they would never hear of it. Instead Mick listened and watched in disbelief as an exhibition by Gilbert and George got coverage on *Newsnight Review* and *Front Row* that, as it obviously didn't generate the required footfall, was repeated almost identically a fortnight later on both shows. *What the fuck?* He reflected that the BBC don't have the same commercial pressures as much of the industry but still conform to all the safe little rituals with their dodgy handshakes and dinner dates, maintaining the rule of the bloated and self-satisfied.

One thing that the BBC producer had said to Russ lodged itself verbatim in his head: 'Those dinner dates have been booked months in advance.' Mick couldn't compete on those terms even if his conscience would allow it. Slots lazily filled by old school ties and favours necessarily excluding new stuff that was only allowed coverage if it was something that couldn't be ignored, something that had already 'broken', the one band in a million that genuinely breaks through myspace – an option not open to writers. A cosy industry regulated by the safe, risk-adverse cultural producers who want more of the same to defend their margins, and the audience will eat whatever it is fed, it has no choice. Some lass in Carlisle writing a staggering stage play, novel or screen play, the name unrecognised by the Londoners so ignored. Left deep in a pile of other work given at most a cursory glance before being discounted on the grounds that the reader has to be somewhere else, probably with a recognisable name. Some lad with a gift in Doncaster has the craft, the imagination, the insights, the determination, but is overlooked. Even if one of the ants battled through their prejudice, the queen would simply reprimand them and their attention would be commandeered by the latest rehashing, by the re-arrangement of the same words and ideas, by the same commodity that sells in a safe manner in the closed market. If The Pistols had come from and stayed living in Dundee, would punk have happened? The publishers, the BBC and the cultural commentators have got their Prog. Literature, their Stadium Authors, so why try something new? In the immortal words of David Bowie singing a John Lennon song, *Nothing's gonna change my world*. Mick wanted to say that it's our world too but realised it really isn't, it's their world. We're only allowed to view it and consume from their fixed menu – oh, and fund it obviously.

There's little fresh art in 'the arts', just mortgages to be paid. Egos and hygienic, professional pride being protected from the germs by prescription and procedures tested and secure, keeping the practitioners safely locked away in the sterile bubble that is the London media village, no dangers there.

Mick came off the phone swearing and settled in the kitchen to a coffee and a hasty fag. The clock showed five minutes until he had to set off to pick up Billy. He was sure the industry people weren't bad people, perhaps they went in with good intentions and a spark, maybe even an aim to battle against their boring and controlling industry. Whatever their objectives, they slowly get eaten up by the beast; unnoticing, they fall into the age-old, prescribed habits.

Perhaps some of them do their best but are not in a position to effect change, and by the time they are they've lost their spark and have acquired too many close industry friends. There must be time pressures pushing them toward the safe and easy, the less complicated decision and the feature perfectly packaged and plonked in their lap by professional and competent floggers. Is their sense of achievement simply the production on time and within budget, no matter what dull bullshit they are flogging? Can they just dress it up and make it look pretty, make it sound interesting and 'worthy'? As long as they don't lose punters, are they safe?

As for the artists, who could blame them? But they don't need to fill the whole cultural space. They don't need blanket coverage week in and week out, reviews and interviews throughout the print media, TV and radio, to squeeze every last sale or punter out of their work. It's not the artists' choice; it's the publicist with a machine gun, doing their job, carrying out the hit by spraying the whole of the London mob. It almost goes unnoticed to us that we see and hear about the same cultural products everywhere and that the media are honoured to be offered them. We switch off as we hear the third review of the same play, we skip to the next book as we see the top seller reviewed for the umpteenth time filling dead space with the dictated because it is simply expected that everyone covers the same stuff. If it is deemed 'important' enough, everyone wants to bask in the association and give their product, their programme or publication, the required gravitas or irreverence. Even if it isn't deemed that 'important' the industry floggers will make sure their mates cover it throughout the industry; it's just more likely to slip us punters by.

5

Daydreaming through a floor, the physical bits bending his back and John Wayneing his gait as he dumped the edger and stepped away, stretching and loosening his arms, shoulders and back like a weight-lifter who's just improved his personal best. The edger small, about the size of a squared basket ball, packed a whole lot of friction and was a solid, weighty bit of kit, constantly pulling away, chasing industrial-thickness electrical cord and feet that were necessarily close to the spinning disc that would slice through a foot as easy as look at it. Sweat dripping from his head, wiping salt into eyes, no time to acknowledge the slight discomfort, just a lot of squeezed eyes, blinking and eye-wiping in between the bursts of energy – whole body slightly damp. *I'm getting too old for this game.* It was weird though, he'd been doing it so long that he suffered less than he did as a kid, better pacing, little tricks to tame time. That was the thing about doing the floors, if it was a single floor it was a constant race against the clock, against needing the machines an extra day and nipping away at his margin. Simple frustrations like the paper discs not getting fully under skirting-boards, leaving a shadow of white or dark that he couldn't live with – everyone else would accept it, customer, builder, decorators, and joiners, but not him – meaning that he'd have to try and recycle yet more fabric discs, to take the edge of the floor right the way under the skirting. People may not notice this one thing as a mark of excellence but it was a combination of things like this that made his floors outstanding, things of beauty.

As opposed to his past office-based stuff, he liked the head-space, the time to think through ideas, let his head run free through meditative thoughts that reared up fresh and new, unannounced and shocking. He'd get giddy with the sparkle of them but often they were untouchable, too much technical knowledge, gear, time or money needed. Time or money – surely they are the same fucking thing.

'What the fuck you listening to now?' Barry comes in for no other reason than to banter and play with Mick.

'Always the same thing, Barry.'

'Fuckin' Radio Four.' Mock female posh voice, 'Ooh, these flowers are particularly beautiful. Put some fuckin' music on, y'soft get.'

'I can't stand Radio One and all the others play the same old shite on a fucking loop.'

Barry made him laugh. He'd take up the banter later but now he needed to get on. Time for a fag. Tapping his mask on the ground to get out the fluid swimming around beneath the seal, not even noticing that the ritual had no effect, he moved on to the next ritual, drying it out with the bottom of his T-shirt, his multi-functional T-shirt. He loved the fucked-up T-shirts, clearing his sinuses on them, not green, yellow or transparent but always brown, more sawdust than snot. Wiping varnish off brushes and hands onto the 100% cotton of his skirting-cleaning T-shirt. Half a fag accompanied by half a plastic cup of coffee from his thermos. A moment for fresh air unchecked by the latex mask and fibrous filters that should stop him from getting the traditional cancers enjoyed by thousand of unfortunate joiners over the years and the centuries of tiny particles of wood. The hot sun which through the window inside had illuminated millions of tiny atoms of wood now lit up he didn't know what but thousands of molecules danced above the grass, they moved to the same tune. Clear light and heat hazy and one-dimensional, warming his being, bleaching his mental processes and bringing him right into the moment.

Back inside via the kitchen patio windows that, through lack of steps, were three foot off the ground.

'Ey, Barry you'll love this next bit, they're following an all women's five-a-side football team from Birmingham to the Muslim Women's Five-a-side World Cup. It's right up your street, mate.'

'Fucking Paki birds playing football, that's not right.'

Barry was trying to get a rise out of him. He'd heard Mick's opinions often enough, although they'd never discussed them. Barry was a really good lad with a heart of gold, no matter what poses he pulled. He reminded Mick of a hyper-active fifty-odd-year-old school kid, always laughing, joking and recounting tales. Worked his socks off mindst you, he didn't stand around chatting, just at lunch time and breaks he came to vibrant life.

The deep, multi-tonal drone of the machine occasionally shifted chord but most often held a constant combination of notes that backed his thoughts, dancing over the top, and providing the melody. The machine passed the negated current through the wooden handle; the all-frequency vibration made his body tingle and removed full feeling from his hands that took on unreal sensations when he broke to pick up a hammer or other tool melting into his palm and fingers that no longer had the clear definition between flesh and object. A large, cylindrical drum with the power to remove limbs, no problem. Although he could daydream as he fought it forward and pulled it back – trying to keep it in line like an over-active colt – he was constantly aware that it may run away and do serious damage: never happened. Most likely was that it would hit a nail or the sheet would become too loose – usually preceded by a definite shift in tone and feel – and shatter into thousands of pieces of varied sizes, breaking his rhythm with the need to sweep up every last grain of gritted paper which, were he not conscientious, would stud the wooden floor with tiny black diamonds.

It was the edger that required the sweat and sinew, and as he'd taken it so far this morning he was rewarding himself with an extended session on the big machine. Nearly home time, or rather, nearly time to pick up Cal, drop in and get Billy and then head home, so if he kept it moving he'd get ahead and have a less frenetic morning.

'See y'later, lads.'

'You done yer hour then, Mick?'

'Fuck off, I got here an hour before Jimmy an' 'ee'll be off soon. Anyway, what y'talking about, mi hour? I've done a full hour an' 'alf today.'

They all did the same laugh they did every afternoon and Mick headed for the door. He loved it when he could just up and go, when the room was his and he was midway, no point in cleaning up, nothing to carry out to the car, just chuck all his tools back into the box or neat pile or neither and away he could go. Weird sometimes how you arrive with no memory of the journey, you get in your car and arrive. You could recount happenings and parts of the route but you were never really there.

41

Turning into Holt Park supermarket car park, he could see his spot, clear and easily accessible. Right up against the bus lane that was right up against the path that in turn was right up against the shopping centre. It should be illegal to park here really but there were no yellow lines, no zigzags, no markings at all. A small space just enough for a car and enough away from the crossing for it to be safe. Sometimes he had to reverse slightly to let a motor or push-bike get to their parking spot, but usually he'd just listen to the radio, watching the shoppers and kids until Cal arrived. If he was a bit sharpish he'd pick up Cal quick and they'd be away good and early. If he was on time he'd lose Cal to a bottle of Lucozade from Asda under the pretence that his dad wasn't there when he came out – which technically speaking he wasn't – but often he'd be in between and just in time to see Cal disappear into the shopping arcade, which was frustrating. Kids, bags, shirts, ties, women, men, silly hats and inappropriate shorts, babies in push-chairs, lives all around.

'Come on Cal, let's get going.'

Cal lurching along sucking on a bottle and smiling. Grinning face up to the gap for the side window of the car.

'Ey, Mick, have you written a book?'

Elijah, one of Cal's old mates from junior school that Mick knew well; back in the old days (last year) they'd play footie for half an hour at a time, every evening as they waited for Ez, sometimes ten kids and another adult, but always Elijah and Jeremiah, his twin.

'I have, yes.'

'What, like a real book?'

'Yeh, like with pages and everything.'

'Cool. See y'later.'

'See y'.'

'Hi, Cal, how y'doing? How was your day?' The age-old question; each afternoon he alternated it with the question all school kids throughout the world and history hate. 'How was school?'

'OK, thanks.'

They chatted and glided through the half-reality that is a journey so routine that it only just exists. Mick trying not to eye up women too obviously, Cal noticing every glance. Hanging a left from

Otley Old Road onto Spen Lane, a broad and less busy hill. The panorama of the south west of the city stunning with light clouds glowing over the horizon, playing hide and seek with the light, bringing troughs and peaks, sparkling off high-rise windows. Every evening he wished he'd brought his camera, every night the memory was gone. Easing off the accelerator as he approached a bus pointing the opposite way on the other side of the road and picking up passengers.

'FUCKIN' 'ELL.' He slammed down on his brakes as a car appeared at speed across his front bumper. Missing it by a foot, it pulled away at speed. 'Tosser.' An elongated beep and flashing of lights. 'That was so dangerous – he couldn't see a thing. Let's just risk people lives, shall we? Cunt.' Mick flashed and beeped him again, hoping for at the very least a raised hand to acknowledge a moment of madness, but no, the driver was slowing down and eventually stopped, opening his door and getting out of his car to rage.

'Fucking cheek. Yep, I'm in, let's fucking go y'cunt.' Mick stopped and jumped out of his car, fuming, determined to go as far as need be to get an acknowledgement of cuntdom.

The bloke was already shouting, 'What fucking speed were you doing? I'd get back in y'car if I were you, mate.'

'Er, twenty, twenty-five, y'cunt. You can't just fly out into a blind spot on a main fucking road. . .'

The bloke, as usual a bit bigger than Mick, and a bit unkempt, was starting to look less confident as Mick moved towards him. 'You weren't, you were going a lot fucking faster than that. Y'coulda killed someone.'

'I could've killed someone? It wan't me driving like a complete twat; you just pulled out blind onto a main fucking road.'

The bloke's body language had changed as he mumbled swear words, stepping backwards. Mick was enjoying the back down. 'Listen, mate, I haven't got all fucking day. You know you drove like a cunt, so apologise or let's go.'

The man backed to his door, wittering, and drove away. Mick gazed over at a voyeur at a bus stop, pulled an 'oops' face and returned to his car.

The situation had wired Mick, and all Callum was saying was, 'Don't know Dad. . . I can't drive.'

'But you could see that he appeared from nowhere and couldn't see what was coming?'

'Yeh, s'pose.'

'When you join a road from a junction, you're not supposed to affect other cars, and if I hadn't slammed on we'd have crashed, definitely.'

'Yeh.'

'Do you find it a bit embarrassing when I get out of the car like that?'

'Yeh, a bit.'

'Sorry.'

A memory flicked through Mick's mind of Ez egging him on in such situations: 'Dad, he's there, go on, look, he's there.' Funny how different kids can be. Another quick memory flashed through Mick of Ez being disappointed that he didn't get out of his car to four road builders in a huge wagon, even though he'd made them back the big fuck-off wagon back through the space they shouldn't have taken while taunting them – not enough for Ez. Did he really think his Dad would have stood a chance? If the non-drivers in the wagon hadn't been so embarrassed by the tossy behaviour of their driver, they'd have battered him instead of looking the other way sheepishly; *they looked like fucking monsters.*

'Well, I'm trying to do it less, Cal, but that bloke is going to kill someone and he needs to realise that.'

'Hmm.'

Mick was aware that Cal found it slightly uncomfortable and changed the subject.

Mick justified this behaviour in his head with some grandiose idea of facing up to dangerous drivers who would bully other people on the road. He went through his most recent encounters and ticked them off in his head to vindicate himself and normalise his psychotic behaviour. That fella that he'd followed into the video shop on Town Street and threatened to remove his head and ram it up his arse. When he first saw him, the guy had been out of his car – which was on the wrong side of a major road, with no plausible excuse – screaming at a young woman shaking in her car, which was positioned in a way that exonerated her from any possible misdemeanour. He'd then proceeded to do the single most dangerous piece of driving that Mick had ever witnessed, a major pile-up, including Mick's car full of his kids, only being avoided by the fantastic driving of a third driver. In another incident the gangster had:

1) flown up his arse beeping and flashing doing at least fifteen to twenty miles an hour over the limit for a housing estate;

2) taken a blind corner at at least sixty where just around the corner was a crossing place for school kids, meaning that it was pure chance that he didn't kill one or more of the kids;

3) done it at half past eight when kids were rushing to school, so he either didn't know the road or didn't give a fuck.

He moved on through his list in the same black-and-white manner. Although the mad driving gangster was probably three or four incidents ago he'd clearly illustrated to Mick the insanity of his crazed, defender-of-the-road routine. No matter how in his face Mick got, no matter what he said and with what venom, the gangster was at all times calm and fully in control of the situation and no doubt could've ended it at any time. Mick got lucky in that the fella was on his way to break legs for money or perhaps the gangster couldn't see enough of a pay-off. Had he encountered him in the gangster's leisure time, Mick sensed that he would have been lucky to end up in hospital.

'What do you do? Just let nutters risk kids' lives?'

For various reasons, not just the certainty of at some point getting battered, he'd resolved not to do it anymore, but there he was this very day willing to enter into violence with a young, fit-looking man. Mick reminded himself that his head was out of step with his body. In his head, he was mid-twenties and fighting-fit, yet the reality of his body was that of a comfortable forty-odd-year-old man with a distant memory of fighting and a liking for cake and leisure. Obviously he'd have chinned the cunt anyway, but perhaps he should retire. . . undefeated.

Digital stalking in Leeds, Yorkshire, England

6

Billy on his first day of school looked like a right bobby dazzler in his miniature school uniform, the proud parents delivering him to school together for possibly the only time in his school career. Billy entered his school life saying 'Hi' to all the older kids, the mid-aged kids and the younger kids in the playground, not phased at all, just walking around introducing himself to people. Returning home he was talking about playing footie with the big kids.

'He's only four, for God's sake, where does he get all that confidence?'

Taking Billy for his second day at school and all the big, middle and small kids greet him: 'Hi Billy. . . Billy how y'doing? . . . Did you walk to school Billy?' They knew he'd be OK, from the moment he started walking at nine months they knew it, he just got up and on with the world, no shyness, no fear just a little confident human being open to the world. It wasn't some remarkable genetic gift that the two of them automatically passed on; Callum, their middle child, had been very different. Cal finally settled into his senior school after strong hints of bullying, the polar opposite of Billy, reserved and careful, assessing situations before engaging. Mick and Lesley agreed that neither approach was right or wrong, just different. They hoped that both would take a little of the other's attitude and learn when and where to use it. They didn't want Billy jumping into the middle of a bunch of feeding Great White Sharks shouting, 'Hi, hi, hi.' Callum gradually started to settle in, make friends and to shine with his school work. After going to a very competitive junior school, kids reading Harry Potter in the womb; he'd hidden in the class, there was no space for him to expand. He now appeared to be gaining confidence and expanding. Very sensible lad, and he hadn't fussed at all about getting the bus home from school – well, to a halfway point anyway; not like Ezra – he'd squealed like a pig.

Ez had thickened out even more, a couple of inches taller than Mick, and in the words of the kids upon the street, 'he's ripped' – can't get into Mick's T-shirts anymore. Mick found it a bit strange, slightly homo-erotic the way in which Ez and some of his mates would have as their avatar their own torso, the jeans hanging low and showing the top of their Calvin Kleins below their six-pack. 'Eeeee, bloody kids today, I don't know, posting semi-naked pictures of themselves on t'internet, it's a scandal – they think they're bloody Grandmaster Flash or one of those other young bloody rapters.'

Ezra had got a part-time job at Wilkinson's and was becoming more and more independent with every week that went by, although he'd still rush in from college every so often, shouting, 'Dad I'm late, can y'give us a lift into work? Is mi tea ready?'

'Yes, it's in the oven, Ez. If you're quick, you'll get there y'sen.'

'Da-a-ad, look at the time. . . . Well, fine, I won't have mi tea then, I'll just have to have it when I get back.'

Mick looking at the clock, a quick calculation showing that it wasn't simply emotional blackmail, a gene carrier threatening the gene giver with bodily abuse.

'Aw, but Ez. . . . OK, we'll be ready by quarter to. Billy, are you coming with me to give Ezra a lift to work?' It wasn't really a question, Mick knew the answer.

'Yes, Dad, comiiiiing.'

'Get y'shoes Billy, and we'll get you ready. We don't need to go yet so you'll have a bit of time to play first.'

That evening, on his way to running the bath, Mick came up the stairs to see Billy hurling Graham Bear into the air and shouting. He was slightly shocked: any other cuddly toy, fine, but Graham Bear? Graham wasn't an ordinary bear, you could sit him with all Billy's other cuddly toys and he was probably the least remarkable, but he was the one that Billy had picked out. Like all parents, they'd tried to get their child to form an attachment with a cuddly toy from a young age – hopefully one of the cuter ones. While he was still a baby, Lesley had named some of them and some had become the preferred attachment cuddly toys. The absolute top of the aspirational list was a medium-sized panda bear that had been to hospital for the birth of Callum. But as Billy grew and quickly imposed his will on the situation it was clear that he wasn't interested in the cuddly toys. Just before his first birthday Billy had jumped over to the gang of assorted stuffed animals at the end of his bed, ignored all the big ones, all the cute ones, all the unusual ones. He deliberately pulled out a nondescript small grey bear from under the pile, shuffled back to the top of his bed, cuddled up and started to settle down to sleep, clasping the bear to his chest. This pattern repeated for a number of nights until the bear every evening lay on the pillow waiting for Billy. Billy later named him Graham Bear.

As he gazed at Billy launching Graham Bear into the air, Mick visualized a horrible image of the mass murderer as a child, chopping the legs off frogs in his back garden.

'Billy what are you doing to Graham Bear?'

'We're playing.'

'No, you're throwing him down the stairs.'

'Look how high I can throw him, Dad, hurrrYARRR.' Graham Bear spinning through the air, slightly pathetic and undignified, with Billy bounding after him.

'Billy, are you sure you should be throwing Graham Bear around like that?'

'Why? NEOOOWN. Look, look how high he goes.'

'Well you might hurt him.'

'No I won't, Dad.'

'Well, the way you're throwing him around. . .'

'No, Dad, I won't because Grahams Bear's not really alive, you know, Dad, he's just a toy, a, a, a cuddly toy.'

Mick was slightly lost for words in the face of such pure logic.

'But. . . but I thought he was your friend.'

'Yes, he is, he's my friend who likes flying. WEEEEEEH.' Graham Bear hurtling off towards the ceiling.

'But—'

'Dad, it's just made up. I make it up. Graham Bear isn't alive, you know, but I pretend he is. He doesn't really like flying but I pretend he does, y'see? And if I pretend he's hurt I'll give him a cuddle but he's not really hurt because he's not really alive. . . see? And I'm only cuddling him because I'm pretending he's hurt. He's not really hurt because he's not really alive. . . see?'

'Ah, I see.' Mick made a hasty retreat. He was out of his depth. On his way down the stairs he shouted, 'You're jumping in the bath soon, Billy. Billy, you're getting a bath soon, OK? Did you hear me, Billy?'

'Yes Daaad.'

Billy assembled a bunch of cars to take into the bath and flew up the stairs, just winning the race to the bathroom.

'You're too fast. It's all that apple that you ate – it's made you too fast.'

'I won, didn't I Dad? I won, didn't I?'

'Yeehh, but you were lucky. I'll kick y'butt tomorrow night.'

'No you won't because tomorrow I'll have some carrots aaand some apple.'

Billy jumped into the bath talking constantly. Mick pulled the nit comb out of the bathroom cabinet. Nits, every child's introduction to school. Throughout the UK, children rich, poor, dirty and clean, they get nits in their first year of school and more than once. 'We'll have a quick check through your hair.'

'But Da-a-ad.' The thought of having to sit still for more than ten seconds doing Billy's head in.

'Yeh, but we need to give it a quick check.'

'Da-a-ad, no one else in the house has got nits, have they?'

'No, not so far, that's why I need to do your hair.'

'You get them off other people, don't you, Dad?'

'Yes you do. You'll get them when you touch heads with people at school.'

'You've checked me, haven't you, Dad?'

'What? Yes, I keep checking you.'

'But you've checked me since I've been to school, haven't you Dad?'

'I have, yes.'

'And I didn't have them, did I, Dad?'

'No, you didn't, Billy, but you see they lay eggs and it can take a week for the eggs to hatch.' As Mick was saying it he realised that it'd been a teacher-training day on Thursday, they'd been off Friday and, with it being Sunday, it was likely that any eggs would have hatched and Billy's hair would have already been combed outside the gestation period.

'But I haven't been to school, have I, Dad?'

'I'll tell you what, Billy, I'll just have a quick check. Really quick, without the conditioner. Just sit still for a minute.' Having had it explained to him by his fucking four-year-old son that it was

50

a pointless exercise, Mick went through the motions trying to work out why.

'Da-a-ad.'

'Yes, Billy.'

'If you get them off other people's heads. . .'

'Yes.'

'Where did the first person get them from?'

'What?'

'The first person who got nits, where did they get them from?'

'Well, that's a very complicated question. It's a fantastic question, Billy, I'll have to check.' Mick knew he wouldn't check, he'd have to think it through and come back to it later if Billy remembered, which he probably wouldn't. Mick thought on it a little longer: nothing, other than Thomas Aquinas and that wasn't really relevant.

'Bloody 'ell, Billy, that's a good question, it's a right belter. Things like animals develop and change but it's really, really slowly. A bit like they change to fill in spaces. It's like when you practise at things and get better at it bit by bit, like when you're six you'll be so good at riding your bike that you won't need stabilisers. Animals change a bit like that, but they kind of grow new bits, and lose bits, but it's really, really slowly, over thousands of years. People will be slightly different in hundreds of years' time. It's like people, right? Human beings came from monkeys that kept changing a bit at a bit at a time. Millions of years ago there were no people like there is today, just big monkeys, apes that were slowly changing into—'

'Da-a-ad, this car's cool, isn't it?'

'What?' Mick laughed to himself. *Tonight I cannot win.* 'Yes it is, Billy, really cool.'

One of the things about the arrival of Billy that they were aware of was that he stretched their life as carers out those extra years. He'd been planned and this matter arose at the planning stage; they loved the plan. Their middle son was eight when Billy was born, *ergo* an extra eight likely years of having to be around. They'd probably be around for the other two anyway but it was a fact nonetheless. The main thing that concerned them about the age thing was that they'd be nearing their sixties by the time he was twenty, although they decided that older parents weren't that rare and that the percentage would increase with time. They also worried that their energy levels might drop as he grew, and a baby with so much energy, walking by nine months and into everything, played a memory-based trick on them that this was indeed the case. From his birth, their experience of Billy was joyous, the birth itself smooth and relatively easy – well, compared to the traumatic birth of Callum, where, had Mick not been a stroppy and gobby get, they were both convinced that mother and baby, especially baby, would have died. That was one of the reasons that Callum was so treasured, the other being that they'd been told years before his birth that conception was highly unlikely, then after one unprotected and particularly loving, passionate sesh, Mick rolled over and announced that Lesley was pregnant, he knew it. After a couple of weeks of Mick's certainty, Lesley was handed a pregnancy-testing kit by someone at work with the words, 'Here, just check and see if he's right.' He was right and they were ecstatic.

7

The north-facing kitchen often needed artificial light but it was always the case first thing on a winter morning. They couldn't remember the last time they'd sat together at half past seven. The daze of hideously interrupted sleep left them wordless, but the comfortable presence made the silence relaxed. Quick few tokes on a fag and Mick was ready to hassle the kids into increased action.

'What the fuck?'

'What?'

'What's the time?'

'What?' Lesley more animated. Surely Mick realised that some obscure guessing game and a sudden burst of tension were the last things she needed first thing on a morning. Mick stood up, looking out through the window, and moved towards the lobby; she followed his movement with her eyes and clocked the gang at the door. 'For fuck's sake, half past seven on a Wednesday morning? They've got to be kidding.'

The gaggle of police entered the room, covering the exit, the boss woman stepping forward.

'Mr McCann and Miss Jackson, I have to tell you that you are both under arrest, on suspicion of making malicious phone calls.'

Mick went for his moisturiser in rage. 'Whaaaat? This is absolutely scandalous.' Patting his cheeks with his slightly perfumed fingers. 'It's unbelievable. What have you been doing for the last six months?' The question hung in the gulp-filled air like a crow in a linen factory.

She continued. 'Anything you say may be used in evidence against you. You have the right to remain silent but anything you don't. . .'

Mick neighing like a horse. 'Unbelievable, absolutely unbelievable. Are you serious?'

Lesley coming around. 'You're arresting us? You are seriously arresting us?'

The flustered policewoman, 'Can I get through this?'

'Oh, very sorry, don't mind us.'

Mick chuckled at Lesley's caustic wit.

'Anything you don't say whilst being questioned and later rely upon in a court of law may be held against you. Do you understand?'

Silence, broken by a series of front-of-mouth tuts, slow exhaling of breath and snorts.

Billy flies into the room in the manner of a high-powered four-year-old. 'Hi, hi.' Looking up at the male officer. 'Who are you?'

Mick jumps in all matter-of-fact for the first time this morning. 'Just some mates come around to see us.'

'Yes, yes, we're just some mates of y'dad's.'

'Come on, Billy, out y'go.'

Billy is out of the room as quickly as he entered it, a ball of inquisitive energy. Later, as the police searched around him, Billy realised that these weren't friends at all.

'We also have a warrant to search the premises.'

'Fantastic – keep an eye out for mi memory stick, will y'?'

'What?'

'I'm joking. I really don't believe this.'

The Detective Constable trying to disguise her squirm. 'Look, we'll make it quick. We're not going to take your house apart, we'll put everything back and we'll make the interviews as quick as possible.'

'Oh, that's OK then.' Lesley still corrosive while Mick tries to steady his shaking head.

'What about the kids? Can I take them to school first?'

'No, you are under arrest.'

'So what about the school run? What about the kids?'

Four blank police faces had obviously not thought this through properly but still looked unconcerned. Lesley, interrupting the collective 'Oops' with 'I'll phone my mum', gets up to find the phone.

'Where are you going?'

'Y'deaf? I'm going to get the phone to call my mother. I wouldn't want to leave a four-year-old in the house on his own; that'd be breaking the law. You should know that.'

'You'll have to be accompanied by an officer.'

'What? Just in case I do a runner? Bloody ridiculous.' A wary officer follows Lesley out into the hall but not too closely. 'Look I'm still here.'

'Michael, we'll get this done as quickly as we can and we really won't make a mess.'

'Yeh, thanks.'

'Are you dressed and ready? Do you want to go down and get booked in now? Get it moving and get it over with?'

'Don't mind. Aren't we going down together?'

'No, we have to take you down in separate cars, it's just procedural, but if you want to get started there's a couple of colleagues waiting outside. It's totally up to you.'

'What? There's more of y'?'

'Yeh, we had to bring a couple of other officers with us. They're waiting outside. Don't worry, they're non-uniform, no one will know it's the police.'

'Not bothered about that. Yeh, might as well get it moving.'

'Y'sure?'

'Yeh, I'll just wait 'n' make sure Lesley's mum's OK to come round then we can get moving.'

'Mi mum's on her way.'

The Detective Constable makes a quick call on her walky-talky and within seconds yet more police arrive at the door.

'Michael, if you'd like to go with the officers.' *Like there's a fucking choice.*

Lesley went to get dressed as they awaited the arrival of her mother; she looked back and swore as one of the female officers followed her up the stairs. She went towards the bathroom, the policewoman a couple of steps behind.

'Is it alright if I shut the door?' Lesley didn't ask but stated.

'Oh, yes, of course.'

'Are you sure? You don't want to come in? This is bloody ridiculous.' Lesley closed the door in the face of the woman. Knowing that she wouldn't have chance to do her hair or make-up, she gazed at herself in the mirror and swore, aware that this morning she would have to face her greatest fear, the phobia of curly hair. She returned downstairs to find DC Strangelove rummaging through drawers and being distracted by things that were obviously nothing to do with 'the enquiry'.

'So are the kids looking forward to Christmas?'

'Yeh, that's what kids do, get excited at Christmas.'

'Have you got it all organised?'

Stop trying to normalise it, this isn't fucking normal. The stallion words held on the end of Lesley's tether rearing up and kicking, fighting hard to enter the real world. Strangelove chatting to a colleague on the phone as she rifled through a cupboard. 'Ooh, it's a right Aladdin's cave in here.'

'IT'S A FAMILY HOME.' Lesley could hold it no longer, her wild, feral words breaking down the mental corral and heading for the open plains. 'THIS IS A FUCKING FAMILY HOME, NOT SOME SCUZZBALL ADDICT'S HIDEOUT.' Lesley started to sob uncontrollably. 'We're normal, honest, working people trying to get on with our lives' – Strangelove, bowed her head slightly and continued her conversation in more hushed tones – 'not some scumbags with criminal records as long as your arm. We've never done anything. Nothing.' Overcome with the power and freedom of the emotions, Lesley struggled to fight back the shaking, the gulps for air, the fluids and running mucus. 'How many times have I called the police? When have you ever done anything about crimes carried out against us? What have you ever fucking solved? Who have you ever caught? No one. You're a set of useless fucking bullies. YOU WANKERS. YOU SET OF USELESS FUCKING WANKERS.'

'I'll call you back. Yep, yeh, bye. Lesley if you have complaints about previous. . .'

'Yeh, yeh, complain and you'll do fuck-all.'

'. . . police enquiries, you can complain, you know.'

'I know, and a lot of fucking good it does you. I've even contacted my MP a couple of times but nothing happens.'

The hairs on the back of Strangelove's neck start to pay attention.

'Have you? Well, I'm very sorry; I know this can't be pleasant.'

'You're not sorry. Are you sorry you haven't been doing your job?'

'We have. Look, I can't talk to you about the specifics of the case obviously, but we have been making enquiries.'

'Not enough enquiries or you wouldn't be here pushing around my family. What the fuck are you doing here? Six of you – it's crazy; I thought that you had no time; I thought you were under so much pressure. Why does this stupid case get so much attention?'

'Wait a minute, it's a serious situation, we have to do something.'

'No it isn't, it's a fucking simple situation. Well, what you've told us is simple.'

'I can't talk to you about the specifics but if you were getting malicious—'

'I'd change my number or get the calls blocked. DER-ER, it's fucking easy.'

'I can't get into the case, but I assure you that we're doing all we can.'

'No you're not, you're not doing all you can and you're messing with the wrong fucking people here, Missy.'

'Look, I can understand why you're upset.'

'NO YOU CAN'T FUCKING UNDERSTAND, DON'T YOU DARE. . . YOU THINK IT'S FUCKING NORMAL. THIS IS FUCKING ROUTINE. JUST THE ROUTINE FEAR OF A FOUR-YEAR-OLD SEEING HIS PARENTS GETTING TAKEN AWAY. THE ROUTINE TRAUMA OF A TWELVE-YEAR-OLD HAVING ALL HIS STUFF ROOTED THROUGH.'

'I know. . .'

'GET IT INTO YOUR THICK HEAD, YOU DON'T KNOW. Don't speak to me now, you can't justify this.'

'OK.' Strangelove continued her nosing; there'd been some unexpected shift in the power relationship. Lesley suddenly snorted, making Strangelove jerk. *An 'Aladdin's cave'?* What she found so exciting about a cereal cupboard was completely beyond Lesley, and surely the condiments weren't that thrilling.

The superior male officer enters the kitchen. 'I think I've got something here.' Holding Lesley's diary like a long-sought-after, prized trophy.

'What is it?' They huddle together in a conspiratorial ruck, heads nodding triumphantly like they'd cracked the case. Breaking, Strangelove threw a 'you almost had me then' look at Lesley and tugged on both collar-ends of her power coat. 'Bag it.'

'Are you serious? You've found what in my diary?'

'Can't say at this point Mrs Jackson, but it's certainly very interesting.'

'It's Miss Jackson. What's interesting?'

'Oh, just some of the tone, it's very. . . similar.'

'What tone? I thought the person had been making malicious phone calls.'

'I can't get into that Miss Jackson, you must realise that.'

'Yeh, but surely these calls are at the very least threatening.'

Strangelove shuffled her facial muscles. 'I can't talk to you about the case.'

'Have you never felt really angry with a situation and written it down to get rid of it?'

'I don't keep a diary.'

'There's a surprise. You'd be too paranoid that it may be used in evidence against you, ey?'

'Look, the quicker we get this search finished, the quicker we can get to the station and get it over with.' Strangelove continued her mandatory rooting.

8

Two detectives led Mick to the unmarked police car parked up the lane. In the back of the car halfway to the top of the lane, Mick patted his pockets.

'I've forgotten mi fags.'

'You won't be able to smoke anyway.'

'I could sneak a couple of drags on the way from the car to the station.'

'Hmm, we can't turn back.'

'I'll phone Les and get her to bring them.'

'You're not allowed to make any calls.'

'Well, you could call her for me.'

'You won't be able to smoke anyway.'

With that, he sat back and chuntered about owt or nowt, they chuntered back. There were no handles and the winder had been removed from the panel, meaning the windows stayed closed. *Where the fuck's she going?*

'Are we going to the Bridewell?'

'Yeh.'

'You do know we're going the wrong way?'

'Yeh, I'm just looking for somewhere to turn.'

'I should've given you directions; it'll take another twenty minutes from here.'

They chatted all the way into town about the state of policing, interspersed with the odd 'I can't say anything about your case'. 'Anyway we don't know anything about it. We were only called in for the arrest.' They returned to the discussion about the state of policing, the two officers getting Mick to guess how many police officers would be on duty for the whole of Leeds city centre on a Friday and Saturday night.

'Don't know. Somewhere between twenty and thirty?'

The two officers held back slightly before giving the amount to raise the tension and render the amount with an increased 'wow' factor.

'Six. There are six officers for the whole of the centre of Leeds, and that's at the beginning of the evening.'

'Six? Are you kidding?'

'No. Six. And by the time a couple of arrests are made or someone has to accompany a member of the public to hospital, that kind of thing, there'll be no officers left. The whole of Leeds city centre on a Friday, Saturday night, completely unpoliced.'

Mick rolled the information in his head slowly. Six of them had turned up to arrest them – CID, therefore they'll be better paid and more qualified than the ones doing the Leeds city centre weekend shift: most of those will be constables. An interesting use of resources.

'Why six of you today? Two per car, per person, only needed four. Why CID? This is surely a job for uniform.'

Subject changed, he felt weirdly relaxed in the midst of the snaking traffic hissing its way into town, catching up and pulling away in a curling line, one body of traffic full of strangers. They probably looked like three office workers on a car-sharing scheme, except he looked very casual; they all looked casual, but he was more comfortable with it. They arrived, and the two officers had forgotten they were on an arrest until Mick quickened his pace to enter the building between them. Surely that was the custom.

In the Bridewell, the two detectives' demeanour had shifted slightly. More on edge, they led Mick to a holding-area-cum-waiting-room, a fairly grim caged and boxed room, completely visible, like the end cell in an old Western movie, and Mick stayed away from the back wall in case it exploded into a shower of flying bricks. Within minutes, he was ushered out to the desk and asked a series of questions by an officious and very competent woman.

'Do you know why you have been arrested?'

'Er, no, not really.'

The Desk Sergeant looks over concerned. 'Did they read you your rights?'

'Oh, yeh, and they said something about. . .'

'Suspicion of making malicious phone calls,' one of the arresting officers steps forward nervously to fill the gap.

'Oh, sorry, yeh, they explained what we'd been arrested for, I just didn't know why.'

The Desk Sergeant makes an instant and correct assessment – lack of experience, not smart-arse. The Sergeant asks one of the arresting officers a number of questions, some of which will have to wait until the boss arrives. Mick wonders why the Desk Sergeant makes everybody so nervous. He's certainly got an air, and I'd trust him with a tenner and a shopping-list. He got good vibes from him, like he was some ancient buffer between policeman and quarry, only interested in the concept 'right'.

'Name?'

'Michael McCann.'

'Date of birth?'

'Fourteenth of the twelfth, sixty-three.'

'Do you suffer from depression?'

'No.'

'Mental illness?'

Mick recognised a question for debate but instead offered, 'No.'

The questions continued; the forms got filled and signed. Finally Mick had to empty his pockets, remove his jewellery and shoes. There was a slight discussion about whether his jogging bottom ties constituted a chord. Mick thought not but the refereeing Sergeant decided to err on the side of caution and Mick changed his jogging bottoms to regulation Bridewell pants with no chord for hanging.

'One pair of Adidas trainers, one jacket, one mobile phone, one silver necklace, one silver sleeper earring and five Tic-Tac mints. Can you sign there please? Thank you.'

They tried to photograph him on the way to the cells but after a few minutes they realised that they couldn't work the computer. Mick offered to have a look but they declined.

'It's OK, we'll do it later when the operator arrives.'

The female officer escorted him down to the cells. Once away from the main desk she became more chatty and relaxed again.

'Won't be long. As soon as your wife is down and booked in, they'll get on and question you.'

Booked in? It isn't a fucking holiday. Michael was pleased with himself for restraining the words in his head and not allowing them to spill out into the space between him and the pleasant young woman. It'd all been very pleasantly done; well, he wouldn't choose it as a way to spend a November morning but it was painless enough. He wasn't even craving a fag, although the thought brought on a craving. *Tit*.

They hadn't gone far but with the seemingly endless turns it would have taken Mick five minutes to find his way back to the desk, although he suspected the plan was loosely circular, so maybe not. Into the cell, and initially Mick thought she was leaving the door unlocked, but after a silly delay it slammed shut and he was left with his feet, thoughts and penis. The room was so bare that how to arrange himself on the tatty red mat-cum-bed became a decision: squat crossed-legged, lie down, perch on the side or sit on the floor against the bed Steve McQueen stylee? A cinematic scene he'd dozed through so many times. Calm and relaxed, he played with the ideas in his head. Should he knock on the thick metal door and request a glove and baseball? Perhaps smearing shit on the walls was the only logical response to the absurdity of the situation. Or was it Paul Newman? *Cool-Hand Luke* and *The Great Escape* – two classic films in their own ways but who was in which? *Who gives a fuck?*

He was quickly bored. The regulation shutter slid open, unseen eyes checked that he wasn't smashing his head against the solid metal toilet with no lid or paper. Can you hang yourself with toilet paper? Surely the perforations render it a less than ideal tourniquet. Anyway, they could supply that stuff that comes out in single sheets. Mick chuckled out loud at a vision of someone trying to choke themselves with toilet roll, manically ramming sheets into their mouth and then being unable to say – but attempting to and with comic effect – 'Bollocks, I'm breathing through me nose.' Prodding nosebleed-related plugs of tissue up their nose, in an attempt to cut off the final supply of air. 'You can't choke yourself with toilet roll.' FACT.

Mick chuckled again at the thought of a hidden camera catching his madness on tape. 'Well, when you're in an empty room you make your own amusement,' he said to his audience. The room had a fantastic acoustic quality so he started to whistle *Summertime* with a jazzy lilt. It seemed hugely appropriate but he couldn't fathom why. After a while he heard the fairly frantic shouting of what sounded like a young woman. No, two young women. So although it was unrelated to his whistling, he stopped –

the idea of having neighbours hadn't even entered his head. The room was obviously not sealed air-tight as he was still breathing.

ANY PERSONS CAUSING
DAMAGE TO THIS CELL
WILL BE PROSECUTED

Big black letters on a dirty white, edging towards cream, wall. How many words could he get out of that then? Fucking hundreds. He got to five and stopped. He couldn't be arsed. It was like this short period of time in a blank room had stripped him of inquisitiveness. For dramatic effect he decided that he would later lace the story with the fact that he sat and got hundreds of words out of it – not true, but it could've been. In reality the only mental exercise he could manage with the letters was to work out that the only missing ones from the alphabet were F, J, K, Q, V, X and Z. *That's half the fucking alphabet then.* The regulation shutter slid open and shut for a third time, the unequal gaze checked that he wasn't carving his initials into the wooden base of the bed with his fingernails. The time before, they'd checked that he hadn't smuggled in some ladders to climb up and out of that skylight that was at least twenty-five foot above him, maybe more. *That's high, that is, and I bet it's locked anyway.* Maybe some really wiry kid could ascend the north wall – in the slight alcove that housed the toilet – using the 'feet against one wall, back against the other' technique, but where would he go once he got there? Well, he could let his back and feet go and fall and maybe smash his head open on the toilet. *Fuck me, I'm bored.*

A minute – perhaps two hours – later he heard the key in the door being fiddled with for days. *Fuck, they can't unlock the door. How will they get food in*? The door swung heavily open.

'Mr McCann.'

He jumped up or rather slid up, no formal invitation required.

'Shall we get you interviewed?'

Cockshot led him to a small interview room just like you'd see on *The Bill*, where Strangelove joined them. There was a slight tension in the air that Mick thought was weird. Surely they'd done this hundreds of times.

'Right, Michael, it shouldn't take blah blah blah, something about relying on in court, blather, blather and two tapes one sealed yatter, yatter, yatter, then you state who you are.'

He managed to say his name at the appropriate moment.

'Have you?'

'Yes.'

'Did you?'

'No.'

'The SIM card?'

'Yeh, wasn't it stolen? Not sure, waffle, waffle, waffle.'

'Do you recognise any of these names?'

Mick paused slightly on the first one but only because it was the first one. 'No.'

'OK. Thank you, Mr McCann, this interview was terminated on the moon in the presence of Winnie Mandela.'

'Right we'll get you printed and blah fucking blah. . . .'

The interview finished, something was really bugging Mick. 'You know Paul Newman and Steve McQueen? And *Cool-Hand Luke* and *The Great Escape*? Who was in which?'

'Sorry? Who?'

'Paul Newman and Steve McQueen. I get them confused. Who was in which film?'

'Don't know, never heard of them.'

Fuck, how old were these women? Twelve?

'If you'd like to follow me, we'll get you photographed, DNA'd and printed.'

'If you'd like to. . . ?' 'Do you mind if. . . ?' 'Can we just. . . ?' – like there were options. Commands presented as requests, some dumb pretence that this was fucking normal, done with consent, almost civilised. This wasn't normal – *eeh, y'never know what the day'll bring* – there was no consent, this wasn't routine. . . . Well, it was, it was absofuckinglutely routine to them, but not to him. Some unacknowledged deception, the institution bearing down on the body of the accused, really fucking badly accused. Was there a sovereign hiding away somewhere in an office, pulling strings and gloating? Standard, routine, normal, habitual. It'd be an *ordinary* restraint if he didn't play ball, his arse encased in an *average* prison cell if he kicked off and said, 'I'm off home now, I've had enough.' If he chose to not take his socially defined role, his trained individualisation, in this fucking farce, if he fought and kicked, it was his freedom, not theirs, his fucking body and being, not theirs – he'd get the 'legal' kicking. The Jesus fantasy flicked through his mind for a millisecond but it was soon beaten down by reality. The threat was, 'Don't fuck with us, we are in power, we make the decisions, we can do what the fuck we like – not you, you are the absolute opposite, you are helpless, weak, just a body to be controlled, and you have no intellectual role to play in your existence at all, none whatsoever, not while we've got ya.' *Ah, the Desk Sergeant: he's not the same level of oppressor as the rest of them. Ah Lesley.* They slid a sly smile across the now buzzing desk area of the Bridewell.

Poor Les, she's just not cut out for this sort if situation, this institutional imposition, she'll kick their butts in the interview, but she won't like all the formalities, the taking of details, removal of items, the sitting in a cell – she'll hate it, it's just not her bag, it'll do her head in. He'd not been that fazed by it really, he'd faced worse than this, but she shouldn't have to go through it, he should be defending her from it. But how could he? Kick up a routine fuss and be routinely restrained by the abundance of police officers and routinely held for a few more hours, maybe days, for fuck's sake. Couldn't they hold him for up to a month? He had no real idea what all this was really about, seemed a bit heavy-handed going by the bits of information he did have. *Ninety days would've been so much better, Mr Blair.* Mr Blair whom he'd defended so many times, even now that he was the last non-affiliated Labour Party supporter left standing in the whole country.

'Mr McCann, this is blah blah blah, she'll be taking your yatter, yatter, yatter.'

'OK.'

'Right, Mr McCann, we'll start with the DNA. Is it OK if I take two swabs from just in here, the inside of your cheeks, both sides?'

'Ah, so there's a choice?' Surely his Labour government had built in some defences for the non-criminals, for the 'no convictions of any kind in over forty-three years on this Earth'-ers, for the good honest citizens, the 'not even had a speeding ticket' brigade, for you.

'Yes, Mr McCann, there is a choice. You let me take two swabs from the inside of your mouth or I, with the aid of more officers, will forcibly remove at least ten strands of hair from your head by the root.' Such dead-pan delivery, so honest, the first bit of straight talking he'd heard all day.

'Can I have a minute to think about it?' he said, smirking, and opened his mouth. The young woman twisted the medically advanced Q-tip around the inside of one cheek and then the other and placed it into its cap to avoid contamination, all very scientific. The only problem that crossed his mind was when they mixed up the records, mismanaged them, or the database got hacked, lost or corrupted then they could be fucked. But no, it's 2007, that could never happen, the mismanagement of records or samples by a government institution. . . never. *Fuck. Bring on the ID card.*

Suitably medicalised and genetically tagged, he was moved on to the fingerprinting suite. As he was obviously not capable of holding down his fingers on the glass screen and rolling them with slight pressure, she did it for him, every one, one at a fucking time – all ten, held down and rolled, and his palms. Lesley won't like this, she won't enjoy this one fucking bit. He was quite confident that when their names were cleared, all this data, all this personal info, all the marks of his body and his existence on this planet, would be kept on the biggest criminal DNA database in the whole world. Forget Iran, Russia and fucking Korea, Britain was a world leader. At last, top of a list, something to make a nation proud: Britain was a world leader in the Orwellian stakes. *Don't give a fuck. I've nothing to worry about.* But some ancient principle, some battled-for by good honest working-class northern folk liberty, had been removed, and he along with millions of soporific bastards like him had let it happen without a fucking whimper. There was something going on here that Churchill, Washington, Lincoln, or more likely Samuel Bamford or John Stuart Mill, would be ashamed of. The politician in him stepped forward: *Well, it's this sort of info that nabs murderers, rapists and thugs.*

Lesley's journey downtown was spent listening to the two women detectives chattering away like a couple of young office girls. Pathetic. A wedding, thirteen grand, clothes, make-up; the only thing that differentiated them from Sharon and Tracey was the cars discussed, they were high-powered, aggressive cars instead of Puntos and Polos, but that was just for their *Spooks* pose, they'd prefer a pink Fiesta, Lesley was sure of it. Lesley had no problem at all with Sharon and Tracey. At least they were honest, not like these buffoons, all big pose and no class.

The detectives' demeanour shifted when they entered the station, putting away their girly yattering. Lesley observed that they'd been watching too much *CSI Miami*, really into the power, the long black coats, black trousers, high-heeled black shoes for that extra height, not girly stilettos but big Cuban heels, CSI power dressing. They *would* be taken seriously; they've got a collar and they *will* be noticed. Posing around the Bridewell, striking a stance and scanning the uniform with disdain: 'Everyone, look, we're not uniform. We are C - I - D.' A Sister Sledge song skanked through Lesley's brain and made her smile as she started arranging a daft dance for them in her head to maximise the foolishness of the two women, all very Potteresque.

We are C - I - D, Yeh yeh yeh yeh-i-er
I got all my colleagues with me.

During the booking-in session Lesley looked over to see Mick at the internal desk having swabs of saliva taken from his mouth. *He does look like a dodgy get.* The thought made her smile and the reassuring presence of someone she loved, someone she trusted, made her feel a little stronger. Lesley snapped out of her protective thoughts as the woman on the front desk asked her a series of routine questions. After the first couple, Lesley entered cruise mode, only re-entering the situation as her belongings were being listed and bagged.

'Three silver rings.'

Lesley had an urge to scream, 'Are you stupid? You're not very observant for a police officer, are you? It came off my wedding finger y'stupid get. Der-er. It's a wedding ring, der-er, it's white gold, y'daft cow. I just don't like your kind of gold, you cheap, orange tart,' but subdued it to a pleasant judgemental smirk and said nothing, confident that what went into the bags would come out of the bags when they were released.

Concentration in the Bridewell was a battle for Lesley; the whole situation took on the guise of half-reality and a full and fantastic recce – she almost asked if she could have a pad to take notes. Situations and scenes played out that she'd often helped to recreate through her work and would have to create again and again. It underlined for her that her suspicions of their police adviser having been too long off the force were correct. *Why does no one ever listen to me?* She spent time taking mental notes. *Ooh, we do that wrong, that's not right.* The two that flagged up most alarmingly in her mind were perfect examples of how quickly things change and how their police adviser should either be an acting police officer or someone with the access and energy to see the little changes, the everyday evolution, but more importantly someone who would know about the big developments.

The first one they may never recreate again, but they had quite recently, and got it, under advice, so wrong: the end of the taking of the personal details – name, address, etc. In the recently aired episode of *Emmerdale* they'd got the character to sign the bottom of the form – pen and paper – but here she was getting arrested for real and what did the over-tanned woman offer her? Not a form but a small and compact electronic pad just like the ones used by couriers when getting someone to sign for a package. It'll go automatically onto the computer, no doubt. It was silly little things like this which really annoyed her. Not only was it right but it would've looked good on screen. Also it was so twenty-first century, and on a contemporary show like theirs, supposedly set in the present, it would've grounded it in the now. Another daft little thought made her smile: any other drama makers, upon seeing the electronic pad, would have gone, 'Ah, so that's how they do it nowadays,' just like she does when she's spotted properly carried-out research on TV, which was often.

As she was led to the cell, she deliberated on the second one. It made her so angry that she could spit – *the* classic televisual representation of a bad 'un getting nicked or an innocent suffering injustice. Used over and over again, the taking of the fingerprints, and they'd got it wrong, and probably would've done for another few more years were Lesley not getting arrested. How could they get something so important so wrong? It was as bad as having Charity Dingle squeezing her clothes through a mangle. As the young lady explained the process, all Lesley could think was *It's crucial that we get such basic things right, we have to be bang up to date.* It was so annoying. They'd use, as they always had, the fingers being pushed onto an ink pad and then pressed across a fingerprint form specially designed for the task. As Lesley looked at the light-box, she swore under her breath: again, the process was electronic, no ink involved, a digital image of her prints going straight onto a computer.

In her meticulous mind these were fairly glaring errors. She was fighting hard enough day in, day out to maintain the quality of the programme. Did it matter? It did to her; she was proud of her work. She was proud that on one of her sets no one would ever be seen putting a knife into an obviously unused jar of marmalade. She would never fall into the lazy *Neighbours* habit of constantly having tables full of untouched things, bread always a full loaf, virgin margarine never been touched by a knife, bottles of milk always full; that cup being drunk out of would not suddenly appear full in a close-up. She'd prided herself that, unlike in many big-budget BBC dramas, characters would not be shown in pouring rain under umbrellas and then entering a room dry – *although they might've done the internals first* – they would always have wet coat-sleeves, wet shoes, perhaps a slight dampening on the back of the coat.

She knew it was entertainment, not art, but whatever anyone said, it was still one of the top three rated shows on TV, and it being accurate and believable was one of the factors that kept it at the top. The audience included smart people, people who would spot inconsistencies, ridiculous plots or wobbling sets, there was a quality to *Emmerdale* that was certainly missing from *EastEnders*, and she was determined to keep it that way – well, in her input anyway.

Her questioning had only been remarkable as Lesley saw the gradual realisation in Cockshot and Strangelove that she was an intelligent, articulate and powerful woman, not the screaming harpy that they'd first encountered. At least after the questioning they seemed to have recognised that Lesley had an aversion to the cells. Rather than place her back in the cells, as they had with Mick, Cockshot joined her on a bench near the front desk. They chatted about *Emmerdale*, the only thing they had in common, Cockshot telling Lesley about her role as a police extra on the show. Lesley knew she'd recognised her from somewhere. Strangelove joined them for a moment and entered the conversation, saying that she wouldn't mind doing some of the extra work herself; Lesley took great pleasure in pointing out, while watching Cockshot's face all the way, that only average, unremarkable-looking people were suitable for extra work, tall or attractive people weren't allowed. 'Don't want any competition for the cast, you understand.' The insult hit home beautifully, especially when Lesley pointed it out again by saying, 'Oh God, that sounded awful, I don't mean that. Well. . . .'

Strangelove went off with a spring in her step.

Don't worry, I'll have you as well, lady, you can count on that.

Cockshot was being all nicey-nicey. Lesley thought that it had finally hit her that they'd just traumatised the family of and arrested two completely innocent people. More interestingly, Lesley saw that the penny was just beginning to drop. Not only were they innocent but they were smart, credible and determined people, from a class just beyond hers. Well, she definitely was anyway. Lesley decided to give the coin a further little shove.

'Yeh, it's not just the First Aid that I do at work, I'm also a union rep.'

'Oh are you? That must be interesting. We don't really have a union.'

She watched Cockshot shrivel. It was pathetic. She was a union rep, therefore not stupid, therefore not as easy to take advantage of. Pathetic and unjust. Lesley imagined how they'd treat the slightly stupid and the young. Their world was dominated by power, by subjugation, by race, by class, by first impressions, by position and by scare tactics. She could see Cockshot's brain scrambling to find context, to find perspective. Cockshot's brain was reflecting on the fact that it'd been a very dubious collar. The last thing they needed were people with the attitude and in a position to highlight that, to take advantage of their questionable behaviour.

Lesley had enjoyed very much showing them a different side of herself; she took pleasure as the person they thought they were dealing with transformed into a whole new beast. Their scare tactics – Lesley reflected on Mick's attitude with a new perspective. She was almost feeling pride towards him. *Steady on girl, get a grip, he did it by chance.* Not only was he sharp as sharpened shit – which must be a worry – but he also wasn't fazed, not afraid of them. It clearly wasn't just bravado but an absolute confidence that they were innocent and that the police had to be a bit stupid. He'd told them that to their faces. He'd shown no deference and no respect beyond what he would show to the postman. It was only through seeing how the police worked that Lesley got an insight into how disconcerting Mick's calmness and straight talking must have been for them, although, being almost intelligent women, they must realise that it is her that they should be truly afraid of.

Digital stalking in Leeds, Yorkshire, England

9

While in the cells, and now on the way home from the station, Mick drifted off into some half-understood Michel Foucault and the way that society classifies and uses these classifications, of how power structures take out their will, their power, their discipline on the body of the individual. *Was that lad fucking psychic?* He kept interrupting it to jab questions and half-pleasantries at the two policewomen. There was so much to go at, Mick was scrambling around his very personal relationship with the dead Frenchman. There was some quarter-memory buried deep that he was trying to dig out that he knew was really interesting in all this. For some reason – he couldn't remember exactly why but had an idea of the area – fifteen to twenty years earlier he'd decided that Foucault had bottled it, but in the intervening period his ideas just kept resurfacing and nattering away at Mick. He cleared his brain of the search, confident that when he did this, the more interesting theft of Michel's ideas would come forward.

'So I bet y'shift patterns play havoc with y'body clock.'

The processing continued while Mick tried to ignore both it and Cockshot's response to his shift question. The subconscious combinations of links being pulled out and discarded. It'd first struck him in the cells – or was it during his classification, or perhaps when they were initially arrested? Whenever he sees people of authority, Foucault seems to be hanging around, up to no good. That was it: the cell and something about his work on prisons, about cell arrangements, about the vantage points of some penal systems. Mick had always linked it to the corner sentry-points in old war films. He knew that that wasn't Foucault's chosen vantage point but it was always Mick's, maybe because the threat was more pronounced, the big machine gun always visible. There it is, the Panopticon, the idea of one person representing the power structure being placed to be able to view the cells of many. The one or few controlling the many and the many never quite being sure when they are being surveyed. Not really relevant to this situation but his brain was gnawing away at a hidden idea and it was as frustrating as fuck; Foucault was always one for the process, for the structures which, probably because he didn't really get it, annoyed Mick.

That's it, there it is, here we go, there's the link: it was kind of a combination of all the things, the arrest, the classification and the cell. *Fantastic*, thought Mick, *I can bastardise it, write it in a book and claim it as my own.* Society was, with a 'new technology', refining and developing the ideas and mechanisms that Foucault had noted and was bringing them into the twenty-first century. The fucking data, the fucking storage of the data, the industrialisation – nay, the computerisation – of the control mechanisms. Just as Foucault's prisons had, say, fifty people being stored in such a way that one person could keep an eye on them, so modern society was entering people onto big databases – exactly as Mick and Lesley's bodies had just been processed. So thousands of people, maybe millions, could be watched, monitored and to some extent controlled by a very few geeks and operators with computers and databases. A classic modern Panopticon, with the unequal gaze: you can never quite be certain if the system is looking at you – well, not until it exerts its power. The expected reaction of the individual stretching from wariness to out-and-out paranoia and an inclination to stay in the line of the hegemon.

He chewed on a more mundane example but one still backed by the law, by society; how many times had the TV-licence people been to their door thinking they'd nailed a villain, and just because they were incapable of noting that in the real world theirs was the only house on the street? 'It doesn't matter that your records say that there's a number five and a seven and a two and a four. There isn't; there's just the one house and this is it, and here is our licence, and there's no point in looking at me like I'm lying to you. Go and check. I can't hide six houses.'

He spent thirty seconds trying to decide if he could think of any adverts more threatening than the TV-licence ads. The visit of the licence inspectors was always preceded by the reflex aggressive letters with threats of legal punishments, financial and perhaps even custodial. Here was the process, the control mechanism, trying to be efficient in an attempt to monitor and control vast numbers of people with the minimum wastage. Upon calling the supplied number – and in the process, entering freely into the system – the accused and monitored were carrying out an advanced, labour-saving function of the structure in monitoring

74

themselves. Being told that the reason that there were three or four non-existent houses on the lane was that the Post Office records showed there were, the accused were then expected, by the institution, to carry out the maintenance of the process by contacting and correcting the Post Office.

'No way, do it yourself.'

'Well, Mrs McCann, if you don't, you're going to have this problem year after year.'

'Fine. I'll just ignore you.'

'But then you'll have to go through this every year.'

'No I won't, I'll have a licence, so you can waste as much of your time and energy as you like, send your inspectors, I don't care.'

It struck Mick that this was a step further and a sign of the twenty-first century, of a 'new technology', the body of the individual monitoring itself under the scrutiny of the beast. Foucault would have loved that, the individual, under threat, being expected to monitor themselves as well as ensuring that the monitoring was correct. *Ah, bollocks. Perhaps the knob would've just raised his eyebrows sarcastically.* Mick had an inkling that this was already built into Foucault's theory – almost central, *yeh, but not in such a concrete and modern way, you elusive twat.* The Frenchman frustrated the fuck out of Mick, always had and always would. So the dance with the TV-licence people became an annual sport, and once Mick and Lesley had got pissed off with it they'd simply explain to the TV licence inspector that the lane carried on just the other side of the flats four hundred yards away but it was really hard to find it if you didn't know it. Didn't Michel say summat about there always being a likely and unpredictable opposite reaction to any power? *Thank fuck for the delinquent's ey Foucault?*

Mick shook all the theoretical bollocks out of his hot head and tried to focus on their predicament. Perhaps a geek's mistake or an institutional lack, or the inability to change a record on the DNA database, may have more worrying results. *Not only does Britain have the biggest citizen DNA database in the world,* he thought – slipping back into irrelevance – *but just look at any CCTV-littered high street in the country. Britain truly is the surveillance capital of the world.*

On this journey home from the station Cockshot and Strangelove were chatting away to Lesley and Mick like new best friends. Mick and Lesley were reciprocating it to a certain extent due to a combination of factors: an injection of nicotine after going cold turkey, in Mick's case for four hours – he could've got to Greece, f'fuck's sake – the relief of being out of that place and the complete shift in tone from formal to informal. Probably the most telling factor in the combined lift of spirits was that until leaving the station, all they'd seen of the day was the mug and half-light of an early November morning. Now, around midday, the world was bright and crisp. Mick couldn't help fishing, and now, with the Foucault sorted, was trying to understand the situation and get his head around how they could've been arrested and be out on bail due to a five-year-old SIM card.

'So surely you can just put a trace on a SIM card – work out when and where it was used, or y'know, record the voice, that kind of thing.'

Cockshot, possibly carried away in the flowing truce and clear sky, was surprisingly candid.

'No, not necessarily, it's not that straightforward with mobiles. Land-lines are different, they're easy, we can do lots with them.'

Lesley threw Mick a knowing look. Hadn't she mentioned to Mick a couple of times that the house phone was behaving strangely? She'd put it down to switching to a wireless connection so that Callum could play X-Box live and they could have different computers online at the same time, but Lesley's look contained a whole new idea.

Ahhh, she did mention that the she thought the phone was behaving strangely. She thinks it's tapped. Off Mick sank into more theoretical bullshit, his head barely keeping above the stench, it was just too interesting, too enticing. The systematic violence where the perception is that no one is responsible, but someone or some group of people always is. Violence? Is it violent to invade someone's private space by listening in to their private conversations without their knowledge? It is certainly some kind of violation. Is it violent to forcibly remove someone from their house first thing in the morning, to search the house around the young children in shock, to remove items, to throw them in a cell, to forcibly take their DNA, their photos and their fingerprints? OK, so there was only the slightest physical violence involved but the clear understanding was that all 'reasonable' force would be used should they not passively have the drama played out upon their bodies, should the delinquents not come quietly, should they not give up their possessions and have their personal physical markers isolated and placed on a criminal database. There was certainly psychological violence; there has to be to fully objectify the accused. They were objects, not people, the whole family being passed through the system as a chunk of data, a series of questions, a sequence of objectifying impositions, a gaggle of physical intrusions, a corruption of classifications. And one big underlined reminder that in twenty-first-century Leeds, Yorkshire, England, they, the whole family, were a collection of powerless fops, but without the fine clothes. The power of the police was final, engrained in the dominant discourse, the techniques of power embedded and safe.

*

After dropping them off, Strangelove indicated left, reflecting on the fact that – as planned – she'd just executed the politest arrest and interview in modern policing history – well, at least on their part anyway. That posh lass had a right gob on her and he was just weird. She couldn't fathom him at all. After the initial bluster and aggressive use of his moisturiser, he just fell in like he'd been through it a thousand times, and yet he had no record at all, not a bean. Something's not right there. Although there was no match for his prints on the database, so he hadn't been arrested before. Perhaps if it'd been him that had got gobby, they may have been able to get a bit more strong-arm, apply a bit of pressure, but that would have defeated the object. They had to just get in, get it done, no mess, but she could almost hear them whimpering and whinging from the top of the road. Ninety per cent of the general public have no idea, not a clue, about the real world that her and her colleagues have to deal with day in day out.

Flicking back into the here and now, she leant her head in the direction of Cockshot while still facing the windscreen. 'You know what's worrying me? That while we get bogged down in this sort of nonsense, we miss something small in the Matthews case that turns out to be big. That we end up with a young girl's body when we could've saved her.'

'She'll turn up, we know that. The family's at the heart of it and whatever we think of them, she's not going to have her own daughter killed.'

'Yeh, unlikely, but you never know. They're not that smart, and if they feel cornered, they might get desperate and do something stupid. We've seen it before.'

'Well, you never know, but all we can do is get on with it and hopefully without these stupid distractions.'

Strangelove had a nagging, something not right, something missed. 'What did you think of him?'

'Who? The brother? The boyfriend? The uncle?'

'Not the Dewsbury lot. McCann. What did you think of him?'

'Seemed alright, quite straightforward. Bet he's a laugh in different circumstances.'

'Didn't you think he was. . .'

'What?'

'I don't know. . . not quite right?'

'How do you mean?'

Strangelove wished she knew; she just couldn't quite nail it. 'So nothing struck you? You had no doubts?'

'Well, I don't know, we'll probably see, but nothing stood out.'

'But what did your gut say?'

'Mainly that it wished I'd had breakfast.' Strangelove growled soft frustration. 'Sorry. No, nothing.'

*

Over the next few days Lesley and Mick became convinced that the land-line was tapped. They weren't sure if it was all too *Spooks* but there was certainly an alarming amount of unusual clicks on the line that both felt sure were not standard. Halfway through a conversation the phone would simply give an engaged tone or cut off. Sometimes, a couple of presses of the big button and you would be reconnected, others not, and on redialling, neither parties had done anything to cause it. They both noted that it seemed to happen when they were discussing the details of the case. Paranoia? Possibly, but, they thought, with grounds. With this development, both found themselves trying to be careful on the land-line not to discuss their theories too much. With the wireless, and a deal to get free calls to any land-line, came a need to use one phone for calling out while incoming calls were received on a separate handset. The old phone was easy to remember, it was big and old – made sometime at the beginning of the twenty-first century – but the new handset for incoming calls was small, felt just like an old mobile, and as they didn't make the call or dial a number, it was easy to forget on that handset and speculate for fun. Usually, when they realised what they were doing, they couldn't resist calling the police a set of cunts.

They mulled over the chances of their phone being tapped. Surely after all these years they, the authorities, would be good at it and wouldn't allow all the clicks, the engaged tones or the phone suddenly going dead halfway through a conversation. But Lesley and Mick didn't fully understand the technology. The line to the house was certainly old analogue technology that the spies should be well used to – or was it? Within the house it split off to two phones, an X-box live and any number of online home computers. Did this relatively new technological development confuse the slow police? Could it simply be that the spies were happy with the idea of Mick and Lesley knowing that their phone was tapped? Crank up the pressure, underline the threat? They knew that people at the periphery of society – Foucault's prescribed delinquents – dealing drugs or stolen goods were careful of using their land-line. Isn't that common knowledge? And if dealers didn't know of people getting nabbed due to sloppy land-line etiquette they wouldn't worry about it.

Knowing next to nothing, they speculated for fun. How many phone-taps or bugs are there throughout the UK? How many in the West Yorkshire area? Are the phone-taps simply electronically swept for keywords or in certain situations do the people listen in live, or to tapes of the calls? Hadn't there recently been a debate about using phone-tap evidence in court? How easy is it for the police to tap a phone? They guessed that there would shit-loads more bugs planted than your average person would guess at, but how common is it? Do they have to get permission and justify it?

It'd been very easy for the police to get a seemingly nonsensical arrest and search warrant with one, at a push two, pieces of extremely poor and easily contradicted evidence.

Bollocks. Mick sensed his relationship with that fucking Frenchman getting unhealthy – he was even considering trying to track down a book. But it was textbook: the Panopticon, the unequal gaze – never mind the 'new technology' being employed by the social mechanism to control or shape the individual – the possibility of audio 'observation', a constant stalker in their house, left them like nervous antelopes ready to scat at the slightest movement or sound. Was the possibility adapting their behaviour, making them monitor themselves? They both instinctively fought the role of the docile body but the only way they could was to verbally disrespect the police and work through the details of the case, picking holes and highlighting inconsistencies. He had a quick sweep of the house but it was a big house and time and energy were limited. How small are these things? He felt stupid doing it, like acknowledging a symptom of paranoia, and wasn't it more likely to be a phone-tap? He'd do a proper search later.

This was all outside Lesley's experience, she wasn't used to dealing with the police, and it felt like a sentence. The fact that she was bailed and under suspicion, that fact that she'd been arrested, the fact that her honesty was in question was a sentence. She was guilty until proven innocent and going by the enquiries so far they'd have to prove their innocence themselves. The police clearly had no interest in finding out the truth, just in convicting whoever was in front of them, and unfortunately that was her and Mick. Mick had been so blasé about it initially, had treated it like a bit of a yarn, one of the first things he seemed to do was set up a thread on One Mick Jones[1] – Cancel Old Sim Cards. He thought it was a complete joke – the police were idiots – and that their innocence was easily proved. Lesley wasn't so sure. The police incompetence did seem fairly comprehensive but there must be more, there had to be more that the police weren't sharing with them. It wasn't until Mick saw Lesley sobbing day after day, after

---

[1] www.onemickjones.com/forum/viewtopic.php?id=1916&p=1

80

he saw her visit her doctor, not until the distress of the kids had filtered through to his brain, not until people on OMJ started warning him that perhaps this was more serious than he thought, that Mick started to get angry and show even the slightest amount of concern.

The children's distress manifested itself verbally in a few ways, Callum trying to subtly find out what would happen if both his parents went to prison. Who would look after him and his brothers? Where would they stay? Would Ezra be in charge? If his mum and dad couldn't work due to being in prison, how would the bills and mortgage get paid? Billy was less inquisitive. The very first thing he said to his dad on being picked up from school on the afternoon of the arrest was, 'I didn't like your friends this morning.' Mick tried to talk to him about it but Billy became immediately distressed at Mick's first word and cried hysterically, only saying, 'No, no, no, shush, Daddy, I don't want to talk about it. . . . No, Daddy, don't talk about it.' His small voice building into a shout that blocked out the words, that blocked out the thought, that blocked out the dread. As Mick initially tried to pursue it – just to calm his son, not discuss any detail – Billy simply became so upset that he couldn't hear him anyway, just fight for breath. Mick quickly dropped it, feeling a deep-sitting anger fuelled by a craving for revenge. *You don't fucking fuck with my kids' heads.*

Digital stalking in Leeds, Yorkshire, England

10

Whatever the situation, whoever was making the calls, whyever they were arrested, whoever was implicated in the decision to arrest them, Mick and Lesley still thought that perhaps they should help sort it out. Lesley'd had a frustrating conversation with IT about the emails and the internal message board. The internal message board wasn't backed up and as each post reached 30 days of age it was automatically scrubbed. The IT bloke seemed to show absolutely no interest in checking her backed-up emails at all, the dumb shit didn't seem to understand the situation or simply wasn't interested. Lesley phoned Strangelove to pass on these bits of information and to suggest that she contacted someone in human resources and perhaps her line manager to get IT moving. Strangelove agreed and requested that she give her the name and number of the person in human resources.

Lesley came off the phone frustrated again. She'd tried to point out to Strangelove that there were a couple of periods of time that they were out of the country but Strangelove seemed to just override the fact and move on to the details of human resources. Lesley swore to herself as yet another job to do remained undone. She resolved to dig out the dates and phone again to press the point. She called Helen Wallis at human resources and explained the situation, which was never easy to do – too much detail, too much incredulity. Helen was very understanding and agreed to deal with the police, get IT to act and inform Lesley's line manager of the situation.

Later that evening Mick entered the kitchen for a fag just after bathing Billy, as he did every bath night. Lesley was on the house phone, the chunky one.

'Fucking hell, you are kidding? Yeh, Charlotte, the TV presenter? Are you sure? Fucking hell that makes me angry. . . Yeh. . . Yes, but it looks like we got done just because she goes out with him. Why else would they arrest us?'

Mick was willing Lesley to get off the phone as she kept throwing him 'have I got something to tell you' looks, but she carried on the conversation, going round and round the same information in disbelief, searching for the contradiction that didn't exist. By the time she came off the phone, Mick could guess at the news but he was only partially right.

'Fucking hell, you are not going to believe this.'

'What?'

'Well, did you recognise any of the names that the police asked us about?'

'No, but I paused over the first name only because I thought I should.'

'You mean Charlotte Tompkins?'

'Yes.'

'Ah, so they asked us the same names and in the same order.'

'Yeh, so what?'

'Oh nothing,' Lesley murmured looking distracted, 'anyway it just so happens that she is married to the head of West Yorkshire Police.'

'WHAAAAT?'

'Yes, isn't that interesting? Fuck.'

'Fuuuckiiiing 'ell, are you sure?'

'Yes the Chief Constable of West Yorkshire Police.'

'You're absolutely positive?'

'Well yeh, we think so, but she's going to check with Becky when she gets home. Becky knows her and will know for sure.'

An exquisite mixture of fear and excitement set in, like leaning over a cliff having forgotten your hang-glider.

Lesley chewing her lip, 'Fuck that puts a whole new perspective on it, doesn't it?'

'When can we find out for sure?'

'She's going to ask her when she gets home.'

They were dancing around their own little personal Watergate moment. Mick slowed the pace of the tune: 'Nah, wait a minute, I'm sure he wouldn't get involved.'

'He's the Chief Constable and his girlfriend is getting malicious calls. He's seeing the effects first hand. I bet he would.'

'No, surely not, that is so unprofessional. But I must admit I'm struggling to work out why they'd arrest us without appearing to've done any work, there is so much simple checking out that they could've done that would've removed us from the enquiry.'

'I know. I'll tell you how it sounds to me. They've had it on a back burner not fully realising who's involved and she's had another dodgy call. She's freaked out or maybe they've, top policeman and presenter, had a bit of a row about it and he's phoned CID up, shouted at them and told them to get their finger out and arrest whoever the SIM card is registered to.'

'But surely they'd just explain the situation and tell him that we weren't likely to have—'

Having already been through this thought process, Lesley butts in, 'Not if he's in a rage and not listening. It'd be an order. He's the Chief Constable. Another thing that shows that they didn't plan it was the kids.'

'What?'

'They knew we had kids and for them to turn up at a family home and make no provision for them is really bad. If it'd have been properly planned they'd have brought social workers for them.'

Not even considering the possibility that the police could have simply taken the kids into custody with them, they continued to speculate.

'Yeh s'pose. Aye, imagine if we'd been hardened crims, we'd have just laughed at them, we'd have said, "Well we can't leave the kids in the house on their own, can we, officer? It's your fuck-up, you'll just have to work out which one of us you want to arrest the most and leave the other with the kids," wouldn't we?'

Lesley grabbing the baton, 'Exactly. This arrest was completely unplanned. They knew we've got kids and it must be standard procedure to take a social worker. I bet it was one of those situations where each thought the other had sorted it. I'm telling you, he just phoned them and shouted, "Arrest them now." No thought, no looking at the case, no planning.'

The anger was starting to swell up and race around Mick's chest. 'Bastard. So we get arrested the kids are scared shitless just because he's had a hissy fit?'

'It looks like it to me. Did you notice anything about the police on Wednesday?'

'What d'y'mean?'

'What were they like when they were arresting us and searching the house?'

'Well, I don't know about the search, I wasn't there, but they were alright when they were arresting us – considering.'

'Do you think they were happy doing it?'

'Well, no, not really. If anything, they seemed slightly embarrassed.'

'Exactly. Like they didn't want to be doing it, like it wasn't their choice?'

'Fuck, you're right.'

'Like someone had told them to do it. The search was a farce. And Mick, you keep saying that you don't understand why they didn't look us in the eye when they first arrived and call the phone just to watch for the reaction. Look for the "fuck, did I turn it off?" or "I don't give a fuck, phone it, see if I care" split-second reaction.' Lesley leant forward and lit a cigarette, noticing the one she already had smouldering in the ashtray she docked it immediately. 'That's why; that's why they didn't call the phone or search the house properly. They were just going through the motions, they knew very well we didn't have the phone and they knew that we weren't making dodgy calls to anyone. But their boss phoned them up ranting and they had to come and arrest us because he told them to.'

'Yeh, I mean when they first came round all I was saying was, "Go away and do your job, SIM cards must be simple to trace and to locate the calls." Knowing they were monitoring that SIM card and still making nasty calls with it would be like walking into a police station shouting "Does anyone want to buy some stolen trainers?" while swinging them around above your head. They know we're not stupid, so even if we were making the calls we'd have stopped or switched SIMs.'

Hot-heads, chain smoking with small fireworks exploding behind their eyes, the two of them were trying to take in the magnitude of what they had just found out. They were certainly shook up but how paranoid were they? Just how relevant was it? Were they over-reacting? Mick lit another touch paper.

'Fuck. Someone would have to sign the arrest and search warrants. Someone higher would have to look at the case before they could do that. And if *we* can see what a pile of shite it is and pick holes in it, so would anyone looking at it, unless of course it's sanctioned by the big boss, then no one would question it.'

'Yeh, someone who'd get a phone tapped or a bug placed as easily as tying his shoe lace.'

'How powerful do you think he is?' Mick's face visibly tightening as he posed the question.

'Well, I'd have thought pretty powerful.'

'Fuck, I wonder if they are monitoring One Mick Jones – I've put up that thread all about it.'

'We need to know, Mick, we really need to know, because if someone so high up is involved we need to be very careful. It really feels like they could turn up at any time to arrest us again.'

'I know, and if they think we know he's involved, i.e. if they are tapping the phone, they really could turn up at any time.'

'We need to tell people, cover our backs, just in case we are arrested again and suddenly disappear.'

'Yeh, but not over the land-line.'

Mick had a quick chat with his older brother via his mobile, just to make sure he had a clear perspective. Taking his phone with him, he went straight to his computer, copied the One Mick Jones thread and pasted it into an email, explaining that they'd just found out that the Chief Constable of West Yorkshire Police was involved in the complex situation outlined below, and fired off a bunch of emails. *You see, Marx was right about communication empowering the proletariat,* he thought as he pressed send.

'So when will we find out? For sure like?'

'Well when Becky gets home she's going to ask her and she'll phone us back.'

'Fuck that, why don't I just phone her? What d'y' think, shall I phone her now?'

'If you like.'

Mick picked up his mobile, his pay as you go was taking a right hammering with all the not using the land-line bollocks.

'Hi yeh it's Mick... yeh good thanks. Just a quickie, you know that we were arrested on Wednesday? Yeh, I think Lesley has told Jo about it so she can tell you and we'll fill in all the gory detail when you next come round... Oh yeh, but can I just ask you a quick question? Y'know Charlotte Tompkins is she married to the

Chief Inspector of. . . riiiight. . . yeh OK, but you're not sure. . . but they're definitely divorced?. . . Oh has he? But you're not positive, no? Yeh I see. . . yeh if you could we kinda need to know.'

Mick ran through the barest bones of the story and then came off the phone.

'She was married to him but they're now divorced and he's left the force, set up a surveillance company, although she might be going out with a different top policeman, Becky is seeing her soon and is going to check for us.'

Lesley clinging on to the conspiracy theory, 'Yeh but he'll still have connections, will still be able to pull a few strings.'

'Yeh possibly but I got the impression that the divorce was a bit messy, she didn't say like but I don't think they're the best o' friends.'

The two of them continued speculating, the revelation adding a new excitement and intensity to their conversation, the situation bringing them closer together.

To check the conspiracy theory Mick started to search for crime stats online; his thinking being that the amount of malicious phone calls in the West Yorkshire area must be huge and if the police treated these routinely in the way that Mick and Lesley had experienced then the corresponding amount of arrests would also be huge. Flicking through the pages on the Home Office website it became quickly obvious that it held absolutely no detail, just very generalised catch all figures. 'What a surprise, open Government my arse,' he spat at the computer, 'easiest thing in the world to make these figures detailed and searchable and yet they're not. They tell us they are but they're not . . . cunts.' With that he noted down the number for the use of people who actually want figures on crime rather than to blankly stare at pages of PR motivated bullshit and retired to the kitchen for a cigarette and a rant.

Through to a pleasant young man who listened to Mick's enquiry and then told him to call one of his colleagues who then listened to Mick's enquiry and then asked him to put it in an email. 'Cunts, another hoop to jump through ergo less information shared, it's a fucking database and should be easily interrogated. I could set it up in a fucking morning.' He explained to the kitchen table. Moving over to the ash tray he added, 'and another thing, how many people are employed in this country to send bullshit over complicated emails to each other when picking up the phone would be quicker and more effective? In turn the recipient has to respond, the initial sender reply to the response and so the justification circle continues and shitloads of extra bullshit positions are created, cunts. I wouldn't mind but they impose it on us in the real fucking world with actual things to do.'

Mick had gone, 'Dear Timothy, it has come to my attention that there appears to be an issue in third floor utilities that requires urgent consideration. Our colleagues roles are stressful enough and it is incumbent upon us to facilitate a clean, safe and well equipped environment within which employees can explore their down time activities to the full. If this issue is not focussed upon I fear that departmental moral may sink further.

On visiting the communal dispensary area this morning (9.30am) it emerged that the coffee jar is not full, indeed the level of the coffee in the jar has dipped well below the top end marker of the label. It may even be possible that capacity filled is below half! I do not need to spell out to you that should this situation continue unaddressed it may transpire that the jar ceases to fulfil its initial brief. Please could you reiterate my concerns – without recourse to your cut and paste or forwarding options – to Colin and Lisa at your soonest.....Bollocks, I don't want to get dragged into the email economy, I haven't got time, I don't get paid for it, I'm not part of that job creation scheme.'

Why do they do it? The only reason Mick could see was to have a record of everything they've ever done, to be able to spend the odd hour tracking down that crucial email and the rest of the time looking busy. *Ooh now then,* he thought, *the Panopticon, the workplace and individualisation, the nervous and paranoid filling the slots and covering arses should their behaviour be questioned. The fear of easy monitoring, of their role and performance being questioned – oh please Foucault, fuck off I've got stuff to do and in this particular situation it's useful.* Mick over powered the babbling Frenchman and opened an email.

From: mick mccann
To: justice.statsapollo@homeoffice.gsi.gov.uk
Sent: Friday, Dec 07, 2007 3:23 PM
Subject: Malicious Calls Statistics

Dear Sir/Madam,

I am looking for the most recent statistics regarding the offence of making malicious phone calls - improper use of telecommunication networks.

I would like to know national statistics and, if possible, those for West Yorkshire over the same period:

1) How many reports of malicious calls were made?

2) How many arrests were made for the offence of making malicious calls?

3) How many prosecutions/convictions happened?

Thanks very much for your help,
Mick McCann

11

For the next couple of weeks Lesley worked too hard and under too much pressure. The first couple of days after the arrest she'd returned home from work early unable to function, some smart-arsed comment or plain ignorance that she would normally rebuff being the last bit of confusion that her head could hold. She hated bursting into tears at work, but she was bursting into tears everywhere at the moment, people would just have to live with it. Possibly as a consequence of her heightened emotional state, news of her position appeared to have travelled quite quickly amongst the *Emmerdale* staff. Lesley wasn't trying to conceal it anyway, and she was buoyed by the amount of support she was receiving. Just that morning Lucy, who played Chastity Dingle, had sat and listened, almost counselling Lesley, and offered, if it ever went that far, to go to court with Lesley as a character witness. They'd laughed as Lesley asked if she'd do it in character. As Lesley walked away Lucy mumbled under her breath, just loud enough for Lesley to hear it, 'Crim.'

'Y'bitch,' Lesley moved away smiling. She loved the fact that her friends were so certain of her innocence that they felt comfortable taking the piss, and also knew her well enough to be able to gauge when and where it was appropriate.

Lesley was really struggling without her mobile, the police having confiscated it. She'd borrowed Cal's – he didn't really need it anyway – but it was hugely complicating her life just at the time when she needed as few complications as possible. She gradually realised just what a lifeline her mobile was. It contained almost all her contacts and without it she had to scramble around for numbers, checking sheets at work that didn't usually contain them or contained old numbers, having to phone people who she did have a contact for who may have the number that she required. At first she avoided entering the numbers onto Cal's phone. Being aware that it was his phone, she didn't want to clutter it up, but she soon regretted it as she'd have to re-find a number for the third time, and started to programme them onto the SIM, or was it his phone? She told herself that when she had hers returned, for the sake of Cal and the privacy of the people she needed to contact, she would remove them all. She'd have to remind herself to check the numbers against her SIM/phone as some numbers had been changed or were new and would need copying across.

Among the many questions that circled in Lesley's thoughts one of the most puzzling was: why had the police told her to cancel the SIM card after the arrest? Why do that? Why hadn't they told her to do it six months ago when they first came around, or at any point after they realised that the malicious calls were still being made? That could have easily concluded their part in the enquiry, no fuss, no mess, the calls being stopped; but now after the arrest, *after* all the trauma they ask her to cancel it. Now that the SIM card was cancelled, they had less chance of tracking it and catching whoever was making the nasty calls. If they already *had* tracked it, why make the arrest? It just made no sense. Why the sudden rush to stop the calls now? They must have been aware that they could have stopped the calls six months ago – or at least that SIM card's involvement – by telling her to cancel it. They obviously either didn't want it cancelling or didn't think it was that important. So what was different now to then? Why the sudden, bogus flurry of activity? There were two possibilities and the least paranoid one – on their part – was that there had been a sudden and scary development in the case. Maybe the bloke was physically stalking one of the victims or had tried to abduct them. But then if the police thought that she and Mick were involved in that, their search would have been thorough and not apologetic. Unless of course it was simply a way of planting a bug. Could they do that? And who would rubber-stamp it? Surely it would have to be the Chief Constable.

The only thing that made any sense to her was that CID, with no doubt a large work-load, had been doing very little work on the case – that much was obvious – and that someone had told them in no uncertain terms to stop the calls. But again why not simply phone her and tell her to cancel the SIM rather than come and arrest her and Mick? They were obviously embarrassed to be making the arrest, they didn't properly search the house to find the guilty phone and they didn't try to call it, which was the obvious thing to do. They knew it wasn't there, so if they knew it wasn't there, why go through the pretence of searching the house – it was doing it around her kids that really got to Lesley, the abuse of the safe family home – and why arrest them? Someone must have got to them, someone must have ordered them to do it. So how could this top guy, who everyone including Mick was convinced wasn't involved, not be involved? It didn't make any sense.

Another frustration was that Orange wouldn't allow Lesley to cancel any of the numerous old SIM cards in her name. She explained to them that the only ones she needed active were two, her own and her son's, and she could supply them with both numbers. But even though she phoned them on her mobile, supplied them with the security information they needed to prove who she was, her password, date of birth, postcode, a previous address and postcode and her debit-card details, they said they couldn't cancel any SIM cards in her name unless she knew the numbers. 'It was five years ago for God's sake, I've proved who I am. Have you any doubt that I am Miss Lesley Jackson? . . . No? Good. Do you have on your records my previous numbers and old SIM cards? . . . You have? Good. So I want to cancel them. . . . But you have the numbers. . . . No, I no longer have the numbers or I don't have them to hand.' Frustration rising, Lesley kept pushing it. 'Look what are the numbers? . . . They are my numbers and you know that I am me; could you please tell me my numbers? . . . This is ridiculous. It's very important, it involves the police. . . . Why not? I just want to cancel all but two records, all but two SIM cards. . . . OK, I'll go and find them then, but this really is a lot of hassle for no reason.'

She and Mick rummaged through the house looking for the numbers, something once so fundamental as her phone number now lost, now a meaningless stream of digits. Why would she keep it? Well, the numbers should be irrelevant but now they are not, now they are important. Swearing at herself, *I'm usually so good at keeping records*, she phoned her mother and friends. No one who she could get through to had a copy of her old number. 'No, they won't tell me what they are. . . . I know. I thought it was my information but they won't give me any of the numbers registered in my name. . . . Don't know. Maybe if the SIMs are still being used they don't want them cancelling, they'd lose money. . . . Yeh, I suppose if it's thirty SIMs per day it'd soon add up. . . . I know.

Do they belong to me or not? The provider doesn't seem sure but the police are.'

After much pulling out of hair there was only one option left: she got Mick to call Strangelove to get the rogue number and finally managed to cancel the SIM card. While on the phone to Strangelove, Mick offered that either he or Lesley would be quite happy to have their taped interview played to the victims of the calls. If that wasn't possible he'd supply a tape of himself speaking or leave a message on a mobile or land-line answer phone to play to any of the women.

The thing Lesley really struggled with the first day at work after the arrest, the Thursday, was seeing the collection of fuck-wit police officers working as extras and taking a break in *her* canteen. A couple of them she recognised from the previous morning. One of them, the man, had spotted her, he was obviously trying to keep an eye out for her. He looked at her like they shared a secret, like he held the power, like she was a piece of shit, where in fact *he* was the insignificant little shit. The thing that really got to her was that within that look was contained the threat that men in power have bullied women with since the dawn of time. She gradually realised that her police adviser – the one who'd been too long off the force – knew all about it. Not only was he avoiding her eyes, he was avoiding contact. Well, at least he looks embarrassed and perhaps even slightly ashamed.

Lesley was so disappointed with herself. All the things she should have said, her preferred demeanour, were pointless now but circled the carcass of the situation, getting higher on the warm air of regret. The wanker, the insignificant little man, was now full of self-worth of self-importance. But how was she supposed to know? It just happened so quickly, so unexpectedly, how was she to know that he would be at the other side of that door? He'd obviously seen her coming, he was killing time, but she was too busy thinking about work to be fully concentrating on her surroundings. His bullying face filled her head; she felt like she'd missed the last bus, his eyes all judgemental, condemnatory and threatening. 'Go on then, love,' as he held the door open for her. Why hadn't she thought to say 'Don't call me "love"'? Why had she done exactly what he'd told her to do and gone through the door? She should have said, 'No, you first.' But the thing that really wound her up was the look of satisfaction as he saw her flap, as he witnessed her discomfort; he knew he'd intimidated her again. *But what he doesn't know, what he doesn't fucking know, is that I'm not scared of him, I'm not scared of any of them, I'm innocent and **you** are guilty, all of you, it's you who should be afraid, not me.* Lesley sat at her desk and sobbed. 'I shouldn't have to fucking take this.'

This policing by fear thing is scary, she thought. If you're innocent you have nothing to worry about, right? Nothing to fear. Nonsense. I'm scared, we're scared – we're innocent and scared. Scared that we don't know for sure what the crime is – it could be big – scared that they're only looking at us, scared that they'll frighten the kids again. Scared that they'll swoop at any time, legitimately skewer their red-painted claws into the backs of our necks, rip our skin and carry us away, their dead eyes craving supper and sleep. Scared that they are totally incompetent – that's all the evidence we have – and that this randomness, which is what it is, will throw up something random. We are scared of the unknown, which is all we face.

Twelve days after the arrest a list of the things removed from the house arrived through the letterbox. Having no idea exactly what had been taken, Mick had got pissed off and called Strangelove two days previously to request details that he thought should have been left with them – and surely signed for – or sent routinely, the automatic response of the system. The beast at least pretending to behave properly. They knew some of the items that had been removed from the house and found those confusing enough but Mick wanted a comprehensive list. He'd been on his way to the station or in the cells when the material had been removed and had he not, he felt sure that he would have insisted on an itemised receipt. In reality he wouldn't have done; the arrest was so unexpected and exceptional that after a while he'd stopped thinking and just fell into a matter of fact apathy, not questioning very much at all.

Here it was, a comprehensive list, although they had no way of knowing if it was comprehensive. There had been no checks or balances, just items removed from the house by the police, and the delivery – when requested – of a list from the police of the things that they stated had been removed. Looking at the list, he saw Lesley's signature, so there had been a procedure. Obviously Lesley couldn't remember it as she'd been in a state of shock – in the same daze that Mick had been in – and had in no way checked the list but just signed. He could hear Strangelove saying, 'That's your problem, not ours.' Mick wondered if, as some of the material was his, he should have been required to sign for it also, but he had too much on his mind and forgot this little procedural question instantly. *So what did they take then?*

RECORD OF PROPERTY SEIZED DURING SEARCH
OCCUPANTS COPY

Entry No.	Exhibits (include condition when seized)	a) Where found b) Who found by	a) Time seized b) Exhibit Ref. No.	a) Where sealed b) Who by c) Seal No.	a)Place deposited b)Person depositing c)Form 52 entry
1	Box/Packaging Re: Mobile Telephone. Motorola V31 GSM IMEI No. 357883-00-7-570299	a) Top Kitchen Cupboard b) DC 5052 Strangelove	a) 0750 b) TS1	a) b) c)LA0212672	a) b) c)
2	Box/Packaging Re: Mobile Telephone. Toshiba TS608 IMEI No. 359229-00-4268282	a) Top Kitchen Cupboard b) DC 5052	a) 0750 b) TS2	a) b) c)LA0212598	a) b) c)
3	T-Mobile RAZR V3i Mobile Telephone Instruction User Manual	a) Top Kitchen Cupboard b) DC 5052	a) 0750 b) TS3	a) b) c)ME0284118	a) b) c)

RECORD OF PROPERTY SEIZED DURING SEARCH
OCCUPANTS COPY

Entry No.	Exhibits (include condition when seized)	a) Where found b) Who found by	a) Time seized b) Exhibit Ref. No.	a) Where sealed b) Who by c) Seal No.	a)Place deposited b)Person depositing c)Form 52 entry
4	BLACK AND RED INDEXED NOTE BOOK	a) Kitchen worktop b) DC 5052 Strangelove	a) 0755 b) TS4	a) b) c) ME0284276	a) b) c)
5	'Orange' SIM card 895948971343118144	a) Kitchen table drawer b) DC 5052 Strangelove	a) 0830 b) TS5	a) At scene b)DS1914 Steal c)SM0242992	a) b) c)
6	'Orange' top up card Card No. 8914421 9909 7329 07327	a) Kitchen drawer b) DC 5052 Strangelove	a) 0830 b) TS6	a) b) c)SM0242990	a) b) c)

RECORD OF PROPERTY SEIZED DURING SEARCH
OCCUPANTS COPY

Entry No.	Exhibits (include condition when seized)	a) Where found b) Who found by	a) Time seized b) Exhibit Ref. No.	a) Where sealed b) Who by c) Seal No.	a)Place deposited b)Person depositing c)Form 52 entry
7	4x Mobile Telephones as listed. 7A Philips 7B Nokia 7C Siemens 7D Orange Alcatel E80	a) Kitchen table drawer b) DC 5052 Strangelove	a) 0835 b) TS 7A-D	a) At scene b)DS1914 Steal c) ME0284117	a) b) c)
8	BROWN NOTE BOOK	a) Kitchen table b) DC 5052 Strangelove	a) 0840 b) TS8	a) b) c) ME0284296	a) b) c)
9	Orange Statement Re Account No 53044191 Dated 1/9/07	a) Kitchen table b) DC 5052 Strangelove	a) 0840 b) TS9	a) At scene b)DS1914 Steal c)LA0212601	a) b) c)

RECORD OF PROPERTY SEIZED DURING SEARCH
OCCUPANTS COPY

Entry No.	Exhibits (include condition when seized)	a) Where found b) Who found by	a) Time seized b) Exhibit Ref. No.	a) Where sealed b) Who by c) Seal No.	a)Place deposited b)Person depositing c)Form 52 entry
10	Typed account re Job Working / Environment	a) Coat pocket in coat hallway b) DC 5140 Loyal	a) 0845 b) CL1	a) b) c) ME0284116	a) b) c)
11	Orange note-book containing handwritten entries re grieviences at work	a) Kitchen table b) DC 5052 Strangelove	a) 0845 b) TS10	a) b) c)LA0212683	a) b) c)
12	ORANGE TOP UP CARD	a) Purse b) DC 5052 Strangelove	a) 0858 b) TS11	a) b) c)SM0242993	a) b) c)

RECORD OF PROPERTY SEIZED DURING SEARCH
OCCUPANTS COPY

Entry No.	Exhibits (include condition when seized)	a) Where found b) Who found by	a) Time seized b) Exhibit Ref. No.	a) Where sealed b) Who by c) Seal No.	a)Place deposited b)Person depositing c)Form 52 entry
13	SILVER MOTOROLLA MOBILE PHONE	a) Kitchen table b) DC 5052 Strangelove	a) 0900 b) TS12	a) b) c) ME0284114	a) b) c)
14	Box/packaging Re Mobile T/phone no 07970 403 559	a) Dining Room Floor b) DC 5140 Loyal	a) 0900 b) CL2	a) At scene b)DS1914 Steal c)LA0187686	a) b) c)
15		a) b)	a) b)	a) b) c)	a) b) c)

There was some blurb across the bottom of the forms that read, 'I have received a copy of *Statutory Powers of Police to Search and Rights of Occupiers.*' Mick was sure they had not but who knows for sure? It was a while ago and the paper-work didn't seem that pressing at the time.

There were a couple of things that puzzled them. The first was that if Mick was supposedly the one making the threatening calls why had they removed Lesley's mobile phone and left Mick with his? The second was that they'd thumbed the first couple of pages of Lesley's address book and left it but then decided to take Mick's phone book and his brown note book that contained material relating to *Coming Out As A Bowie Fan In Leeds, Yorkshire, England.* Yes, it contained media contacts but it also held lists of pre-publication amendments for his book, notes on how to convert digital files, kid's' doodles, contacts for book shops, accounts departments, costings. If Lesley was supposed to be the one holding the vendetta, surely they'd be interested in her address book that also contained names and phone numbers. But no, they didn't even look at it properly, they picked it up looked at the first couple of entries and put it back down again. Were she and Mick thinking about it too much? Were the behaviour and decisions of the police completely random or was there some method? An obviously flawed method but a method nonetheless.

Something else was bothering Mick. DC Cockshot – or whatever her rank was – had on the day of the arrest suggested that the police had difficulty tracking mobile phones. Mick had quizzed Strangelove as well, separately, who also assured him that it was no easy task, involving gaining permission from high-ups, and that each mobile provider charged different but exorbitant rates and gave varied levels of information – the whole process being a drawn-out and comparatively complex and time consuming job. What was bothering Mick was that his mate Lol worked in the mobile industry and had checked with a friend who worked for a company that sold software to the police. This software did just what the two policewomen claimed they couldn't do, find out when and where – to within a few streets – a mobile was used. The guy who worked for the software company was being a bit cagey and wouldn't say whether or not West Yorkshire Police had the software but it was certainly available to them and Mick couldn't imagine them not having it.

12

Mick had just sanded a few floors for the guitarist of the Kaiser Chiefs and his better half but his head and snippets of time were concentrated on *Hot Knife* and the arrest. He'd even forgotten to give his own book a plug to the lad – he really was distracted. John had persuaded his London agent to release him, and he and Mick had agreed that *Hot Knife* would be the second title released by Armley Press. John had decided that having the book out and available was preferable to waiting more years for the majors and possibly never having the novel in print. Mick was excited at having another book and one of such quality, written and ready to go straight into preparation.

Hot Knife – what a fucking book, like a finely tailored suit. The space in-between the dialogue and plot development inhabited by the tightest writing, almost perfect – you never get perfection; well, maybe 'Sweet Thing' or moments of Rodrigo Y Gabriela, but they were the exception. Vividly evoking a scene, sentiment or dilemma and holding the reader captive as it hurtles towards another development. No wastage, precise word selection and placing, not like his babbling, overlong sentences and paragraphs careering off into complication and verbosity. He'd even made up words, f'fuck's sake. How the readers managed to keep with him fuck knows, but they often do. How could publishers ignore *Hot Knife*? It could easily be mistaken for a simple, fast-moving thriller about a collection of Leeds-based druggies and scamps but it was so much more than that. It was a slice of reality with all the colour and depth of that reality. Mick thought it was a brilliant piece of writing produced by a brilliant craftsman.

Knowing that the print on-demand business model was unbreakable, they were going to publish *Hot Knife*, and with more time to consider and plan the PR and marketing. Punk Publishing – that was what they were going to tag John's book with. It'd been formulating in Mick's head for a while, a slow foetal process where bits fell into place until the final piece created a 'Eureka' moment that served to obscure the mental processes of a year. While designing the press release and after consulting a journalist from *Metro*, they realised that the Punk Publishing idea deflected attention from the book. They resigned themselves to a normal press release with the Punk Publishing idea as one of the 'notes to editors', just as the helpful and correct journo had suggested. They could flog the Punk Publishing idea if they had any serious bites.

Mick's book had been a success – a minor success but a success nonetheless. Firstly, he didn't want to lose money; he couldn't lose money. Sales were well over what he expected but he always wanted more: Hollywood adaptation leading to a bestseller or even just a three-part series on Channel fucking 4 leading to decent major-like sales. He consoled himself with the fact that he'd made more money than many people selling over 30,000 copies through a major. They must give their authors less than 3% of profits – had to be about that figure, the cheating bastards – and if it wasn't less than 3% of profits they were stupid as well as cheating bastards. Famous, gifted writers such as Jodie Marsh or Jade Goody may get a huge advance and a better deal but they deserve it, they put the meaning and depth in many people's lives. The perfect spokespeople for the large chunk of society in Britain 2007. Anyway the punter reviews of *Coming Out As A Bowie Fan In Leeds, Yorkshire, England* on amazon[2] had been more numerous than he'd expected, and reassuringly good. The only person not to give it five stars had been John Lake, *Hot Knife* author. Contrary to what many people suspected, Mick didn't know all the people who'd reviewed it. There was also a good review thread on One Mick Jones[3] although it wasn't as big as James's *Mick McCann's Bowie Book* thread. He'd got positive feedback from obscure places, from complete strangers who'd loved it, and it gave him a warm buzz. He had no idea what it was like; he'd been too close to it for too long and now it was too far away.

Mick had later decided that he received over 100 times the amount per book as many authors who were published by majors. He considered that the majors' economies of scale must mean that they make more per book than he did, but perhaps with them being so firmly rooted in the old world, their 20th-century structure may

---

[2] www.amazon.co.uk/Coming-Bowie-Leeds-Yorkshire-England/dp/0955469902/ref=pd_rhf_p_t_1
[3] www.onemickjones.com/forum/viewtopic.php?id=4614

cut their margins below his. Whatever the situation, it appeared that the majors were shockingly miserly with their average author. He wasn't sure how the advance worked, mind, whether it was similar to the music industry where it's reimbursed to the record company via sales. Or is it a big chunk of money given to predominantly boring but famous people to write (or pretend to write) boring books about being famous and slightly boring? But this new economic element gave the whole idea a Factory Records feel and he liked that.

While trying to work out the cost of publishing *Hot Knife* his mobile started dinking out its tune.

'Mick. Hi, it's me. Listen, you're not going to believe this.'

'What?'

'How many years have I worked here?'

'Dunno. Six, seven years.'

'Right, and we've never in all that time, never once, filmed in the *Calendar* studios. Well, guess what I found out this morning?'

'You're kidding; you're filming in the *Calendar* studios?'

'We're filming in the *Calendar* studios. My next block has a few scenes there. How mental is that? And it gets even more ridiculous.'

'What? That's just unbelievable.'

'I know, but listen, it gets worse. We're filming a news report and guess who's down to do it?'

'What, who?'

'The news presenter they've got down to do it is Charlotte Tompkins.'

'Fucking' ell, you're kidding mi, you—'

'I know, our life is just full of the most ridiculous coincidences at the moment. We've never, ever filmed at *Calendar* and as for the presenter. . .'

'You can't do it; surely, you're going to have—'

'Well, fortunately, it's Mickey's block and he spotted it straight away and—'

'No way, no way can you do it.'

'Listen, I may be able to do it because Mickey has told Scripts that he would prefer a male presenter.'

'Brilliant, good on him, but they wouldn't have been able to allow that to happen, surely.'

'Well, you'd have thought not, I've told John and Helen about the situation so I'm sure they'd have seen my point.'

'Yeh, you'd have thought so. So did you have a word with Mickey then?'

'No, he saw the script before me and had already requested a male presenter.'

'What are the fucking odds on that?'

'I know, we've never filmed there before and for it to happen within a couple of weeks of getting arrested for making malicious calls to Charlotte and for them to cast her as the newsreader as well . . . it's unbelievable. Our life is pure madness.'

'Ee, lass, if you wrote it no one would believe you.'

Realising that he was only half listening and that this was important to Lesley, Mick left the washing-up, dried off his hands and sat at the table, concentration up to 90 per cent.

'I know, but I've got even more news, and this one really will blow y'socks off.'

'What? Do I need to sit down?'

'You might do, but listen Mick, this one's a classic. Well, you know we got our knickers in a twist when we found out that Charlotte was married to the Chief Inspector of West Yorkshire?'

'Yeh.'

'And we felt a bit daft when we found out she was no longer married to him?'

'Right.'

'Well, she may be divorced from him but guess who she's going out with now?'

'Don't know. Who?'

'The Head of Homicide and Serious Crime at, wait for it, West Yorkshire Police.'

'WHAT? FUUUCKIIING 'ELL.'

'I know.'

'Are you sure?'

'Absolutely positive. He's a guy called Rob Thurston, so we're already convinced that they've behaved really badly, but this shows again that we're likely to have been bullied because Mr Big-Wig has been doing things he shouldn't have been doing.'

'Fuuckiiing 'ell. You're absolutely positive?'

'Completely.'
'What's his name again?'
'Detective Chief Superintendent Rob Thurston.'

Conspiracy or incompetence? Paranoia or apathy? Anger or acceptance? Make an accusation or be afraid?

When recounting the detail to friends Mick only once mentioned his bastardised Foucaultian ramblings about the body of the individual, classification, the control mechanisms, the Panopticon and the unequal gaze. As his understanding was limited and his self-regard allowed him to slope off into a redefinition of something he barely understood, he wished he hadn't and didn't again. But there's that fucking prowling Frenchman again, popping up uninvited and distracting Mick into woolly-headed cul-de-sacs. Rob Thurston, the 'sovereign' that society had reigned in to stave off social unrest, meting out his revenge, the unpredictable, arbitrary and whimsical punishment, ignoring the procedures. Mick reflected that Thurston even fell into his own 'individuality discipline' – bang in his discourse – the socialised role. The top of the structure, so much on his desk that he made a quick and ill-considered judgement that – through the power relationships – he could be confident wouldn't come back and bite his arse. Mick snorted at the thought that were it Prince Harry or the relation of a top politician, no way would they have been arrested without due diligence. With the thought of the targeting of them – the seemingly 'powerless' – Mick re-snorted at the perfect example of the coded, structured supposedly egalitarian frameworks that as Foucault had stated, the cunt, simply mask the micro, everyday realities of uneven, skew-whiff power relationships that are anything but egalitarian. He pondered again his mate Dosher's argument that if they want you they'll get you or you'll just get sucked in by the 'system' and no matter how knowledgeable, sussed, articulate or even innocent you are, be it chance or malice, sometimes right or wrong, you're simply fucked, you'll get nailed.

The tale did drag up some of the 'unintended consequences': anger, support, sympathy for the victims of the 'sovereign' behaving unpredictably against the individuals; although the natural response of many people they spoke to was, 'No, it sounds like the police have just been completely useless, but I don't think there'll have been any malice, they're just useless bastards.' Aware that it was a lot of information for even their closest friends to take in, Mick or Lesley would then state their case, would point to the overwhelming, although circumstantial, evidence. How could it be anything other than circumstantial unless they bugged Rob Thurston's office phone the way that the police had bugged theirs? To do that they'd have to move *Doctor Who*-like back in time and steal some of his other magical powers. Lesley and Mick would state their case and the unconvinced friend or relation would go quiet and offer no more opinions or questions but would occasionally assert, similar to someone believing in the existence of God, that the police wouldn't do any of that.

So what was it that Lesley and Mick were suspicious of? They knew that one of the four women receiving the 'malicious' calls was the partner of Detective Chief Superintendent Rob Thurston. They were suspicious that, on discovering or witnessing that she was still getting the calls, DCS Rob Thurston had responded with anger and frustration. This natural response had caused him to quickly phone the CID supposedly investigating the crime and in his angry and emotional state had told them to sort it out **now**. A brief discussion ensuing in which the angry boss instructs the scared underling to simply arrest whoever the SIM card was registered to. They speculated that he was upset and not in any mood to listen to reason from the 'incompetent' detective, that he did not know the case, didn't study it, wasn't interested in understanding the case, but simply in banging some heads together and stopping the calls at any cost. They also argued that the action contained a certain level of malice or the police would have simply phoned them and requested that Lesley cancel the SIM card, instead of making the arrest.

This led them to their central and most important question on the morals of the situation which was: Is it OK in principle for Mr. Rob Thurston, Head of Homicide and Serious Crime for West Yorkshire, to have his officers arrest them and scare an innocent family because his girlfriend is one of the however many thousand people in West Yorkshire receiving 'malicious' phone-calls?

If their theory were correct his only possible defence could be the human response. It must have been extremely unpleasant for him to witness his partner receiving malicious phone calls, but does that justify him getting personally involved in a case that impacts his personal life or should he treat all equivalent cases in the same way? Should he not have studied the case before making an important decision that he was clearly not equipped to make? And once involved, didn't someone so powerful, a public servant, owe Mick and Lesley a duty of care? Where was his human response towards their family? It is not OK for him to appear to want revenge and to use his public office to possibly exact that revenge.

Is it normal for people in authority to abuse their power? A Home Secretary wouldn't be stupid enough to fast-track a visa application for his lover's nanny, would he? And what would be the consequences of a powerful individual using his public powers to improve his private life? Mick was sure that according to that wittering Frenchman it was a likely consequence of power that it would be used in an aberrant way. *Surely not*, thought Mick, *that sounds too useful, too much of a concrete statement, for that vague tosser. And another thing: how can power be fucking neutral? Its very presence is an action, its existence a threat or hope.* Mick wished he still had his old books and maybe shake Foucault off so that he could focus on the here and fucking now.

The case of the police was that Lesley had become angry and frustrated with four women, some of whom were from Granada Media – who worked in completely different buildings to her and whom she'd never met – and that she'd asked Mick to make malicious phone calls to them. Mick simply said yes and proceeded to make the calls.

So what evidence did Mick and Lesley have to justify their suspicions? Well, as they saw it, more evidence than the police had against them – and they weren't going to invade his family home – if he has one – and scare his children half to death, confuse the information that they'd given the children that the police are friends, that they are to be relied on, that they are good people. Their children now had a fear of the police the same as that of any child of a petty criminal. They were not going to inject a huge shot of stress into *his* life.

Considering the possibility of making a formal complaint, Lesley and Mick made a list of the very basic things that they believed the police should have done in the six months that the case, or their involvement in it, had obviously been put on a back-burner.

In the six months between the initial visit by CID and the arrest, they asserted that the police had not:

1) contacted Lesley to see if she could provide proof of the emails or SIM card exchange.

2) contacted IT at Lesley's place of work to see if her story of passing on the SIM card could be verified.

3) checked if Lesley worked in the same building/department as any of the women – Granada Media employs 10 to 11,000 people who are very clearly separated and have little contact outside their department.

4) asked the four women receiving the calls if they knew Lesley.

5) contacted anybody at Lesley's place of work to see if she had any history of harbouring grudges or had had any serious disagreements with anyone.

6) asked Lesley and Mick their whereabouts at any time.

7) traced the phone/SIM card making the calls.

8) asked Lesley to cancel the card – she didn't have the number and wasn't aware that the calls were still being made; they told her to do this after the arrest.

9) asked any of the victims to record the calls – very easily done.

10) asked the victims to alter their phone number or contact their providers to block calls from the number making the calls.

Lesley and Mick believed that the police had had the opportunity to investigate and very simply remove them from their enquiries, but had not. Why was that, and why the sudden and apparently unplanned arrest?

Having being startled into a state of fear, paranoia and obsession they made another list of questions regarding their arrest. Although it was more offensive it felt like a line of defence:

1) How many people live in the West Yorkshire Police area? It is approximately 2,500,000.

2) How many malicious phone calls are made per year in this area?

3) How many people are arrested per year in West Yorkshire for making malicious phone calls? (One of our friends received malicious phone calls and emails from a man who wasn't trying to hide his identity – he received a warning.)

4) Why, when people can be easily shown to be making malicious phone calls, are they only warned, while we were arrested?

5) Why were we arrested under suspicion of making malicious phone calls when the police had clearly not investigated the case with any thoroughness?

6) Would we use a SIM card registered in our name to make malicious phone calls?

7) Being intelligent people, would we continue making malicious phone calls using the same SIM knowing full well that the police are investigating it and suspect our involvement?

8) Who OK'ed the arrest and search warrant?

9) Why were six highly paid members of CID used to arrest us when they told us that there are only six lesser-ranked police officers for the whole of central Leeds on a Friday and Saturday

111

night, decreasing to none as arrests are made and hospitals need visiting? Is this a good use of resources?

10) Why CID and not uniform?

11) When we are shown to be completely innocent, why will our DNA, fingerprints, etc., remain on the Criminal Database?

13

'Hi Lesley it's Helen, have you any spare time to pop in to see me this afternoon?'

'Possibly, what time are you looking at?'

'Well, other than 3.30 for about half an hour, anytime really, I'm flexible, but if we could organise a time that —'

'What's it about?'

'I've had a response from IT, not very good news but I'd like to discuss it face to face.'

'What are you doing now?'

'Now? Well yes, give me 15 minutes.'

'OK, I'll see you at half past.'

'Yep, that's fine, I'll see you then.'

Lesley gave Mick a quick call to tell him; he'd suggested that she takes notes, der-er doesn't he realise that her whole job is about taking notes?

Lesley's heart was pumping: not good news? She saved the setting list she was working on and grabbed her coat; she needed a cig before she went up. It was weird that a lack of news in this situation was bad news. Well it kind of is news – sounds like the news is that they've found nothing. She felt certain that they would have moved to emails, they wouldn't have carried out the whole transaction on the message board. How could there be no records? As Mick had said, the techies may be shit at searching databases. Fuck she didn't need this, she needed Helen to say 'Yes we've found them, there's this one on the third of February 2002, discussing the SIM card and this other one on the seventh of February 2002 arranging how to send the SIM card and money'. Lesley was at the outside door now. *Shit, it's raining.* She hadn't brought her brolly. She quickly nipped around the corner where the roof extends beyond the building by a few feet and affords some cover. One of her favourite directors popped out of the door and joined her.

'Les, how are you, how's it all going?' Even though they were doing the next block together, she knew he meant her personal life and not work. She loved Mickey.

'I'm just off up to see Helen in a minute, sounds like there's no sign of any emails.'

'Shit, you're kidding, I was sure you'd have gone to email.'

'I know, so was I. I'll know more after I've spoken to Helen but it doesn't sound promising.'

'Oh I'm sorry, Les, that could've cleared it up, couldn't it? Well, at least backed up your story and removed you from suspicion.'

'Yeh that was the idea – I'm sure we'd have moved to emails.'

'Well, wait and see what Helen has to say, it might not be that bad.' Mickey squirmed slightly: the emails were either there or not, it wasn't levels of. 'Are the kids alright?'

'Yeh, they're fine – seem to have forgotten all about it.'

They chatted for a while and after Lesley had docked her fag they entered the building together, separating at the stairs. People at work had been very supportive but none more than Mickey.

Making her way up to Human Resources, Lesley couldn't stop the predictable thought of how departments were separated at work and ones that should communicate didn't. She cleared her mind as she stepped into the small open plan office and up to the end desk.

'Could you let Helen know I'm here, Lesley Jackson? Thanks.'

She took a seat as the secretary phoned a phone that could be heard faintly ringing on the other side of the partition wall. It stopped and a couple of seconds later:

'If you'd like to go through Lesley.'

Helen was at the door as Lesley went to open it. 'Come in, sit down. How are you coping?'

'Oh, you know, getting on.' Lesley was chewing her lip and fighting back tears. She hated the way that this happened at completely inappropriate moments, she hated the way it would hit her suddenly. She could be fine and then bang, in floods of tears. Lesley was surprised but relieved that Helen hadn't spotted the oncoming flood. Helen was obviously trying to collect her thoughts about IT. The lack of acknowledgement of the imminent outburst made it easier to control. The simplest 'Ooh are you alright?' would have been the finger leaving the dyke and the dam burst, room flooded with wasted time, but now Lesley was over it and more composed. Helen looked up from her notes.

'Well, it's not what we'd hoped for. They've carried out a thorough search of your email and come up with nothing. Ooh, before we go any further I should tell you that we've had to inform the police.'

'Yes, yes obviously.' Lesley's mind had returned to its state of mush, of complete confusion; she pulled out her notebook and placed it on the table.

'It is OK if I take notes, isn't it?'

'Yes of course it is Lesley, I'll give you a print off of what they search for but the email is backed up for 7 years and I must say they appear to have been very thorough.'

Lesley looked at her blank notebook and stricken pen. The list of search terms was all she needed really.

'What did they say?'

'Well, they searched—'

'No, sorry, what did the police say when you told them?'

'Oh I don't know, I didn't call them that was Terry, head of IT. But he said they just took the information, no real reaction. The thing is Lesley it doesn't prove anything. You could still have passed the SIM card onto the person via internal mail and simply organised it on the board.'

'Well, it does make my version of events a little less plausible.'

'No I don't think it does. It was a long time ago and you're obviously very unlikely to remember something so trivial in detail. It simply shows that you and the man didn't exchange emails, nothing more, nothing less.'

'I don't understand it, I felt sure that we would've switched to emails.'

'Yes it would seem likely but...'

'So what did they search for? I mean, I'm sure they know what they're doing but I'd like to know anyway.' Lesley flushed suddenly and unexpectedly at the thought of someone rooting through her personal emails, not that it matters, people root through her personal stuff all the time... bastards.

'Yes, of course. They searched for SIM – card – £6 – 6 – the pound symbol – money – send, erm... exchange – Orange – spare – internal – mail. As I said, I'll print the list off for you but there was nothing at all relating to a SIM card.'

'Shit.' Lesley was fighting back the tears. She didn't know Helen that well and she hadn't expected this. 'When is something going to go right? Fuck.'

Helen could sense the distress and for professional reasons – for Lesley as much as herself – wanted to defuse it. 'I know it could've pretty much cleared you but it doesn't make it any more likely that you are involved in anything.'

'It will to them, to the police.'

'How can it?'

'It'll undermine my word.'

'No, how could they expect—'

'Honestly Helen you don't know what they are like, they are so stupid, so suspicious. Even when something makes no sense they seem to ignore the obvious and go for the ridiculous. They are not interested in clearing our names, in finding out the truth. There's so much that they could've done to show that we aren't involved but they are not interested in solving the case they are only interested in proving our guilt however they have to do it.'

'Oh I'm sure that's not true.'

'It is Helen, it really is. I thought like you six months ago, but not now. They're a set of useless bastards who just want a collar – any collar. I mean, look at the stuff you know. For example, before they arrested us they didn't even check if any of the four women knew me. Why not? I'll tell you why not, because that may have removed a possible motive. Did they contact here? Even now, have they contacted her to see if I've any history, if I'm the sort of person who harbours a grudge, if I've behaved vindictively, if there have been any incidents? Have they checked out my character? No, anything that may remove us or circumstantially reduce the possibility of our involvement is ignored.'

A mischievous glint entered Helen's eyes. 'Well, don't worry, if they do, we'll put them straight. There are many examples of how you deal with grievances head on, of how you speak your mind and stand you corner, even other people's corner for them.'

A solidarity laugh was exchanged between the two women and Helen was pleased that she may be helping in a purely bleak situation. 'The thought of you making malicious phone calls, or getting your husband to do it, is just ridiculous to anybody who knows you. You're the last person I'd expect it from, you'd just go piling in and state your case. Air your grievance and leave the managers shaking in fear.'

They were laughing together, a hint of hysteria but laughing all the same. Lesley couldn't afford to wallow too long. 'Even this checking of the databases, I'm the one who has pushed for it, not them. Oh sure, they want to know the results, but only so that they've got any information that I've got.'

'Yes, it would seem sensible to check out your story with our IT department before invading your house and arresting you in front of your children. You told them about the SIM card months ago, didn't you?'

'Yes, when they first turned up at the door I told them I'd passed it on to someone at work, I even offered to look for the emails, but they weren't interested. Honestly, Helen, they think they've got their villains and all they have to do is build a case. I see them here, you know.'

'What?'

'They work as extras on *Emmerdale*; I've seen two of the ones that arrested us.'

'You're kidding – that's awful.'

'No, one of the men and one of the women... and the looks they give me, it's so intimidating. One of them opened a door for me with a sarcy comment. He looked at me like I was scum, like he knew all about me – like I was a criminal. It was hideous.'

Tears began to well up in Lesley's eyes and it looked like the long-avoided over-familiarity was about to arrive.

'Oh Lesley, I am so sorry. We'll have to see what we can do about that.'

'No, no, don't worry. I mean, those are just the things that you know about, all the stuff with the police at work, but there's so much more, so many other things that I could tell you about. So much that it just fills your head and you can't get a handle on any of it.' Lesley regained her composure, happy that she'd kept it together, and decided to leave before she pushed it too far. 'Anyway, thanks, Helen, I really appreciate your help.'

'No, that's OK.'

'And I'll leave you to get on with your job now.' The second Lesley got out of the office and into the corridor she was overwhelmed with suppressed emotion. Feeling exposed, she headed for the nearest toilet and sanctuary.

Helen decided to do a couple of things herself to try to help Lesley. She'd obviously done nothing wrong and the more this drags out the more her health was going to suffer. From a professional perspective, it was the right thing to do, but more than that, she liked and respected Lesley.

'Hi, is that Paul?'

'Yeh.'

'It's Helen from HR, regarding Lesley Jackson. I know you've had a good look through her stored emails but if there's anything else you can think of just do it. With the police being involved, it's quite a serious matter.'

'Well, yeh, but I've done all I can.'

'No, I understand that but if you think of anything else I'm just letting you know that it is worth spending your time on it. If anyone asks, send them to me.'

Paul came off the phone with the slight buzz of a challenge.

'Hi, John, its Helen. As her line manager, I just wanted to keep you up to speed with the Lesley Jackson situation. We've had a quick trawl through her emails and can find no reference to the SIM card.'

'Oh really?'

'Yes.'

'So she's lying?'

'It doesn't mean that at all, John. There could be a few explanations for it and personally I've no doubt that she's telling the truth. But I just wanted to let you know that she may be a bit distracted and... with your history, she may be a bit unpredictable, perhaps slightly volatile. Just tread carefully.'

'What? She should behave professionally, as I will.'

'Yes but John, make sure you do. Don't forget, as we've seen in the past, she runs rings round you. You need to be careful; she's not likely to bite her tongue.'

'Excuse me; I'm perfectly capable of—'

'Look, John, I'm not sure if you're hearing me, and I didn't want to say this but bear in mind your position.'

'I don't understand.'

'Look, I didn't want to spell this out but you've had a written warning. Think before you speak and try to be supportive.'

'Oh, right, I see.'

'Thanks, John – speak to you later.'

'Yeh, see'y.'

God if that man had a brain he'd be dangerous. One last call and I can get on. Helen was a little nervous about the next one. It was a grey area; although it was obviously work-related, it was unprecedented. Anyway, deep breath. *Answer phone, as I expected...* 'Oh, come on, just put me through to the answer phone... Hi, Charlotte, it's Helen Wallis from Human Resources. Could you give me a call when you get a chance? Thanks. I hope you're well.' Just as she'd decided that it would have to be a couple of days before she could call again, her phone rang. 'Hello, Helen Wallis.'

'Hi, Helen – it's Charlotte.'

'Oh hi, Charlotte, thanks for getting back to me, we've been—'

'How are you and how's Mike?'

'Oh, we're both fine, thanks. And how are you and how's Rob?'

'Yeah, we're good, thank. What can I do for you?'

'Well, it's quite delicate really so if at any point you're feeling uncomfortable about speaking, let me know.'

'Ah, is it about the calls?'

'Yes it is.'

'And how did you find out about them?'

'Oh, well, it has involved someone from *Emmerdale* and the police have been in touch.'

'Oh, OK. They told me to keep it to myself, as much as I could, while they made their enquiries.'

'Ah, I see, well, they've been in touch with us now. As I said, it has now involved someone from *Emmerdale* and I just wanted to ask you something to see if we can shed some light on it. It'd help you and help our other employee.'

'Yeh, what is it?'

'Well, I'm aware that it's a man making the calls and the suspicion of the police is that it's the husband of a member of staff.'

'Ah, I didn't realise that.'

'Well, I just wondered, if we get a recording of his voice, you can have a listen and see if you recognise it. I'll check it out with the police first obviously but we could clear up that line of enquiry.'

'Well, it's funny that you should say that because... wait a minute. I've been advised not to discuss this with anyone, but I will on the understanding that it's confidential.'

'Yes, of course.'

'OK, I think I already have heard his voice.'

'Really?'

'Yes, a soft voice, quite "Leeds" but sounds slightly camp. I mean, I don't know for sure that it's the same person but they did let me know that it was work-connected and it was a police interview.'

'Right?'

'And obviously, in the calls the person is much more aggressive, but to me, and I could be wrong, it sounded very similar.'

'Really?'

'Yes, I'd say 90% that it was the same person.'

'Oh, that does surprise me.'

'Yeh, looks like they've got their man. Well, I hope so anyway. It's hideous. I can't say too much but it really is horrible.'

Helen recognised the pre-crying wind-up and didn't have the emotional energy left for it. 'I'm sure it is and I hope it does all get sorted out. Anyway, thanks for your time – leave it with me and I'll give you a call back if I need to, I mean, if that's OK with you obviously. You don't need to speak to me about the situation if you choose not to.'

'No, that's fine, I appreciate that you're trying to help. I just want the calls to stop.'

'Yes, so do I, and thanks for your help, Charlotte. Bye-ee.'

'OK, bye.'

Helen had not expected that. Her head was buzzing in confusion. Charlotte obviously thinks it's the same man and Lesley's husband *has* been interviewed by the police – that much she knew – but Helen was also as certain as she could be that Lesley would not be involved, and if Lesley isn't involved, neither is her husband.

14

'Fucking phone. Why is it that it rings just as I'm half out the door?' Mick pulls the door closed behind him and goes in search of the house phone, feels like he's got there just in time.

''Ello.'

'Is that Mr McCann?'

'Could I ask who's calling, please?'

'Mr McCann, you and your wife have been making some enquiries and are being indiscreet. May I suggest that you stop?' The voice deep, calm and deliberate. Sounded like Franco when they were visiting Gibraltar, when he's come back from work, back from making all his orders and getting all the salutes.

'What? Who is this?'

'You know what I'm talking about. You've had your fun and it needs to stop now.'

'Fun? My wife's a wreck, mi kids were scared shitless, they're still not—'

'May I suggest that you stop now?'

'You can't just come round and bully us and then make threatening phone calls.'

'Oh can't I? Look, come on, it wasn't that bad.'

'It really is that bad and there's no way we're going to be bullied into silence by you.'

'Right, last time, let's resolve the situation now and you stop your enquiries. Good day.'

The phone dead in his shaking hands, he was buzzing with anger. 'It's like the fucking Stasi.'

1 – 4 – 7 – 1. 'The number was withheld.'

'What a fucking surprise... cunt.'

On the way back from school Mick was trying to decide how to tell Lesley about the phone call. Billy running ahead like he always does, fine hair doing strange, solid, almost animated flicks as he runs. Mick getting butterflies as he hears the low rumble of a car moving past him. 'BILLY, KEEP AWAY FROM THE EDGE, DARLIN'.'

Billy's little legs going ten to the dozen, looking so small as he pulls away. Mick had the same thought he did every night. *I know all the other kids are stapled to their mother's side but it's important for them to understand danger, how to do stuff and feel a bit of freedom. I'm educating my kid, not being slack. Billy's smart, he'll stop in the same place and wait at the side of the road like he always does.* The car was slowing as it neared Billy. 'Good lad. I do that; slow down as I'm going past running kids.'

Wait a minute, it's slowing a bit too much. Why's he got cardboard over his number plate? Mick started to run. 'BILLY, COME HERE, COME BACK HERE, BILLY.'

The car was moving along at the same speed as Billy with the driver leaning over and talking to him. 'BILLY, COME BACK HERE, **NOW**.'

Billy stopped and looked around. Mick was getting closer as the passenger door opened and Billy quickly, instinctively, tugged away from a grabbing hand. Billy pulled away fully and ran in a big circle back towards his dad. 'Good lad, Billy.' Mick hugged him close. 'Good lad. You are going to eat so much chocolate tonight that you'll be sick. Well, you can have two extra chocolate fingers. Good lad, Billy, that was so smart.'

Mick's tingling chest said that was real – *Jesus* – should he phone the police now or do it at home away from little ears? *I'll phone them when I get home, I don't want to blow it up in Billy's mind.* 'Billy, don't forget… fast past the leaning wall.'

It was still on his list of things to do, pop round to The Conservative Club and tell them about the leaning, bulging wall. Seven foot of hanging stone right next to the path where mothers roll pushchairs, pensioners walk their dogs, kids return from school laughing and pushing. He'd better get it to the top of list and actually do it. It could fall anytime and it would kill anything beneath it and kill his conscience if he hadn't had a word. Billy pushed past Mick and slowed just in front, bumping and breaking Mick's rhythm. 'Billy, if you're walking ahead, walk fast.'

Mick was turning the happenings in his head. Coincidence? Surely not, but certainly possible. Keeping the information moving around his brain and trying to cut out Billy's constant chattering. 'I'm first, I want to go first – I'm the fastest. No don't you go first, I want to go first. I'm faster than you Dad.'

Mick stumbled against his competing son. 'Well, don't keep slowing down then. Come on , Billy, get moving, I need to make a phone call before we pick up Cal.' *Fucking litter* – he cleared it every night and every day a set of cunts dumped more – plastic coke bottles, polystyrene trays from a chippy, crisp bags. The land belonged to *The People Of Armley* therefore the fucking council don't have to clean it.

'Come on, Billy, let me past, I've got the keys.'

Mick moved around Billy and through the six-foot stone gateposts of the drive. Thud. Something hit him around the back of the head at velocity and part hurled, part folded him to the ground. What the fuck? It reminded him that this was reality, not the dream of life that we float through but pain and the dull, starry thud were the real world. Starting to pull up, a blunt hard pain to his stomach and he was over grasping at air, trying to pull it in and fighting the wooziness in his head. In among all this he could hear Billy scream and forcefully shout, 'Hey, leave my dad alone.' Through a watery haze he could see little legs kicking at full length legs. A split-second of pride was replaced with an all-encompassing, paralysing fear. He tried to shout 'RUN', but without air words are impossible. He tilted his head to see Billy trying to make a run for it and getting scooped up wriggling and fighting for his big life. They were both helpless. Mick felt like he'd been raped – *That's my fucking boy*. He tried to concentrate on the snatched view of the man – something front of his twirling brain told him he had to. More nightmare screams and a dream involving a car starting up.

He levered himself up off the ground. 'Snidey, cheeky cunt, I'm gonna kill him, I'm going to rip his fucking liver out.' His battered male pride abruptly replaced by the real issue. 'Fuck, get in the car, where's mi keys?' Spilling them onto the ground, 'Bollocks – no, think, think, think, think, think.'

He moved quickly to the gateway and tracked the car turning out of the top of the lane. The same Focus but now the number plate was clear. It was far off but Mick picked out a zed. Diving back into the drive and into his car he reversed round the stone posts at speed and, 'Bollocks,' stalled. Re-starting and skidding on the leaves, he was too fucking slow. Proper tyre-skid screech and he's flying up the lane, instinct screaming not to stop at the blind top, brain overruling with the image of slamming into the side of someone or being slammed and stopped. Car coming at him too fast, he pulls out with a second screech. Beep, beep, beep, and flashing lights, acknowledged with a raised hand, muttering, 'You were fucking speeding anyhow, y'Beemer cunt. Keep up with this.'

Flooring it. 'Fuck, I can drive.' Scanning the horizon, instinct pulling him through tight spaces, dodging beams at speed with endless fucking beeping. Jabbing his horn to get the dozy slow-witted fucks out of the way. 'Move, y'cunt. Bollocks, bollocks, bollocks.'

It was dawning on him just how many possible turn-offs there were, how many side streets the bloke could have pulled into to watch him fly by. He could have gone anywhere; he could have even cut up onto Tong Road. Every second was crucial and he suspected the cunt would be driving careful. Maybe he should be taking his time, see if the cunt was parked up and hiding. 'He better have fucking strapped him in. I'm going to fucking kill him.'

He wanted to sort this on his own, make it all alright, but it was smacking him in the face that he couldn't. This wasn't some *Dirty Harry* film, not some scripted bullshit Hollywood movie. This was real life. The adrenaline was losing its intensity and each movement on the clutch was accompanied by a sharp guttural pain increasing exponentially with the fall in chemicals.

He screamed, 'FOR FUCK'S SAKE. Yeh, yeh, I don't want to fucking re-record owt, I want to leave a fucking message, you smarmy cunt. Lesley, you've got to phone me now – right now. Some bloke's got Billy. Pleeeeease phone me. He turned out the top of our street toward Armley about two minutes ago. I'm on Town Street, can't see him. Fucking hell, phone me.'

He's not that fucking smart, not that fucking cool to park up and wait, he'll be on the main roads, he'll be on Stanningley Road going into town. *Concentrate. It's fucking Armley Road there, you cunt.* Beeping through the red light of the pedestrian crossing, he missed a dopey old cow by a foot. 'F'fuck's sake. Get out o'the way.'

Left onto Branch Road: 'Bollocks, no wait a minute...' A queue of traffic waiting to hang a right onto Armley Road. 'He'll be in this fucking queue.'

He cruised down the queue to his right. Nothing. 'Fuck, he's gone another way. I've lost him. Fuckin'ell, Billy, I'm sorry.'

A lump of guilt like a block of un-melted lard sat heavy in his stomach weighing him down with indecision. He then consoled himself with the thought that he wouldn't have come this way to get onto Armley Road, he'd have taken a shortcut. The bloke still might be in front. Right to the front in the wrong lane, he indicated right and tried to get the attention of the driver to his right. 'Stop daydreaming, you bearded bastard.' It hit him that he wasn't daydreaming, just ignoring him. Mick was sliding his window down just as the light changed.

Stupid fucking tune out of his phone.

'Hello. Ah, Lesley, thank fuck. He's got him – you took y'time.'

With a calm voice that seemed all wrong, she said, 'What make of car is he driving?'

'Silver Ford Focus – had a zed in the reg.'

He heard Lesley repeat, 'Silver Ford Focus and it had a zed in the reg.'

'That's what a fucking said.' He cut in front of a dawdling car to jump the queue. So much fucking beeping – 'What's wrong with these people?' Unable to hang the right due to the stream of cars crossing the junction, small gap, he risked it through to one elongated, concentration-sapping beep.

'What does he look like?'

'Phone the police.'

'Mick, what does he look like?'

'Maybe five foot ten, white, 30ish, short dark hair maybe receding a bit, clean shaven, wearing like a khaki jacket and jeans. Phone the fucking police.'

'Five foot ten, white, 30ish, short dark hair maybe receding a bit, clean shaven, wearing a khaki jacket and jeans.'

'Lesley f'fuck's sake phone the...' Ah, she was repeating what he was saying to someone else. 'I'm on Armley Road going to town, but it's all snarled up for some reason. Can't see him, might've gone another way.'

Lesley repeated him word for word. 'Yep, bye…. Mick I'm off the other way toward Kirkstall, phone me back if anything happens. I've given the police your mobile number and this time don't worry about speaking to them while you're driving.'

He screamed and thumped his steering wheel. 'PLEASE GET OUT OF THE WAY, PLEEEASE.' It then struck him again that this wasn't just slowing him down, and he wasn't trying to be anonymous. *Thank fuck for the traffic. What's going on? Well, thank God it is.* He could see all the cars before the chicane – no silver Ford Focus. He could cruise the outside of the traffic again but he'd better do it now, the cars coming the other way weren't far off. He put his hazards on and floored it, jabbing his horn. A car coming straight at him, flashing its lights but well off.

'I'm on the wrong side of the fucking road, so you'd better move over, y'cunt.'

Not enough space to safely fit a fourth lane of traffic. He slowed and flicked across the line of cars – nothing. With the tosser beeping him as he got closer, Mick looked up and started gesturing for the driver to move over, but instead they rolled collision course toward each other as Mick continued to scan the cars in front. 'It like fucking New York with all the fucking beeping, this is.' Cars ten feet from kissing bumpers, the red faced bloke stopped and got out. Mick got out too – he might be able to persuade the cunts to get out of the way.

'What the fuck y'playing at?' the suited bloke called out as he approached. 'You're gonna kill someone, y'stupid bastard.'

'Someone's snatched mi kid. I think he'll be here.'

'What?' replied the commuter.

'Ey, y'cunt, what the fuck are you on?' Another voice unnerved him from behind. He spun round and there was a brick-built builder. 'It's cunts like you that kill people.'

'Who's got y'kid?' asked the commuter.

'A bloke's just snatched mi kid; I think he's going towards town.' It suddenly struck Mick that upright he could see further along the traffic, and he started to jog along, looking ahead.

'What's he driving?' the commuter shouted.

'Silver Ford Focus, had a zed in the reg.'

126

'What's up, mate?' Another voice coming from the window of a car.

'Someone's nicked mi kid.'

Instead of cars creeping forward feet at a time he was getting to the point where the convoy was starting to build up a bit of momentum and pulling away. He turned to return to his car, four or five blokes milling around chatting with drivers, three systematically looking at the cars.

''ERE, MATE,' came a shout from one of them pointing at the traffic halfway between the two of them. Mick's pulse quickened further but he'd checked these cars. He tried to home in on where the bloke was pointing and running towards. 'Fuck, it looks right.' The closer he got, the more right it looked as it, feet by feet, got closer to the point of the flowing traffic.

'IT'S HIM,' Mick screamed. He'd found the cunt. 'STOP HIM.' Mick sprinted through the cars, some of which were still rolling forward, soft cunts. Fair play to the suited bloke, he was pulling at the door, banging on the window and hurling threats at the driver. Billy was shouting and crying in the back.

'FUCK NO— GET THE CAR IN FRONT TO STOP.'

They could box the cunt in but he was still easing forward and getting close to the sneaky little turn-off that goes down past the sex shop.

'GET THE CAR IN FRONT TO STOP.'

The bloke heard him but as he moved forward to get to the bonnet of the car in front enough of a gap appeared for the wanker to pavement it through to the turn-off. For a moment he could see the white of The Cunt's eyes and Billy looking him straight in the eye, crying. Mick gestured for him to strap himself in and blew him a kiss.

By the time he'd got back to his car and along the line of traffic – which was now more accommodating... cunts – the Focus was gone. He and probably the other bloke who'd got to the car were following the trail in vain. No more silver Focus, no more Billy, just dim wet streets and head-lights; people with normal lives, on the way to the pub or home. Home to their safe houses all standing separate from the madness, from the nightmare. He'd never forgive himself if owt happened to Billy and if they don't find him in the next couple of hours he'll end up dead. Tears rolled down his face and he wanted to phone his dad, his dead dad who would have sorted it, were he alive. 'FUCK.' He phoned Lesley.

'Hello.'

'I've lost them.'

'Yeh, but y'know I've got the police onto it?'

'Yeh, like they'll fucking do anything.'

'Of course they will. Someone's kidnapped a child, it's not a break-in.'

'Bollocks, Callum. He'll be waiting for me; I've forgotten to pick him up.'

'It's OK, I'm on mi way now. The police said you'd, well, we'd better go straight home.'

'They can phone me. I'm going through this fucking city street by street.'

'Mick they've got more chance of finding him—'

'GET OUT OF THE FUCKING WAY, KNOBHEAD.'

'You need to tell them everything you know.'

Mick distracted by the fucking car-cum-fucking pushchair in front. 'JUST DRIVE Y'FUCKING CAR. What?'

'If you give them all the information, they'll move more quickly.'

'Bollocks to'em, they'll do fuck-all. Anyway, what information? I've told you everything I know.'

'Mick, please, go home and let's get them moving.'

'Just tell them to phone me.'

The call finished. He was up by the side of YTV and pulled over. He was trying to decide whether to go from Burley Road towards and past the dental hospital or work his way along towards the Burley Lodges.

In his rear-view mirror he spotted a squad car turning up the road. 'Bollocks.' *Drive or sit tight?* A quick spin of the lights and the car pulled up behind him. 'What are the chances of that? Cunts – they find *me* easy efuckingnough.'

An officer arrives driver's side as Mick presses the button to slide down his window. 'Mr McCann?'

'Yes, who are you, fucking Yuri Gagarin?' Mick laughed hysterically. 'Or some other cunt who can read people's minds?'

'Step out of the car sir and watch your tone.'

'Don't you even fucking think about talking to me about my fucking language. You got kids?'

'Switch off the engine and step out of the car Mr McCann.' The police officer looks puzzled. 'No I haven't got—'

'Well, if anybody's ever fucking stupid enough to shag y'and y'not firing blanks, come back and tell me about y'fucking language when some fucker kidnaps one of your kids.'

'Kidnap? Sorry, Mr McCann, we've just been alerted to the fact that we need to escort you back to your home. We don't know any of the details, just a rough location and that you're needed home urgently – so if you'd like to follow us.'

'No, I wouldn't like to follow you. On what fucking bollocks grounds are you arresting me this time?'

'We're not arresting you, and anyway, we thought you had no previous.'

'Look, I'm not going anywhere; I'm looking for mi kid.'

The second officer steps forward. 'We can arrest you for all the abuse you've been spouting. Now switch off the engine and get out of the car.'

'Fuck you.' Mick floored it again, his *Whacky Races* driving going to his head. Flying up the road, he could see in his mirror the two coppers scrambling back into their car. Straight left, no looking, no searching for gaps. He heard the screech of applied brakes but miraculously no beeping, followed by a low glass-smashing thud. 'Stupid cunt, should have kept a proper fucking braking distance. Well, at least it might slow the police down – bollocks.' Hanging a right onto Woodsley Road, he could hear the siren and see flashing lights behind. Calculating that he couldn't get involved in some juvenile police chase and search for his son at the same time, he snatched a straight right, left again, lights off.

'I'm that fucking cool, y'cunts. Look at your options now. I could be anyfuckingwhere.'

Four possible options and Mick had taken the first that arises before you realise it's an option.

The police car flew by, all noise and excitement. Into reverse, he pushed around the corner and started to systematically cruise the streets and eye the car parks back towards town. Not a fucking sausage. Back towards Woodsley Road, he crossed over to

Alexandra Road to check all the Burley Lodges. The futility of it started to hit him. 'He could be halfway to fucking Harrogate by now.' But Mick was going to do a systematic sweep of the city anyhow. What else was there to do? He couldn't get Billy's eyes out of his mind, full of fear and betrayal. 'I'm going to fucking kill you, I swear I'll track you down and I'll fucking rip you limb from fucking limb – stupid fucking phone.' The daft tune startled him – Cal – which means Lesley after those dopey bastards had confiscated Lesley's phone. 'Yeh.'

'Listen, you're making this worse. Apparently, those bobbies wanted to arrest you until CID sweet-talked them. Come home and speak to them. Look how quickly they found you, y'stupid get. Come home. I mean it, Mick, come home. They've got all sorts of ways they can help.'

'Yeh, yeh, but after I've spoken to them I'm off back out again.'

'Whatever, but come home now.'

'I'm coming – you there?'

'Almost – d'y promise?'

'Yeh, I'm on mi way.'

'Try to think back through what happened and don't get distracted. Straight home, yeh?'

'Yeh – be about five minutes.' He pulled out of Carberry Road left onto Cardigan Road and headed towards Canal Road and home, frustrated and scared.

15

Fuck, Mick was getting tired, getting ground down and worn out by all the fucking swearing in his head but it was all that was fucking appropriate. A reflex fucking rat-a-tat-tossing-tatting, a constant fucking stream of swear words through his head. He remembered times when he swore less with fondness. If he never fucking heard the word 'fucking' again he'd be a happy fucking man. He felt like he had fucking tourettes. It reminded him of when he'd started spitting as a kid and once the habit kicked in he spat so much and it was so strong a reflex that he could only stop when his lips got so sore that they couldn't spit anymore, too painful. Another time, as a young dandy, he'd started to blow sarcastic kisses to red-necks. It happened so often that it developed into a kiss-blowing twitch. He couldn't help himself; he walked around or sat in class constantly blowing kisses at bemused people. His phone rang again, breaking his train of semi-thoughts.

''Ello.'

'Where are you?'

'I'm on mi way.'

'You should have been here by now, where are y'?'

'Yeh sorry, it struck me that all those scrap yards, industrial stuff and offices—'

'COME HOME NOW.'

'I am. I'm just on Canal Road. I just wanted to check—'

'Just come home.'

'Look, Lesley, every second is crucial; this is the sort of place he could hide up.'

'COME HOME NOW.'

'I AM. I'll just check the industrial museum and I'm home.'

'NOW – FORGET THE MUSEUM.'

'I'm coming, just thought—'

'NOW.' The phone fell dead with a commanding monotone buzz.

Mick pulled into the lane. There was a squad car parked halfway down and around his house there was a gaggle of unmarked cars. *Fuckin'ell, a'they doing summat?* A man in a car talked into his hand as Mick went past and Mick parked up behind a car sitting in his spot. 'Cunts.' As he put his key to the door it was opened by Lesley.

'Did you see anything? Did you get anywhere?'

'I saw him on Armley Road but he got away.'

'What? F'fuck's sake, how did he get away?'

'He was—'

'Mr McCann, if you'd like to step into the kitchen.' Strangelove again and a couple of extra blokes that Mick didn't recognise but she introduced... he wasn't listening.

'No I wouldn't like to – I will but I'd rather be out there looking for him.'

'Right, Michael, you need to leave that to us. Can I just check some details and then if you want to tell us what happened from the beginning? Right, so far, we've got that the car was a silver Focus that had a zed in the registration and that the man was around five foot ten, white, 30ish, short dark receding hair, clean shaven, wearing a khaki jacket and jeans. What else can you remember?'

'Not a lot, what else is there? Oh, yeh, that was it, the car had a sticker in the back window, some car place in Barnsley.'

'Can you remember the name?'

'No, it happened too fast.'

'Any of the writing at all, part of the address or postcode?'

'No.'

'Are you sure?'

'Yes, of course I'm fucking sure, I just caught it as he pulled away.'

'Can you remember what colour the writing was?'

'Red text.'

'Just red text?'

Mick nodded. 'Yeh.'

'The man – anything else that you can remember?'

'No, don't think so.'

'What colour shoes did he have on?'

'Black, kinda heavy-duty, not boots, shoes, but you know, like Doc shoes, Doctor Marten shoes?'

'Any marks on him?'

'Not that I saw.'

'Colour eyes?'

'No idea.'

'His build?'

'That kinda skinny-stocky build, you know? Looks kinda skinny but you know underneath they're quite built.'

'Anything else at all?'

'Don't think so but if anything else comes back to me I'll let you know.'

The room rang with confusion, a grieving process just kicking in with Lesley as the lack of practicalities created the space to mourn. Mick was too wired to mourn, too fired up, too angry – like a eunuch in a room full of surgeons with his finger twitching on the trigger of a shot-gun.

'OK, Michael, could you go through the events from when you picked Billy up from school?'

'Billy runs ahead every night – it's OK, he's learning about danger and stops down at the bottom to cross the road.' Mick drifted off into reflection, trying to justify a decision that now seemed rash and careless. He should have stapled Billy to his side like all the mothers.

'Which road are you talking about?'

'Just down there... Theaker Lane.'

'Yeh, carry on.'

'A car slowed down and the bloke tried to grab him but Billy pulled away and ran to me.'

'What? Was this before he'd been snatched?'

'Yeh, I was—'

'And you didn't call the police?'

'No, I didn't want to scare—'

'When something like that happens you act straight away, you don't wait until the right opportunity to call the police.'

'Yeh, but I—'

'So did you have your mobile?'

'Yeh, but I was going to phone you as soon as we got back home.'

'Someone's just tried to snatch your son and you wait until you get home to phone the police?'

'Yes, it's literally a couple of minutes away from our house and I didn't want to have a huge discussion in front of Billy and make it into a big thing in his head that someone had just tried to grab him.'

'You should have phoned straight away.'

'YES— I realise that now.' Mick was hot with frustration and guilt.

Lesley, who'd been struggling to formulate sentences, soon found the words. 'So you're saying that the bloke had already tried to snatch Billy before he actually got him?'

'Yes.'

'F'fuck's sake, Mick—'

The domestic broken up by one of the men who had been quiet until this point. 'Mrs McCann, we need to focus, you can bollock him later. Now we need to find out exactly what's happened.'

DC Strangelove, unable to decide who to throw the look at, asserted her position. 'Was it the same car?'

'Yes.'

'Are you sure?'

'Yes I'm positive; it's unlikely that two kidnappers would be operating in the same small area of Leeds on the same day.'

'Did you see that car? Did you see that it was the same car?'

'Yes, yes I did.'

'What time was this... the first attempt?'

'Twenty past three.'

'So what happened next?'

'So we walked up the hill to home and just as I came round that corner,' Mick stood up and pointed through the window to the tall gate-posts, 'someone clouted me on the back of the head and—'

'You're saying that he was driving the same car that was down on Theaker Lane?' Strangelove struggling hard to mask her difficulty with the story. 'I thought you said that it only takes a couple of minutes to walk up the hill?'

'It does. Maybe we dawdled a bit.'

'Someone's just tried to snatch your son and you're dawdling?'

'Well, don't forget that Billy ran back along Theaker Lane to me, I took a few moments to make sure he was alright – but it wouldn't take long in a car to get along Theaker Lane and up and around to our house.'

'What, you think you could do it in a couple of minutes?'

'Yes... definitely.'

One of the men stood and left the room.

'So in the time that it took the two of you to walk a couple of hundred yards, someone drove down Theaker Lane, up onto Armley Town Street, through the traffic, back along, down your lane, parked up, got out of his car and hid around that corner?'

'Yes he must have because—'

'Also someone has just failed in kidnapping a child, has been spotted doing it and he comes back two or three minutes later to have another go?'

'F'fuck's sake, what is this? That's what fucking happened. I knew this'd happen. There's a kid out there that needs finding and all you want to do is question me as if I'm lying. Let's have a nice little suspicious chit-chat while you try and trip me up and we'll forget trying to find Billy for a few hours, shall we? The crucial first few hours spent getting fucking questioned instead of looking. So I did it, that's what you think, that I did it?'

'Nobody's accusing you of anything, Mr McCann, I'm just trying to work out what happened.'

'Listen, you don't have to work out fuck-all cos I'm telling you exactly what happened.' Mick hadn't been fully concentrating; he was clinging on to a question, waiting for a gap. He quickly threw his question at the slight pause. 'Have you got onto the press yet?'

Strangelove looked down at her clip-board. 'No, we need to get the details first and then alert them.'

'I've got fucking the details, you've got the fucking details, there's a bit of a rush on here, y'know. We need to let people know before he goes to ground. Get it straight on the telly and then people might spot him.'

'It doesn't work like that, Mr McCann. The local news doesn't start for a while and people who see them now or in the last half hour are still likely to be travelling. We will ask if people have seen them.'

'Oh, yeh, s'pose.'

'Look, we need to decide what the relevant details are and then get a press release together or make some calls. So let's get back to what happened – as he hit you, did you see him?'

'No, I went straight down and he kicked me a couple of times but I snatched a look just before he went.'

'Did you pass out?'

'Don't think so but if I did it was only for a couple of seconds.'

'You should get yourself checked over, y'know. It's hard to tell how long you've been out for. I'll tell you what, we'll get a police doctor to come down later and have a look at you if you like.'

Mick stretched his jaw that suddenly felt stiff and became aware for the first time that his right eye was seeing less than it should. 'Yeh, yeh, fine, but if I was out it can't have been that long because I was conscious as the car started and got to the lane in time to see it out the top.'

The man who had earlier left the room returned and whispered something in Strangelove's ear that seemed to confuse her and left again.

'What? What is it?' Lesley asked.

'Nothing. We need to get on with the questions,' replied Strangelove, trying, badly, to mask an important thought process.

'Look, if you've got some news, you'd better tell us,' Lesley demanded, strong and uncompromising.

'No, it's really nothing, we mustn't get distracted. Michael, so you got up from the floor?'

Lesley interjected. 'If it is something, you must tell us.'

'It's not relevant, Lesley, we need to get moving. Michael, so you got up from the floor?' Just as Strangelove posed the question her phone started playing a tune. 'Hello... Yes... Bugger,' she sighed and widened her eyes. 'OK, thanks.' Strangelove snapped her phone shut with a frustrated flick of the wrist.

'What?' asked Mick.

Strangelove looked over at one of the male officers. 'CCTV at the top of the lane was unoperational.'

'CCTV,' shouted Mick, 'you can check all the CCTV.'

'Yes, Mr McCann, we are,' sighed Strangelove, still frustrated, 'but if you could give us a more precise time it would help.'

'I've given you the time – check for a silver Ford Focus with a zed on the reg.'

'You've given us a rough time and we will work through the CCTV in the immediate area but don't hold your breath. Have you any idea how many silver Ford Focuses there are? It isn't always easy to follow a car. Plates are often obscured by buses or vans; they may turn off into areas that have no CCTV and park up. Especially with something like a silver Focus, it's hard to be sure that you're sticking with the same one and we don't even have the registration.'

'But you'll check?'

'Of course we'll check.'

They toed and froed through the car chase, the exact timings that Mick could only guess at through a tracking of moments that were unreal, manic and outside time. What sort of car was this person driving? That person? What did the builder's van look like? Mick couldn't drag much information up out of the half-remembered nightmare. His focus wasn't the periphery but the search for the invisible car that appeared sudden and missed. The car that now symbolised his complete uselessness as a human being to all concerned.

Lesley couldn't help herself when it came to the questions on Armley Road. 'You had him, you fucking had him and you let him go. I bet Billy saw you run past – how could you have missed him? It was a fucking car in a queue of stationary cars – you must have been checking the cars. Weren't you checking the cars as you ran past? – The cars? – Were you checking the cars?'

Mick couldn't answer, he couldn't speak; she was right, she was so fucking right. In all this he'd made a string of bad decisions and mistakes that could very well have led to the death of their son, their baby. The body-shattering guilt led Mick briefly to think about joining Billy in death, but the nagging hope, the possibility of finding Billy, the thought of taking however little attention away from the search for Billy and the cowardice involved in the idea killed the urge dead in its track. Every so often across the ensuing weeks, Mick returned to the idea, brought about by the notion of Billy scared and alone in some afterlife that Mick wasn't even sure he believed in. As the imaginings brought him to his knees, the certainty that – even though they'd never met – Granddad would not leave Billy scared and alone returned Mick to focus on the here and fucking now. This colossal problem, his huge fuck-up, his inability to carry out the single most important task he had on this earth, the protection of his kids. Anyway if Billy was dead and there was an afterlife Billy would be having a fucking ball – Granddad would see to that.

As the energy started to drop in the room and the endless questions appeared to get less and less focussed, Mick noticed men with cameras starting to arrive at the gate-post. A proper camera crew turned up and the policeman who had earlier twice left the room appeared from nowhere, his face glowing in the darkness, a surreal ghost speaking into a growing number of microphones and small electrical boxes. After a short while two camera crews moved off down the lane, past the house and out of sight.

'Where the fuck are they going?'

Strangelove lifting her non-functioning head up from her notes: 'Pardon?'

'Where the fuck are those cameras going?' As Mick jumped up to leave the kitchen and check through one of the side windows it struck him that the news crews would want some shots of the scene of the crime, of Theaker Lane, that was all, no developments, just establishing shots.

'What the fuck?' Mick gazed out of his window at Theaker Lane packed with vans, and a long line of regimented police with sticks and torches crawling across Armley Moor. 'What the fuck?' Running back into the kitchen: 'What the fuck are you doing? Are you fucking mental? What's the fucking point in that?'

Strangelove, jolted out of her fight to concentrate: 'What?'

One of the men more focussed than Strangelove stood up, almost threatening. 'Calm down, Mr McCann.'

'I'm right in the fucking mood for you, mate. Fucking touch mi and I'll rip your fucking head off.' The man professionally tamed his instincts and sat down again.

'MICK, STOP IT,' Lesley shaking as she entered a new phase of shock, 'WHAT'S WRONG WITH YOU?'

'They're searching the fucking moor, that's what's fucking wrong with mi.'

'WHAT?' Lesley jumped up. Now the policeman looked scared as she rushed past him.

'They're searching the fucking moor – what's the fucking point in that? How many is there? You could do a sweep of the fucking city in about an hour with that lot.'

Strangelove returning to the real world: 'It's just procedural, it's bog standard – for the cameras.'

'BOLLOCKS,' shouted Lesley returning to the room, 'you wouldn't use all those people just for the cameras, and if it's just for the cameras why are they searching the other side of the wall?'

Mick gazed out of the window to see weird and random light bouncing around trees behind the wall opposite the house. 'What the fuck? I just don't believe it. This is the one fucking place in Leeds that doesn't need searching and you useless cunts are searching it.'

'We have to do this, it's routine in this kind of situation.'

Lesley snapped back into focus. 'Brilliant, it's routine, great answer. There's an area containing a couple of million people that needs searching, urgently, and you waste time and all your resources on the one place that quite clearly doesn't need searching.'

'You don't know that, he may have been watching the house. There may be clues of his presence – he may have left something behind. We have to do this.'

'Bollocks, you're looking for a body, aren't you?' Lesley's eyes started to haze up. 'Instead of being out there looking for my alive son you're looking for his fucking carcass. Look, Mick may be a daft, stupid, useless wanker—'

'Steady on,' protested Mick half-heartedly.

'But I'll tell you this, for sure, absolutely no doubt at all in my mind, not one iota. He didn't purposely hurt Billy and if he'd had an accident he'd be too busy mourning to concoct some ridiculous story.'

'I can't handle this, I'm getting out.' Strangelove, looking curiously emotional, moved quickly to the door and out of the house. She visibly straightened as she moved towards the small gaggle of reporters who'd resisted the lure of the search.

She hated it when cases took big unproductive twists – it was a mess with no obvious leads. Surely it was unconnected to the SIM Card. But you never know, and with all that bullshit chuntering from the two amateur sleuths in there, it was hard to focus. 'Of course we're going to search the immediate area, you idiots.' She dampened the words with the back of her throat to make sure they didn't travel. To make it worse, she'd met the little kid: the sort of kid that makes you lose the battle with the hormones. More than cute. She hadn't had that much experience with little 'uns but even she saw that – for one so young – he was vibrant, confident and so alive. A picture flicked through her mind of the little fella – like the adult ghost of a child – coming through into the kitchen, not fazed at all by the four austere strangers. Saying hello and asking them who they were. No nerves, no toddler bashfulness. Maybe that was why it'd got to her – they didn't normally get to see the victims in a happy life, just the blood and guts of fucked-up people. The dad – she still had her doubts about the dad, although she hadn't had him down as a killer. But that's the problem with killers, they're often normal people who – although she couldn't see the situation – react extremely to complicated situations. It's not often that you can see it in their eyes, most of their lives they're not killers – just for that moment. For someone like him his reaction was almost textbook, and the wife certainly knows nothing. It's not like that lot over in Dewsbury, every time you turn away from them you can sense them starting to giggle. When you look back they try to turn the sniggers into sobs like naughty school kids behind their teacher's back. *I haven't seen E.T. for a while*, she thought. *Where did that come from?*

Back in the kitchen, the policeman stepped into the space left by Strangelove's departure. 'Look, we are not assuming anything. We have to check the immediate area if a child has been taken, we just have to do it.'

Lesley spun on him furious. 'No matter what? No matter how unlikely? No matter what a clear waste of time it is? You have to do it because it's expected, it's procedural, you may get reprimanded if you don't. Ooh, that's so much more important than finding a four-year-old boy, isn't it?'

'But we have to do it,' he asserted.

16

There were two different adults living in the house. One manic and fretting, spewing out random, obvious statements, trying to drag something constructive out of his boots, and the other paralysed; a paralysis that sprang from the womb, creeping around the incomplete body and filling it with a dread – prickling and stabbing at vital organs.

She'd wake up in a sweat and stumble through to the bedroom, sniffing the empty bed, holding the pillows up to her nose to fill her being with essence of Billy. If Cal woke, she'd soothe him to sleep, often falling asleep in the empty bed beneath, rapping the smell of Billy around her. Mick's body clock dragged him out of his half-sleep nightmares every night sometime between half-one and half-two, his bodily cogs making it random to properly mirror the waking of a young lad needing the loo. Sometimes as Lesley left the room Mick's cruel head told him that it was Billy opening the door to sneak into the bed; he could hear the soft sleepy breath of the young child refusing to fully leave the womb. One night his mind played a soothing role. His brain forcing more sleep onto the unconsenting body as Mick cuddled up with Billy trying to hold him in as the legs kicked and body wriggled, little fingers grabbing at Mick's ears, the breath slightly stale.

Lesley taking the phone with her everywhere – sitting in the room while it charged. Every time it rang her heart moved, sometimes it jumped with a positive craving, sometimes it dropped a foreboding, sudden and breath-stealing fear deep in her chest. And who is it? Cold-callers or people who think they are so close that they can invade the house with that jolting ring. The worst of all, the absolute worst were the 'Mrs McCann, it's Matt Taylor from *The Sun*' calls. 'It's Miss Jackson, you wanker,' and the phone hammered off, a half-reminder of the satisfying old slammable phones with their two disconnect prongs but a full reminder of Billy. The all-consuming fear for him, the mind-numbing helplessness, fully re-engaged.

Why had Mick tidied away Billy's toys, why did he do that? It was like shuffling Billy's presence out of the room, like getting on with normal life without him. Cars kept turning up in the most unexpected places, dressing-gown pockets, the bottom of her handbag, in the heel of a boot that she hadn't worn for ages, tucked away on floors all over the house under furniture, by radiators and skirting-boards. Little chunks of Billy all around. Every time she saw one she saw him playing with it, she saw his shining face making the engine sound. She saw him playing, not a care in the world, and it ripped her guts out, it bent her over double, howling in pain.

Little sketches were all over the house and it felt wrong to gather them up and hide them away. They seemed to be everywhere, on surfaces in every room and tumbling unexpectedly out of drawers. Billy had for the first time in his life developed a clear style and started repeating a design involving a blue sky and colourful flowers, usually red, which looked like tulips jutting up out of long green grass. He'd started calling them *Love Cards* and had brought them home every day for different members of the family – Mum had the most. These drawings were the most common, and the way in which he'd done it felt like he knew he was going away. The house was haunted, haunted by the lack.

Mick hadn't identified it, he was too wrapped up in worrying about his son and chastising himself for being a useless cunt, but his primary function on Earth had been removed. Lesley was the hunter, he was the gatherer and the nurturer, although obviously all roles were shared. Sometimes he did hunting around the childcare, and Lesley when time allowed, did plenty of nurturing. Even if she rarely acknowledged it, Lesley carried around a genetic guilt, as did Mick.

He couldn't escape the removal of this primary function, these purged nurturing and caring routines extenuated his absolute sense of loss. Every time that the clock notified him of a task to be carried out and then his brain reminded him that the task was now pointless, also reminded him of Billy's absence, of Billy's predicament, of his own redundancy, of his inability to protect Billy and of Billy's possible death. His brain sometimes blocked these habitual assaults out – they were too painful – but it was masking, not curing, the illness that dominated Mick's body. He wasn't a person but a ghost, dead in this world and alive in a life

142

past. A past in which he and Billy exchanged love simply because they loved each other down to the bone.

Now that Billy was gone Mick questioned his whole attitude to parenting. Although society ignored it, he was more experienced than most women, but was it OK to tell your four-year-old to 'bog off'? And was it alright to give him a quick kick up the butt with it? Of course it was, Billy would run away giggling excitedly as Mick chased him pretending that he couldn't catch him, but planting a couple of side-foots first. He didn't hide these kinds of things, he did them anywhere, and took the looks of disapproval without resorting to telling the judges that he probably knew more about parenting than they'd ever know. Yes, it was OK to tell Billy to bog off, it was honest and straightforward; parents do need space, parents do need to able to hold conversations with other adults without constant interruptions. In what way was it different to saying 'Now run along, darling'? Same meaning, different words, and different levels of honesty.

Fucking 'modern parents' – 'Of course, Chloe' – didn't these people understand that their kids know instinctively when the parents want them to piss off and that to make yourself constantly and fully available is fucking up their kids, and dishonest? It drove Mick crazy when some visiting child would enter the room talking. At some ages it's acceptable as long as they are told not to do it and not to think it's acceptable to constantly interrupt any conversation going. He was honest with Billy; their relationship was built on honesty. The nights when Billy sat on Mick's knee to read a story, Billy knew full well that that was their time and that Mick was fully present, enjoying it and not just going through the motions. Billy knew when they were playing or babbling crap together that Mick was happy doing it, but Billy would also understand that when his dad's on the phone and tells him not to interrupt, not to be so rude and to bog off, that his own behaviour isn't good.

Kid fucking gloves. When it comes to parenting, thought Mick trying to justify himself, *there's a social rule book – especially among the middle classes – that you must not step outside. If a parent didn't try to splash their kid with cold water while the kid was in the bath, how would they find out that it was the most fun to be had outside a park on God's earth?... And the kid might like it too. But that's it, it comes as a package; the unexpected, the risk-taking, and kids love it. If they are not used to the unexpected their already closed mind will simply define cold as uncomfortable and not recognise the inherent excitement.* Mick could hear, he could see, Billy giggling so much that he was struggling to breathe. Mick had to pace it as he passed him the toy pan full of cold water, ostensibly for Billy to drink, that just happened to get dropped over Billy as Billy failed to grab it in time. *If Billy had been in discomfort,* he told himself, *I'd have stopped straight away, but he wasn't, he was sat in a warm bath saying, 'Again, again, one more time, Dad, please, Dad, just one more time.'* Mick's being filled with a huge tear drowning his thoughts as he remembered the joy Billy experienced in the warm bath when he introduced cold water to his skin, the memory of the ecstatic laughter an excruciating bliss that Mick couldn't bear but could not live without. When he got him out of the bath, he also shunned modern parenting with its risk-averse bollocks and prissy rules. Wrapping him in a towel and pretending to drop him head-first in the still full bath. Dangling him by his feet as Billy whooped with pleasure, 'Again, again, one more time, Dad, please Dad, just one more time.'

'No, Billy, that's enough. I would NEVER drop you on purpose… Whoops, I dropped you. How did that happen?'

Billy's head dangling by Mick's shins, giggling and shouting, 'You dropped me, Dad, you did, you dropped me.'

It was OK, Billy liked it and that was all that mattered: he was a good dad – almost.

The parenting issue that was really worrying Mick was the constant balancing between allowing Billy to 'know his own mind' and stopping him from being a stroppy little get. Billy was so bloody headstrong and determined, would he natter The Cunt into submission or defy him into extreme punishment? Every time he tried to work through the puzzle to its conclusion, he had to hack the thought down, its resolution too awful, the threat constant.

Memories and reminders littered the house, silent camouflaged snipers, unseen until it was too late, delivering the deadly shot directly and perfectly to the heart. Every day that came and went was a day that Billy was less likely to see and it mattered not how diligently the brain tried to defend against that fact; as soon as thoughts left and a gap appeared, the notion would sneak through the wire and stand up, front-of-brain hideous and naked in the spotlight. Every day that came and went was a day which increased Billy's life lived in the past, his existence in the present becoming paler and harder to imagine, his future dying slowly in the sluggish, rhythmic tick of killing time.

The world was unrecognisable without Billy, like they'd awoken in the middle of a nightmare trip where everything was simply wrong. All the things clung onto to make sense, all the familiars, all the markers, not quite right and unfamiliar. Days went past, irrelevant, wasted and pointless, and yet the only solid thing they had was time, plodding on relentlessly, ticking down to an unknown conclusion or – worst possible outcome – no conclusion at all. They sat in a torturous limbo. Plans of any kind were improper, almost disrespectful – not that they could have planned anything had they tried. Some everyday routines continued but only because they had to. They had to eat, Cal still had to go to school, they had to survive, but only for the slim chance that Billy would one day bound essential and alive down the hallway, spreading radiant joy around him. It wasn't right, it wasn't right that The Cunt should experience that joy; that he should live day after day in the presence of that vital spark of life so easily lost in mundane life. That he should witness his everyday developments, the pure jaw-dropping logic, and if he's extinguished that vital spark, if he's removed that light from the world, if he's sinned against the eternal, he'd better expect an eternity of hell and a lifetime of pain.

Days dragged and days disappeared. It was two days since, five days since, and then a week since, everything measured, everything experienced in relation to Billy and to the moment that he was no longer there. Without him would they ever remember to be silly again? Would they ever be spontaneous? Would they ever look at simply everyday things in a new way? Would they ever be fully alive again outside this twilight zombie existence? Feelings usually closed down were at times so extreme that all that existed was numbness – the numbness of the edge of the extreme and the numbness of the lack. The music had gone from the house, as had the laughter, and they were both followed closely by the future, wrapping a scarf around its neck and heading for the door. All that was left was the now and the next pointless breath.

They lived in the first second, not the automated one but the human one. The one that exists, that should exist but doesn't really. They lived in the one-second gap before the 'one' that is always uncounted, 'one-gap-two-gap-three'; their space was a hypothetical gap so ignored that it's hardly there.

He was so fucking vital that his absence was against nature. He was so fucking alive that the concept of him being dead was like the earth stopping turning, leaving just an absence, a void, an age without existence, space and time barren and extreme. Surely he's still alive: the world is still functioning, the planet is still turning, night still follows day, the moon still drags oceans around the earth, and there's still air to breathe. As for his ability to survive, that was beyond question – *he* is not the problem. Although he is small and vulnerable, throw him in the river and he'll get to the side still breathing. Leave him somewhere too cold and his body will refuse to sleep – he's hard, he's a fighter, a natural-born survivor. Surely even The Cunt could see that to hurt him would leave The Cunt with the same mental turmoil as Pontius Pilate. Nobody who experienced Billy could seriously consider harming him, no matter what a fucking sicko they were, surely?

As for surviving on little food, he'll simply do it. Sleeping in unfamiliar or uncomfortable places, he'll be alright, he'd fall asleep on a sixpence. *He's a right little trooper is Billy* – Lesley's body started to shake at the repeated use of the present tense in her head; silent, tearless sobbing that emanated from the centre of her chest and shook her body, building into an overwhelming, uncontrollable first-time fit. She was so glad that Mick hadn't witnessed this – if the two of them did it at the same time it'd bring their home down, collapsing around their ears and burying them alive in the debris that was once their life.

Immediately that one of them left the house they were followed by the press, snapping away. How many fucking depressing photos did they need? How much grief and desperation did the nation need to devour and wallow in? *If any cunt puts a flower anywhere near my fucking garden*, thought Mick, *I'll kick their fucking head in. Anyone with a fucking ribbon will be found in the morning hanging from a lamppost with the yellow ribbon around their fucking neck.* The press were incessant, following them to work, to drop Cal off at school, to the supermarket, for fuck's sake. At least they didn't follow him in, just stayed with the car and followed him home again. They could have got some good photos in Asda – it was torture. He'd kept meaning to switch supermarkets but habit kept dragging him back there and not until he got over the threshold would he remember the trial that confronted him. He'd considered walking straight out and going to Morrison's but decided it'd just confuse him – might as well just keep his head down and run round. Moving quickly through the first few aisles – that Billy would nag him through constantly chattering about the cow – reflex movements throwing things into bags or straight into the trolley, he couldn't avoid it. It was inevitable. A little lass jabbing the big red button next to the full size plastic cows head and dragging a wire brush across the inside of Mick's chest, filling the corner of the supermarket with the moo, the small child with giddy anticipation and Mick with Billy's smiling face. People looking at him like he was a weirdo, tears rolling down his face, moving along to the Thomas Tank Engine yogurts he couldn't help but pick them up and start to shake.

At first Mick used to take the journos coffee out – if it was quiet and not too many there – but their inane questions were just too much to handle, the only thing they had in common was a missing child and Mick couldn't handle the constant speculation. He'd half expected sensitivity. You'd think they'd switch off and chat about the weather, but no, a constant jabbering, 'Have you heard anything?' 'How are you feeling?' 'What do you think about the way the police are handling it?' 'Has anyone got a grudge against you?' The longer Mick stayed, the more complex the questions got and the more he realised that they, the fucking press, didn't seem to understand the situation at all.

The final straw, the cause of the cessation of contact with the press, was the question, 'So what do you think the link is between Maddie and Billy?'

'Link?' Mick had scoffed. 'There is no link, just pure unadulterated coincidence. All they share is a surname, a rough age and the fact that they've been taken.' Mick's head suddenly and unexpectedly filled with the imagery of the press, the attempts to heighten the drama, the entertaining speculations trying to connect the two children, and his stomach turned. Surely they weren't running with that.

They'd watched and listened to the coverage at first but it simply emphasised their state of despair and helplessness. Trapped on a desert island hundreds of miles from the trade routes, they had no choice but to face their isolation. They'd asked friends and family to monitor the media just in case something came up that they should know about, something solid, not tittle-tattle but anything new, anything that mattered. They had no calls regarding the press. Sair had tried to talk to Mick about how much coverage *Coming Out* was getting but it simply made him angry and she quickly asked if Lesley was in. Mick may find out at the end of the month that over at Lightning Source a printing press had been given over solely to its production, but he'd stopped checking his emails, his address was too widely known and too easily got. There were some sick fucks in the world.

Out in the real world people nudged each other and pointed. People in queues would offer condolences and support. They meant well but it made Lesley and Mick want to wear a niqab, except it was against their lack of religion. Even now neither prayed. They may use words that contain the term 'God' but they were pleading with fate or chance, not a superior being. They prayed just as much to Fuck as they did God: 'Fuck, please'... 'For Fuck's sake'. Up and down the country sad people prayed, unaware that both Lesley and Mick would prefer them to give their attention to the thousands of children dying around the world every day through lack of food or clean water, rather than wasting their time and energy on something they could do nothing about. But Billy was cute, fair and white, he was involved in a dramatic kidnap story – of course he'd get an obscene amount of coverage. At work many people were different with Lesley, although she'd decided that they didn't mean anything by it, and the people that mattered were the same, supportive and sensitive.

17

Mick had been distracted by that stalking fucking Frenchman again. Every time his theories crawled to the front of his brain Mick felt guilty, like he was hiding away in some abstract hole when the concrete world needed his constant attention. That was the problem with the spineless Gallic twat, all abstract and no action, but here were his abstractions again: the unseen gaze had been so unequal and so unseen that its intentions weren't even considered. He didn't care if it was an individual, not an institution/society – although it kind of was society, with its unavoidable delinquents and individualisation – the perpetrator must have done some serious surveillance, looked at the possibilities, studied the patterns, and God knows what stalking or how. The police found no sign in the area around the house, and now, if The Cunt wanted to, he could get Mick or Lesley to do anything, absolutely anything – *All hail the fucking sovereign.* He was such a mess that he couldn't even tell if any of this bollocks was at all useful. Was it just cluttering his brain with smokescreens and bullshit?

Right, fuck Foucault – real world, Mick. So there were no signs of anyone watching the house by physically being in its locale, but surely the police realise that with it being 2008 you can watch a house from the comfort of your own home; there's a global Panopticon (*FUCK OFF, FOUCAULT*). It doesn't have to be like some shitty 80's police drama with the stalker hiding in the bushes, soil rubbed into his nose and small branches sticking out of his hat. Mick's gut was telling him that this cunt was a techy so if he watched the house he could have done it via the internet, via live satellite; Mick would have no idea how to do it but a geek would. So the companies who provide the service would be able to scan their records to see if anyone had been watching the McCann's co-ordinates, and, if so, provide the IP address. Bingo! You've got your prime suspect (*It's a two-way Panopticon, y'cunt*). Surely those CSI-obsessed CID twats will have checked that, but with the way their case had been handled, Mick had his doubts; he'd phone and give them a shove. 'Bollocks, I can't phone, I'll have to email her.'

Before Foucault had butted in he'd been trying to think through the fact that he should tell the police about the dodgy phone call that he'd received before Billy got snatched. The longer he'd avoided it, the harder it had got. If he phoned them now about the satellite stalking thought and didn't mention the phone call it'd just complicate it if he ever did tell them about the call. He felt a bit guilty as Lesley had just assumed that he already had told them and it felt like he was deceiving her. He just didn't trust them, and if it was a rogue officer the delay in reporting the call may frustrate him and make him call again or do something else. He'd also checked with BT, who had assured him that no matter what, the call couldn't be traced, so nothing could be gained by it. He decided to give himself a break from the domestic routine, went into the kitchen for a coffee and a fag, and maybe when he'd got his fix he'd phone the police about the call.

Ezra entered the kitchen. 'Dad I really miss Billy, I miss him so much that I can't stop thinking about him. Do you think he's OK?'

'I don't know, Ez, there's no way to know, but I don't think the odds are very good, not after this amount of time... but you never know, there's still hope.'

'What if it's a paedophile, Dad? Or a bunch of them and they're hurting him? I swear...' The two men tingling with fear, anxiety, revulsion and violence at the thought.

'Ez, you can't think like that. I know it's hard but there's absolutely no point in torturing yourself. We don't know anything.'

Ezra's eye filling up with chaotic tears: 'I swear to God, Dad, if they hurt him,' fighting for the words through a stream of tears and lack of breath, 'I'll track them down and kill them. Forget joining the police, Dad, I swear I'll track them down and I'll kill them.'

Mick's initial frustration that Ez had entered the kitchen just as he was about to light a fag had long since evaporated. He stood up, went over to Ez and put his arms around him. 'I can't tell you it'll be alright because it may not be, but try not to think about it, we can't do anything but wait.'

Ezra nuzzled his face into Mick's shoulder, squeezing so hard that Mick was struggling for breath. 'I swear, Dad, I'll kill them – I miss him so much.'

'I know, Ez.'

The two men sobbed in a long embrace. Mick was sure that if Ez ever did find the guy that he would kill him, he held such a rage. Mick couldn't help but notice that Ez was considerably taller than him; although he was slim, his shoulders were way wider and he was solid, muscular and fast. There was absolutely no doubt that he would kill The Cunt. Ezra'd had quite a tough and difficult young life and was streetwise and intelligent with an extremely well-defined concept of right and wrong. It was a credit to Ezra that he was as honest as the day was long and would never knowingly act against another human being... not without provocation. Mick took this situation on board and silently promised himself that if the occasion ever arose, it would be him that took retribution, and he'd make sure that Ez knew fuck about it until the job had been done.

'How are you going on at college?'

'I can't concentrate, Dad.'

'Do you want me to phone them and have another word? Maybe you should take a year out.'

'No, Dad, I like the routine. I'll maybe just have to do another year and re-sits.'

Mick spent the next ten minutes doing his best to talk him down and Ez left the kitchen to prepare for work.

'I love you, Dad.'

'I love you too, Ez.'

As soon as the door closed, Mick picked the waiting cig up from the table. 'Fuck, I love smoking.'

*

'Ooh.' Strangelove double clicked.

From: mick mccann
To: s.strangelove@westyorkshire.pnn.police.uk
Sent: Friday, Jan 11, 2008 3:29 PM
Subject: Satellite stalking

DC Strangelove,

Bit of a weird one this and if you already have it covered could you let me know.

I was just thinking about the search you did around the house and it occurred to me that if the kidnapper is a geek, which I think is likely, he'd be more likely to watch the house via satellite in real time on a PC. Now I don't know how to do this but I'm sure it's possible.

If he did do this you could contact the companies offering this service, they could do a search on our co-ordinates and if anyone did monitor our immediate area you could get their IP address. You would then know that someone with access to that computer is likely to be our man, may even be his home address.

Thanks,
Mick McCann

Strangelove shook her head and sighed. 'Maybe in five years time love,' she muttered to herself. 'Joe public won't be able to do that and what makes you think he's a geek? Quite ingenious though.' She was getting weird looks across the office. *Why can't they just accept I talk to myself, blokes do it and no one thinks that's weird.* Words safe back behind the eyes. *That Bloody Spooks programme really has got a lot to answer for. The public think it's real. They should try CSI if they want reality.*

From: DC Strangelove
To: mick.mccann@hotmail.co.uk
Sent: Friday, Jan 11, 2008 3:29 PM
Subject: Satellite

Michael we have considered that possibility but it's a long process, I'll let you know if we get any further information.

Thankyou,
DC Strangelove

Strangelove smiled to herself. *As if. They're so naïve, as if we'd share our information with a suspect.*

*

It felt almost futile – as did everything in life – but Lesley was worried that the SIM card and the associated suspicion may be muddying the water. Surely the police could see that there was no connection between the two things, just another bizarre coincidence, but if they could remove themselves from the SIM card situation it would lessen the likelihood of their involvement in Billy's disappearance. Lesley reflected again that she wasn't even sure what 'the SIM card situation' was, but she would do anything that ensured that police time was focussed fully on finding Billy.

'Yes, could I speak to DC Strangelove, please? Yes, it's Lesley Jackson.'

She sensed the woman scrambling to put her through. She'd tell her husband tonight, 'Ooh, I took a call from that Jackson woman today.' Suddenly they were the centre of a nation's gossip and suddenly they were taken a bit more seriously.

'Yes, hi, Lesley, it's Rachel. What can I do for you?'

Lesley wanted to spit at the over-familiarity, the gentle friendliness, and her question was so fucking tempting, Lesley resisted 'Do your fucking job' and instead opted for, 'Yeh, I was wondering why you've never asked us about any dates?'

'Dates?'

'Yes, y'know, where were you on this date or that date? I called you before about it but if we can account for ourselves at given times then your investigation can take on a whole new focus, can't it?'

'To tell you the truth, Lesley, the SIM card enquiry has been put on a bit of a back-burner and...' (*Oh, she can fucking discuss the case with me now then, can she?*) '... our enquiries have been reflecting that.'

'Really, it'd have been nice if you'd have told us that; anyway, wouldn't it be good for all concerned to eliminate us fully?'

'Well, yes, but we've pretty much moved on from the malicious phone calls.'

'Oh brilliant, so what, we stay permanently out on bail? And you don't think the two things may be connected?'

'Well, we've been looking at that and think it's unlikely that we are dealing with some sort of manipulative criminal mastermind. It's more likely to be chance, but obviously we haven't discounted anything.'

'Yes, whatever, but surely you've got a list of when the calls were made. We may be able to tidy the case up a bit – take me and Mick fully out of that equation.'

'Even if you do prove that the calls were nothing to do with you, it doesn't necessarily—' Strangelove stopped herself. This was the problem when you get into discussing cases with a suspect or a member of the public: no matter how careful you are, you end up with too much candour.

'Look, I can show that we were out of the country for three weeks in the last year. If calls were made in that period, you'll be able to show that it either was or wasn't us. No grey area, a straightforward fact – I'd have thought you'd like facts.'

'Well, yes, I suppose we could. I'll have to check. There's costs involved but' – Strangelove heading off the anticipated attack at the pass – 'in this case I'm sure cost won't be a consideration; well not this kind of cost anyway.'

Lesley felt a slight disappointment that she couldn't lay into the bitch with a list of the money already wasted in this case and just what she was aware of; God knows how much other money had been wasted in the background.

'Right, well, we were out of the country from the 18th of May until the first of June and again on the 12th until the 19th of September.'

'You could still have made the calls.'

'Yes but they would come through a Greek or maybe Turkish provider, possibly even Albanian.'

'Ah yes, of course, and I think we'd probably be able to check the whereabouts of the SIM card anyway – y'know, was it in the UK or in Greece?'

'Yeh, but it would've had to have been used in that period.'

'Mm, maybe. Well, we'll check it anyway. It could take a few weeks.'

'Weeks?'

'Yes, I have to get permission and then it may take a couple of weeks for the information to come back.'

'Look, sorry, I'm not trying to do your job for you, or maybe I am' – ooh, she enjoyed that, she simply couldn't resist it, a rare sweet moment in her life – 'but you must have a list from the victims of when the calls were made. They must have kept a diary and if so, why not save a lot of time and money and check that list with the dates we were on holiday?'

'Yes, Lesley, I've got your dates, leave it with me. Was there anything else?'

'No I don't think so.'

'OK, well thank you for the call, and how are you all bearing up?' Strangelove almost bit her hand in frustration. What a question.

'Oh, fucking brilliantly. Goodbye.'

And with that, the phone rang off and reverted to that annoying 'don't put the phone down on me' buzz. Strangelove leaned back in her chair and tossed her pen onto the table in frustration. *Couldn't the stupid woman see that unless the two things are connected – which is highly unlikely – it proves nothing about the abduction and distracts me from the list of things I have to get done before seven? As for the abductor having access to his own personal satellite, well.... And some of the jobs are for their son, and more relevant than these pointless diversions.* The trained list-ticking obsession deep in her psyche was taunting her, *This dates thing should have been cleared up months ago and you never know, maybe there'll be some merit in clearing it up. Maybe something will spin off.* Her empirical head entered the constant battle for clarity and punched her third-level inquisitor square on the jaw. *Don't be stupid, there's only so much we can do and life is full of ridiculous coincidences, I see them all the time, and this is one of them.* Staring at the dates on the pad, she picked up the phone.

The instant that Lesley closed her phone to Strangelove it rang again, like an obsessive boyfriend managing to recall immediately. It couldn't have been Strangelove, not that quickly.

'Hello.'

'Hi, is that Lesley?'

'Yes.'

'Oh, hi, Lesley, it's Helen from Human Resources. Would it be possible for you to meet me at IT? We've got something, something that may help.'

'Yes, of course. When?'

'As soon as you like. I'm there now but if it's not convenient I can meet you later.'

'I'm on my way.'

Lesley entered the room, heart pounding; there were too many balls in the air, too many distractions on top of an overwhelming pain and longing that made everything else seem pointless. It was only the vaguest possibility that they may be connected, that perhaps whoever had the SIM card also had Billy, that drove Lesley on. She couldn't betray Billy by curling up in a ball and giving up on it all.

'Hi, Lesley, this is Paul, he's been looking through your email stuff again and seems to have found something. Paul would you like to explain?'

'Yeh, well, all the emails are backed up for seven years and, as you know, we couldn't find anything that you'd sent containing the search terms. Anyway, Helen explained to us how important it was so I decided to interrogate all your mail, outbox, inbox, all your folders.' Lesley bit her tongue – *Surely you checked everything first time.* 'Anyway, you must have replied to something and saved it to draft and then cancelled it – maybe, I'm not sure. It looks like you did it by mistake because you haven't written anything. But the weirdest thing is that it's saved to draft without a recipient address. Shouldn't happen, that. I don't know how you've done that. I could work it out but it'd take too long and it doesn't really matter, does it?'

'Yes, it does. The address it was sent to is crucial.'

'Yeh, I've just said, the recipient address isn't there. I could work out how you managed to save it without an address but I can't find an address that isn't there.'

Helen butted in, intrigued. 'Could someone have removed it?'

'No, no, no. Well, the rest of the email is unusual as well, so I suppose anything's possible, but I can't see it – no, definitely not.'

The email was open on his desk-top and Lesley leant over to read it. *If you want to check if there's any credit on the SIM card...*

Paul continued, 'And look, you're obviously answering someone that you've exchanged a couple of emails with but you've, for some reason, removed their address and name in the body of the email. Look twice, here' – Paul scrolls down the screen – 'and here. Can't think why you've done that, it's weird, and there's other stuff that doesn't make sense.'

Lesley was stuck in between two things, reading the email and listening to Paul, but accomplishing neither – especially as Paul scrolled down the screen – and it felt so important that the lack of focus was making her furious.

'Can I just read the email and then we'll try and work out what's going on.? Lesley said, polite but firm.

'Yeh, sure, just tell me when you want me to scroll.'

Lesley reflected that it would be better if he just moved out of the way and let her sit, read and scroll, but he was a geek and they defend their mouse like a Pit-Bull Terrier with a baby's leg; it just wasn't worth it.

From:
To: lesley_jackson@granadamedia.com
Sent: Friday, 21 July 03, 3:02 PM
Subject: Re: Re: Re: SIM

Well if you want to check if theres any credit on the SIM I'd be happy to reimburse you for that amount.

Thanks

From: Lesley Jackson
To:
Sent: Friday, 21 July 03, 2:19 PM
Subject: Re: Re: SIM

Hi

Yes it's fine for you to have it, it's spare and of course I can send it through internal mail. I don't know if there's any credit on it though.

Lesley

From:
To: lesley_jackson@granadamedia.com
Sent: Friday, 21 July 03, 2:02 PM
Subject: Re: SIM

Thanks very much Lesley,

As long as you don't need it and you're sure it's OK for me to have it. I'd prefer if you sent it through internal mail, things are, as always, very busy this side.

From: Lesley Jackson
To:
Sent: Friday, 21 July 03, 1:22 PM
Subject: SIM

Hi

As I said I've got an Orange SIM that you can have, I could leave it on the YTV front desk for you if you like.

Lesley

Lesley started to get confused and pointed out to Paul that it would make more sense if she could read from the bottom up. Before Lesley got her head around it, Paul started talking again; no problem, they were just words, just words that showed that she wasn't a liar and that someone else was involved.

'The other person obviously emailed you from a Granada Media address. His format is right. Look, can you see? It's the same as yours. But I don't understand why you removed his name and email address. Look, you've done it all the way through.'

'Well, perhaps that's because I won't have done it.'

'You must have because—'

'And I always use people's names.'

'Well, do you let other people use your computer?'

'We all share the computers.'

'I know but do you log off and keep your password safe?'

'Yes, of course I do, but perhaps—'

'Then how would someone else get into your account?'

'I don't know, but I thought it might be possible for some techy to hack my—'

'No no no, our security is extremely tight, *you* must have removed them.'

From nowhere, Lesley burst into head-low tears. 'Why the fuck would I do that? I'm sorry, I'm sorry, it's just... I don't know.'

Helen head-gestured to Paul, who was already recoiling, and he stood up to walk away. 'Sorry, I was just saying that—'

'It's OK, Paul, she's just upset,' interjected Helen. 'You OK, Lesley? It's good news, you know? It shows that there was a conversation with someone else about the SIM card.'

Lesley starting to regain her composure: 'We need to tell the police and it would be better coming from you.'

'Well, they've been in conversation with IT and it'd probably be better coming from them. They can explain it more clearly.' Helen called Paul, who was hovering over another computer, back into the fray. 'We need to let the police know about this.'

'I already did. That Strangelove wasn't there. I spoke to another woman.'

'What was her name?'

'Don't know.'

'Was it Cockshot?' Lesley asked.

'I don't know, she didn't say, just that I could talk to her about it.'

'And what did she say?'

'Not much, really. I didn't really understand something about it being convenient and they'd get back to us.'

Lesley returned to her foetal position – 'Oh, for fuck's sake. I can't handle this' – and started to sob quietly.

Digital stalking in Leeds, Yorkshire, England

18

One of these days he was going to change the tune on that fucking phone. 'Yeh.'

'Michael, how are you?'

'Wh'is it?'

'I've got someone who'd like to say hello.'

Mick's body exploding into chaos as he heard the silence.

'Hello-o.' He waited, longing for the little voice his whole being had been craving since the beginning of time. The little voice too often greeted with 'In a minute', 'Off y'go', 'Go do y'stuff', 'I'm busy now Billy.'

'Dad, I want to come home now. I don't like it here... there's no *Top Gear*... and, and I want to see Mummy and you and—'

'Billy, how are you?'

He heard an off-phone voice: 'Give me the phone now.'

'No I want to... to...' He could visualise Billy using his body shape to defend the phone – *He's good at that kinda stuff.*

'Dad, it's like *Wonder Pets,* isn't it, Dad? Like your friends—'

Mick sensed that time was up, 'I love you, Billy.'

'Dad, I've eaten some—' Followed by fierce protestations, a sudden yelp and sobbing.

'I love you, Billy.'

'Michael.'

'Don't hurt him, mate. Why have you phoned?'

'Ooh, y'know, I didn't want you worrying or doing any unnecessary grieving.'

'Naah, why did you really phone?'

'Anyway, must dash. Things to do.'

That dead tone burrowed through his ear, leaving a void which was instantly filled with joy.

He's alive, he's fucking alive, thank God he's alive.... I knew it, the world is still turning. He sounded OK as well, sounded fine, calm and settled. He almost wanted to kiss The Cunt, kiss him and then rip out his spleen and force feed it to the vegan squirrels. Relief surged through his veins, tempered slightly by hearing the yelp, but that sound didn't necessarily mean that The Cunt had struck Billy, he would have made that sound if The Cunt had snatched the phone roughly. He didn't give a fuck – as long as he's alive, as long as he's not in serious physical pain, and he *is* alive, he'd just spoken to him and he sounded comfortable. *Thank fuck he's alive.*

He went straight into the call history on his phone; the call was listed but no number.

'Fuck, I thought I had him.'

He called 450 on his mobile, through a few options and to an operator. 'Hi, yeh, I've just received a call on my phone and I need to check the number of the phone that made it.'

'There will be a charge for that of—'

'OK, whatever, I just need the number.'

'Yes, can I just take a few details for security?' They went through a series of routine questions, address, the last four digits of his debit card, the last three digits of the card's security code and the final question, 'Can you give me the first two digits of your Orange security code?'

'Security code?'

'Yes, the four-digit code that you used when you first registered the phone – just the first two.'

'That was maybe 10 years ago, how am I going to remember that?'

'Just have a little think, Mr McCann. Four digits. I only need the first two.'

'What about fourteen– I mean one and four.'

'Thank you, Mr McCann, now how can I help?'

'Yeh, I've just had a call on my phone and I need to check the number of the phone that made it.'

'Have you checked your call list? Numbers are usually listed there.'

'I have, yeh, but there's no number, just the time that the call was received.'

'When was the call made?'

'About five minutes ago.'

'It usually takes some time to retrieve this kind of information, and I hope this call isn't being recorded, but aren't you the man whose son has gone missing?'

'Yes I am.'

'OK, Mr McCann, I can fast-track this and I'm not going to charge you. I'll just put you through to one of my colleagues. He'll have all the details we've just been through, so if you could hold the line, and good luck, Mr McCann.'

'OK, thanks very much.'

After a 30-second pause, a male voice: 'Mr McCann.'

'Yeh.'

'We don't have the number that called your phone. The call has registered on our system – I must say that's very fast. I can see it, but we have no details.'

'How can that be the case?'

'Well, it looks like the caller used an unregistered SIM card.'

'Unregistered? Can you get a SIM without it being registered?'

'Well, not with Orange, but some other providers do allow unregistered SIMs on their network and you can buy them all over.'

'So is there any way of getting the number?'

'I'm afraid not.'

'Could it be taken off my SIM card? If someone interrogated my SIM could they—'

'No, your SIM won't hold the information; an unregistered SIM card is just that, it's anonymous. I'm very sorry but there's no way to get it.'

'Fuck... OK, thanks for trying.'

'You're welcome, Mr McCann, and good luck.'

'Yep, ta.'

Body shaking, hands moving too fucking slowly, he dropped his phone, picked it up, took a couple of calming drags on a fag and, three quick thumb-flicks later, he willed a ring-tone but went straight through to the answer phone, 'Yes, I know how to re-record my fucking message, just put me through, you automated cunt. Yes, Les, listen, phone me, now, it's absolutely urgent, phone me now.'

Aware that a text may break through before a voicemail, he quickly sent, *Phone me – IT'S URGENT.*

Within a couple of minutes the land-line rang and Mick pulled it from the collection of phones at his side, ''Ello.'

'Michael, I've got a couple a pies in the fridge that could do wi' using but I'm off away in a couple—'

'Mum, I've got to get off the phone. I've just spoken to Billy and—'

'Oh thank God.'

'And I've left a message for Lesley to phone me—'

'OK, phone me when you can.'

'I will. He sounded fine considering, but I have to. . .'

'OK, bye.'

'. . . get off the phone. Bye.'

With that Mick cleared the line only to engage it again immediately as he tried Lesley's mobile: voicemail.

He longed to be sitting in the heart of his family, relaxed, warm and secure, all present and correct.

The voice – Mick recognised that fucking voice. It was the same one that'd phoned him to warn him off. Surely not, surely not the Detective Chief Superintendent? One of the most powerful, if not **the,** in their case, most powerful people in West Yorkshire Police kidnapping a kid? Why? The actual kidnap would undoubtedly bring huge attention to the case – the last thing he'd want. Anyway, would it be that serious if they went to the press? Supposing that he had leant on CID because his girlfriend was getting dodgy phone calls, could he not just argue that they should investigate malicious phone calls anyway? He'd weather the storm. He wouldn't kidnap a kid, that's a whole new ball game, unless there's some seriously dodgy procedural stuff going on in the background. But even so, they'd just cover it up, and even if it was a resigning matter that could be proved, would he kidnap a kid? Risk prison, rather than just retire on a big fuck-off pension and package and start up a detective agency or go into security or just dig his garden and take shitloads of family holidays? What if he's a nutter and sees it as personal, something personal between them? Some oik fighting back and being too clever by half, posting references to him and his partner online, not showing him enough respect or deference. Powerful people, especially people of rank, have got weird attitudes to folk; he knew that they felt superior because in their professional world that's exactly what they are, superior.

No way, no way would he risk everything on some spurious bollocks. But what other explanation could there be? Wait a fucking minute; wait one fucking minute – The Cunt. It might not have been the policeman warning him off on the phone before; it might have been The Cunt. That'd work – either just warning him off or knowing that Mick would automatically think it was the police. But how would he get his mobile number? *The Cunt could, he's a techy, I'm sure of it, and he's obviously into all this surveillance bollocks, and anyway, I'm hardly careful with it.*

The incoming land-line phone rang.

''Ello... Ah, thank fuck. I've just spoken to Billy... No I'm not... Just now... No, he sounded fine, said he was missing *Top Gear*.' The two of them laughed and cried at the same time, 'I know, the little bugger, but he did say he missed you...' Mick gave Lesley a moment to sob. 'It was really brief. The Cunt took the phone off him... Yes, I know, he's alive, thank fuck he's alive... Nothing else really, just that it's like *The Wonder Pets* and like my friends... I know, could mean anything... OK, yeh, see you in 15 minutes.'

Although there was nothing else to say, Lesley had to come home and was immediately climbing into her car. A bit daft really as they'd forgotten that Mick had to go out to pick up Cal anyway. Lesley had to be there, had to be as close to the person who'd just spoken to Billy – and by association close to Billy – as soon as possible. Something good had happened and nothing else mattered – she had to be near it.

Mick was pleased with himself for keeping calm during the call with The Cunt; he'd rehearsed that situation endlessly and didn't lose his rag. He was a bit pissed off with himself for asking The Cunt not to hurt Billy but at least he didn't threaten or worse still plead with him. He'd thought through the psychology and convinced himself that either of those two things might make The Cunt rise to the drama of his words and do something rash, or just feed some sick buzz that The Cunt was craving. What did Billy mean, 'like *Wonder Pets*'? 'Like my friends'? *The Wonder Pets*, a fantastic programme for young kids where three animals in a school classroom take on human characteristics as the last child leaves at home time. Incorporating the voices of young children, it has a marvellous haphazard feel. They – the chick, the turtle and the guinea pig – go off to help other young animals in distress, like kids' superheroes, but they are only successful when they use team work.

What's going to work?

Teeeeeeam work.

He couldn't get the damn tune out of his head, but it brought a strangely comforting tear to his eye that built into a line of water. *Is he just telling me that he's in distress? That he needs saving? What else could he mean? It's like* Wonder Pets. *Is he in a school or surrounded by small animals? A vet's? A pet shop? The Butterfly House maybe? He must mean that he needs saving.* The veiled cry for help and the physical stabs of hearing Billy's voice were too much. Mick sank into a mire of desperation, anger and frustration as his face became awash with the fluid and mucus of pure incomprehensible emotion. Like a fighter trying to pointlessly drag himself up from the canvas when he's been out-boxed, over-powered and knows he won't land another punch, Mick tried to awaken his senses, the useful ones, the appropriate ones, the ones that may wake him from this paralysis.

He hated leaving his phone behind at the best of times, but after he'd driven a mile – on the way to pick up Cal – realising that he didn't have it felt like he'd lost a limb. What if The Cunt phones back? He won't, not so soon.

On the return journey, whilst Mick was thinking about what to tell him, Cal opened up for the first time. 'Dad, I really miss Billy. I mean I really miss him, Dad, and when I think about winding him up or trying to get rid of him cos I'm talking to my mates on X-box Live…' Cal lowered his head, angling it away from his dad.

'Cal, you can't feel guilty about having a perfectly normal relationship with him – he's four and you're 12. He's bound to wind you up or tire you out with his constant talking. Think about all the times, and it was every day, that you played with him and made him giggle.'

'But I want to see him now, and when he was around I spent half mi time trying to get rid of him.' Cal's face lowered further, hiding the tears rolling down his flushed, translucent face.

'We all did it and we all feel guilty, but it's really stupid. It's just because our brains can only take so much, they can only hold so much love that's got nowhere to go. It's like we miss him so much that our heads can't hold it all, so it spills out into all sorts of other bollocks. Also we couldn't say "Good bye, I love you, Billy, and I'm sorry for hiding your ball" or whatever, but he knows, Cal, Billy's not stupid and he knows how much we love him.'

'Are you sure?'

'Yes of course I'm sure. He's certain of it – what was he like, Cal?'

'What d'y'mean?

'I mean what was he like most of the time?'

'He was happy, always laughing and messing about. He was really busy, hardly ever stopped...' Having a quick side look at Cal, Mick noticed the dawning of the slightest grin coming up on Cal's face. 'He was annoying.'

They did a unified spluttering laugh, the type that is often accompanied by snot or spit.

'There y'go, he was happy and busy, always messing about. You're not happy and busy like that if you're in a house that doesn't love you. Anyway, Cal, I've got something to tell you. I spoke to him today, he sounded alright and he's alive—'

'What? How?'

'The Cunt – sorry for swearing but that's his name—'

'You swear *all the time*, Dad.' Cal threw Mick a condemnatory look.

'Anyway, he phoned me and let me have a quick chat with Billy and he sounded fine.'

Cal was unsure what emotion to express, everything was happening too quickly. 'That's good news, isn't it, Dad?'

'It's fucking fantastic.' They both laughed out loud at Mick's inappropriate language.

For the rest of the journey, Mick returned to the back of his brain. *'Like your friends'... which friends? Does Billy recognise the guy? Does he look like someone, or is it like someone's house? That could mean any style of house. Ahhh, does he mean like the*

167

police? He'd called them mates and friends just to try to minimise the impact of having Billy's world invaded at seven-thirty on a schoolday morning. *That would start to make a whole load more sense. The police? Why would one of them take Billy? And surely it would just be a rogue officer. Does he just mean that The Cunt dresses like an undercover cop? Surely not, he wouldn't notice that, and even if it is a rogue cop, what difference does it make, other than he may have access to a lot of the information?*

When they got home, Lesley was sat in the kitchen smoking. Before she got chance to launch into the set of cultivated questions, Mick, removing his coat, jumped in. 'I'm a bit wary of phoning the police but I need to, don't I?'

'You do really.'

'OK, I'll call them now.'

'No, no, wait a minute, there's a couple of things I've thought of. Have you checked your calls list on your phone to see if the number's there?'

'Yeh, I have, it didn't list the number and—'

'Well, if you call Orange—'

'I already have, they've checked. They can't get the number either and they think the call will have been made on an unregistered SIM.'

'A what?'

'An unregistered SIM. You can get a SIM that you don't need to register and that makes them anonymous apparently.'

'What? Where do you get them from?'

'He said you could get them anywhere.'

'Y'kidding.'

'No, listen, I should phone the police now. Ohhh, shit.'

'What?'

'I still haven't told them about the threatening call I got.'

'WHAT?'

'Well, I kinda forgot.'

'You forgot? For fuck's sake, Mick, you said you'd phone them – it was important.'

'I know, I know, but there was so much happening—'

'I can't believe you didn't tell them – never mind me – at the time.'

'Fuckin'ell, Les, they'd just asked me four thousand questions, I'd been tear arseing around Leeds searching for our kidnapped son, it seemed the least of my worries. And anyway, it sounded like a policeman, I thought it was one of them, and when I started to phone them I kinda got thinking that if it *was* one of them, they'd know I hadn't reported it and it might tempt them into doing something else. So I decided to put it off 'til I'd thought about it.'

'What the fuck are you talking about?'

'If whoever it was who called me knew I hadn't reported it, well—'

'You think too much, that's your problem – they might have been able to trace it.'

'Look, I tried BT. They said that it couldn't be traced.'

'Yes, but the police may be able to get it. Fuckin'ell, Mick, you have to tell them.'

'I know, that's what I've just said. Anyway, we can talk about this later. Shall I just phone them?'

Lesley nodded and Mick called Strangelove. He told her everything about the most recent call but Strangelove insisted that they needed to visit the house and get 'more details', so he decided it'd be best to tell them about the other call face to face.

Digital stalking in Leeds, Yorkshire, England

19

Within 15 minutes of the call they arrived – which was good going considering the traffic. Lesley and Mick knew it by the flashes and lights going off at the gate. After going back through all the details a couple of times that Mick had already given her over the phone, Strangelove said, 'Now Michael, so what time was the call?'

Why was it that when anyone used his first name it always made him feel ten years old?

'It's Mick. About twenty-five to four.'

'And when did you phone the police?'

'Ooh, about – well, as you know, it was about ten past four.'

'Why didn't you call us earlier?'

'I wanted to tell Lesley first and then I was straight out to pick up Cal. I phoned you as soon as I got back.'

'Yes, but you should have phoned us straight away.'

'Does it matter? Was there something that you could've done?'

'But if you've just had a conversation with your abducted son and the abductor, you should phone the police immediately.'

'Why? Oh, wait a minute, you don't believe me, do you?'

'I'm not saying that. But I did say to you when Billy went missing that you should have phoned the police straight away.'

'No you said that you would've expected me to phone the police straight away.'

'I'm sure I didn't, but anyway, while we're here, is it OK if I clear up a couple of other things with you?'

'Yeh, course it is, but there's something I've remembered that I need to tell you first.'

'What?'

'Well, just before Billy got snatched, I got a suspicious phone call; it just slipped my mind with all the stuff going on.'

'In what way suspicious?'

'Well, it was kind of warning me off.'

'Warning you off? Sorry, when was this call made?'

'Just before I went to get Billy, the day he was snatched.'

'So the same day. What time?'

'About ten past three.'

'Mr McCann, that was ten days ago. How come you haven't told us about this before now?'

'Well, I've had a bit on mi mind, y'know.'

'But it's a very important occurrence – you must have recognised that.'

'Yeh, but on the day of the kidnap it seemed like a very fucking minor occurrence.'

'But it obviously isn't and subsequently, you've had ten days, why wouldn't you give us this information? It could be crucial.'

'No, I checked with BT and they assured me that there was no possible way to trace the call.'

'Oh. So you spoke to BT but you didn't think it was important enough to tell us? I find that very hard to believe.'

'What, so I'm lying? Look, we've got a lot on our minds. Sometimes I remembered, when I wasn't in a position to phone you, but mostly I just forgot.'

Strangelove caught the sigh in the back of her throat and slowly released it through her taut lips; she knew it, she fucking knew it: *He's not right. What's he up to?* She still couldn't nail it. *He's not that woolly-headed; does he purposely keep throwing big piles of confusion up into the air?* She returned to the external world. 'Yeh, but you would've made a note and just phoned us when you could.'

'Good point, but what you're missing is that I was caught in two minds cos I just don't trust y'.'

'Excuse me?' This bullet bluntness took Strangelove by surprise. 'You didn't trust us?'

'Yeh, still don't.'

'In what way don't you trust us?'

'Oh, think of a way and I don't trust you in it. Let's be honest, you're really not very good, are you?'

'You want to be very careful, Michael. Seems to me that you were consciously withholding evidence.'

'Yeh, and it seems to me that you get off on threatening people.'

The mute male officer, seeing a bout of pointless bickering coming on, suddenly finds his voice. 'So even if you think we're not very good at our job, why would you withhold this information? What could we do wrong with it – other than not find the caller?'

'Good question.'

172

'Mmm, could you answer it?'

'Probably.'

'Well.'

'It's a bit complicated but do you know what I'd say if you asked me what he sounded like?'

'What?'

'He sounded like one of you lot, but someone with authority.'

'A police officer?'

'Sounded like it to me.'

'What did he say to you that made you think that?'

'Mainly tone and. . . well, stuff he said.'

'Yeh, specifically?'

'Well, it was mainly the way he spoke and just things like I said "You can't come round and bully us and then give us threatening phone calls to shut us up", and he didn't deny it.'

'But was there anything specific that *he* said that led you to that conclusion?'

'No, not really – just stank of you lot.'

'OK, OK, but what did he actually say?'

Mick, flushing slightly, was starting to feel a bit stupid. 'Just that me and Lesley had been making enquiries, were being indiscreet, and that we should stop.'

After an unproductive silence designed to make Mick continue speaking, the detective added, 'Yeh, and what else?'

'Well, nothing really, he just kept repeating that. Similar to how you'd repeat a question if I wasn't answering it.'

'You need to think. What else did he say?'

'Nothing. Look if any specifics come to mind I'll phone you.'

'Well, yeh, it might be an idea,' Strangelove spat, returning to the fray.

The male officer looked over at Strangelove slightly disappointed, again trying to avoid the bitching, and with a tone that surprised Mick into understanding that he was her superior added, 'Anything else, DC Strangelove?'

Strangelove returned to her notes, head shaking with exasperation.

'Yes, Michael, when we interviewed you, you said that you'd no idea who any of the people were.'

'Yes.'

173

'So how is that the case when Charlotte Tompkins introduced a piece featuring you on the TV?'[4]

'Ah, yeh, wondered when you'd get around to that. I didn't realise at the time you asked me.'

'What? You didn't know the name of the person who introduced you on TV?'

'No, I didn't. It was like a vox pop. Well, not really a vox pop, they came around to the house. I didn't go to the studio – I didn't meet her.'

'But she introduced you on the piece. Surely you knew her name.'

'No, I didn't, I don't watch the programme and she was just the presenter.'

'Really?'

'Yeh, really, that's all.' Mick couldn't resist putting on a mock David Bowie voice from the *In Person* bootleg, and Strangelove looked suitably confused.

'It's come to our attention that you weren't happy with the piece.'

'That's not strictly true. I was very happy with the fact that they did a piece; I just didn't think I came across very well. That was nothing to do with Charlotte Tompkins, it was just silly little technical things and me not handling them very well.'

'But you weren't happy with it.'

'Well, it's a bit pathetic really. I was very grateful to them for doing a piece but while they were asking me the first question I was still thinking about the fact that there was glare and that I had some grease-proof paper in the kitchen and—'

'Pardon? Grease-proof paper?'

'Yeh, the director had just pointed out some glare and the cameraman said he didn't have any gels with him. I was going to suggest grease-proof paper because you can use that like a gel to reduce glare. Then I realised that I should be answering a question and I got flustered and went to pieces a bit. Then we re-took the question and I was more together but one of their phones went off halfway through so we scrapped it and went on to the next

---

[4] www.youtube.com/watch?v=WLVkRS0-wQY

question. So the first take was the one they had to use – the one with me flapping.'

'But weren't you so annoyed that you created a parody and put it on the internet – you were angry about it?'[5]

'Oh for fuck's sake, no, not really. But I'm a woolly-headed perfectionist and little techy things annoy me and I thought that *I* should have handled it better, done a better job, but I let it get to me. And that thing online isn't directly connected to the feature on the TV, it's just like taking an idea to the extreme.'

'But you did it because you were so annoyed?'

'No, I did it because I thought it was a funny idea. Look, this is getting really fucking silly – I wasn't so annoyed that I started stalking the fucking presenter.'

'But you were annoyed.'

'Oh fuck off. No a wan't.'

'Mr McCann I suggest you—'

'And as I've said, ooh maybe twenty times now, why don't you record my voice and play it to her, see if she recognises it?'

'We have, and she did.' Strangelove lowered her head slightly. She really hadn't wanted to disclose that information yet, and Cockshot and her boss were aware of that. The gobby little shit was winding her up. His style of arguing reminded her of her soon-to-be husband.

'WHAT? You've played my voice to Charlotte Tompkins and she thinks it's me? Surely not – surely fucking not.'

Strangelove conscious that she'd let the info slip, thought she'd better pursue it now rather than give him the head-space to create an excuse. 'Yes, can you think why that might be the case?'

'Well, no, not unless it's just the Leeds accent.'

'Your Leeds accent isn't that strong.'

'Whatever, not unless the guy has a similar level of Leeds accent as me.'

'And the same pitch, the same timbre, similar expressions?'

'Don't know, but I certainly haven't been making the calls. Perhaps it's someone who knows me or maybe it's Mike fucking Yarwood and he's been listening to my myspace.'[6]

---

[5] www.youtube.com/watch?v=l0DoybMO3Eg&feature=related

[6] www.myspace.com/mickmccann

'Pardon?'

'There are copies of my voice online. It's possible that someone's listened to those and is mimicking me, trying to make it sound like me.'

'Sounds unlikely. OK, Michael, one last thing. You said when we interviewed you that you thought that the SIM card used was the one that had been stolen from the kitchen—'

'Yeh.'

'Knowing full well that it wasn't that one. We established six months earlier in your kitchen that the stolen phone was not the phone we were looking for.'

'Oh well, fucking lock me up then... looks like you've got me bang to rights, governor.' Mick slipping into a sarcastic cockney accent, the pressure of the new voice-recognition information boiling up in the casserole that was his head.

'Why pretend that you thought the SIM had been stolen?'

'Because I did—'

'What, you thought that the SIM card used was the one stolen even though we'd established that it wasn't?'

'And your point is? What exactly does this prove? Only that I didn't listen to you six months ago and to be honest I'm struggling keeping up with you now. It really wasn't that important in my life, I didn't take notes or anything.'

'This is a serious matter, Mr McCann; I don't think you understand—'

Mick was feeling cornered. 'No, I understand just fine. Do it, do it, then, do your fucking worst, charge me and take me to court. You are not going to intimidate me and my family anymore. Even if you've got what you think is some decent evidence, that I know nothing about, it's all bollocks. Just with what I do know a half-decent brief in court would make you wish you'd never joined the Girl fucking Guides.'

'Mr McCann, may I suggest that you alter your tone?'

'No, you may not, you may suggest fuck-all. Sorry, is it not the case that maybe you could arrest me in the street but I can say what I like in my own home? So may I suggest that if you don't like it that you get out of my house?'

'Mr McCann, I will not accept this threatening behaviour.'

'Threatening behaviour? Just because my voice gets slightly more animated and I chuck in a couple of swear words does not make it threatening. I'm sat fucking down and I will remain seated. I'm not that stupid, not stupid enough to give you exactly what you want – apply enough pressure and watch them crack. And who's threatening? It's you who's doing the threatening. That's all your job is, going around and scaring and threatening people. I'm not threatening anyone, I'm getting slightly agitated like I should've done the first and second time you invaded our private space with your spurious half-baked bollocks born out of the fact that you haven't done your fucking job.'

'Mr McCann, I can assure you that we did and continue to do our jobs.'

Lesley was getting that awful sensation in her gut, the ghost of the horrible, pointless and spiteful arguments that had littered their early troubled relationship rising up from her bowels.

'Mick, calm down, just answer the questions.'

He turned to her, confused and fast-shaking, glaring betrayal; she could see the venom poisoning his angry eyes. 'It's not you who's being accused of killing Billy.'

Mick lowered his head, temples throbbing with hatred, rage and confusion. He focused his malevolence and turned to Strangelove. 'Did you get a call from Rob Thurston then, DC Strangelove? Did y'? Did the head of Homicide and fucking Serious Crime for the whole of West Yorkshire phone you then? Did he, and give you a rocket up yer arse?'

Oh fuck. Lesley lowered her head.

Internally cursing, Strangelove's boss stepped in. They'd talked this through. McCann's volatile and under pressure; they have to tread carefully. 'Mr McCann, this is just wild speculation. We take malicious phone calls very seriously.'

'You did, din't y'? So me and my family got bullied by Rob Thurston because he's the head of Homicide and Serious Crime for West Yorkshire Police and doesn't mind abusing his power. He gets pissed off because his girlfriend is getting dodgy phone calls, phones you up and shouts at you to come and arrest us.'

Strangelove couldn't maintain eye contact. Her boss decided to let it ride; the situation was too sensitive, too high-profile.

'He didn't want to know, did he? Mr Fucking Robert Thurston. He just lost it, didn't he? The boss out of control, man in power using his position for his own personal reasons. He didn't care that the two of us have never broken a law in our lives, did he? I bet he didn't even give you chance to say just how unlikely it was that we were involved in any fucking way, did he? How do you think them lot out there would like to add that to their speculation and conspiracy theories? That Robert Thurston, Head of Homicide and Serious Crime for West Yorkshire Police, fucked over an average, honest, working family just because his girlfriend – a TV celeb: they'd love that – was getting dodgy phone calls?'

Strangelove exchanged glances with her boss. 'But we hardly—'

Mick continued ranting. 'And why are CID involved? Surely 99% of malicious phone calls that you bother to follow up, which will be pretty fucking few, would be dealt with by uniform? Why CID for this one? Obviously nothing to do with Robert Thurston using his influence and getting you to hassle an honest fucking family, is it, ey, Strangelove?'

Her boss tried again. 'Mr McCann, this is just wild speculation. We need to concentrate.'

Mick turned to him. 'Yes, and I really can't believe that you're still asking us about this shite when our fucking son is missing, but seeing as you are, how many malicious phone calls do you think are made per calendar month in the Leeds area? When the students are here and including all the bollocks with a Leeds postcode, Wetherby and Otley and the like, that's a million and a half, two million fucking people. How many malicious phone calls? Never mind the malicious nutters who just choose a number at random and hassle people, but kids getting bullied, blokes threatening their estranged wife or girlfriend. Estranged wives or girlfriends getting their new bloke to phone up and threaten their ex.'

This was what the superior officer was trying to avoid. 'Mr McCann, this is getting us nowhere.'

'Oh, it really is getting us somewhere. The wife or ex phoning the new girlfriend to explain aggressively how she's broken up the happy home and how if she ever sees her she's going to kill her. People owing people money, people disrespecting each other, people falling out. How many fucking malicious phone calls do you think that is per calendar fucking month?'

Strangelove hadn't expected this and was fighting hard to keep a veneer of calm. 'I have no idea. We won't have those numbers. Not everybody phones us and reports it.'

'And if they did, unless it was very fucking serious, you'd tell them to change their number or contact their provider. I bet it wouldn't even go on record, I bet it's only one in twenty that makes it into the statistics.'

'No, Mr McCann, we take malicious phone calls very seriously.'

'Bollocks. That's complete bollocks. How many people per year are arrested in the Leeds area for making malicious phone calls? And I bet not one of them, if there are any, not a single one has evidence half as flimsy as what you imagine you've got on us.'

'That's not true, Mr McCann, I can assure you that—'

'Bollocks, you can assure me of nothing. Why were we arrested? I'll tell you why, because Robert Thurston had a fucking hissy fit completely to do with his fucking personal life. Bit of a row with y'bird? Go and frighten a good family – go and scare the shit out of a four-year-old boy. Leave a twelve-year-old wondering why you're searching his bedroom while he's trying to get ready for school, and send the missus scurrying off to the GP with depression. Good work, DC fucking Strangelove – you should be proud of yourself.'

'I know it wasn't very pleasant but I can assure you that—'

'There you go again with your fucking assurances. Can you assure me that next time you'll do your fucking job? Now I'll tell you what, you get the fuck out of my house, all of y', and concentrate on what really matters in all this – finding our fucking son.... GET OUT.'

'No, Mr McCann, you've got this all—'

'Get out; don't make me phone the police – I will if I have to.'

They headed for the door. Forget a happy marriage and a long life; Strangelove's one overriding lifetime hope was to get that little fucker on his own in a field miles from nowhere.

20

He'd spent most of the day deep in thought anyway but the discussion with Strangelove had really shaken him up and wired him. That night he couldn't settle and, being a writer, he began to tap out all the jumbled observations that he could remember about possible state monitoring and the digital world maybe careering out of control. This and that French lad were cluttering up his head. He just had to get it out, get it down; it seemed that this was the only thing he could concentrate on that didn't involve Billy. He needed to clear his head of the shite to get Billy's seven simple words into perspective. He wrote:

The subjects were objectified and subjected to objective violence. And just in passing, when in your life are you the subject and when are you the object? Can you see things changing, like Billy's image slowly morphing from that of a beautiful and vibrant young lad into a simple signifier of a situation?

So where are we? January, 2008, and within 5-10 years most of us will have lots of personal data and markers stored on a government database – our identity on a card or biometric passport – British subjects becoming digital objects. And once we're all on a digital card it won't be long before the use or the negating of it will be used as a form of punishment or control, denying access to services or freedom of movement. The removal of the validity of the card could be selectively used. Maybe starting with something as obvious as the purchasing of alcohol. Perhaps later, when we've got used to the concept, it'll be introduced at train stations – for security obviously – and in the process recording our movements – but no valid card, no travel. It could record certain misdemeanours or information that then denies access to the individual to a whole range of possibilities. Digital control ... get behind me Foucault, I'm trying to concentrate. They can put chips holding the animals' details in pets' necks, f'fuck's sake.

Yes, many countries use identity cards, but I bet they don't include the same amount of electronically stored data as the one being constructed in the UK, for the database state. But those records are safe, yeh? The seven or eight government databases compromised in late 2007, early 2008, were just glitches, and does it matter that personal records involving over 25 million people are compromised? Half the country is secure anyway, well, as long as they weren't on any of the other databases. And when someone low down the structure behaves badly or someone higher up has their laptop stolen or leaves it in the pub, the politicians come out to squeal, 'We can't be everywhere, we can't police everything.' The statement in itself a simple admittance of the inherent insecurity of the data.

Thing is, the bigger these databases get – and it's in their very essence to grow, in their programming – then the more people required to maintain them. Hundreds, maybe thousands, of people altering and inputting records, the databases accessed by more and more people, and with each person, the security of the databases decreases a tad more, the database becomes a little more vulnerable. The Child Benefit records concerning the 25 million people were initially reported to have been lost by 'a low-level' operative sending out discs that they'd copied – apparently without getting permission – and sending them out in the ordinary, non-traceable, post. There's a worry, thousands of relatively poorly paid people having unlimited access to information that could be worth millions to unscrupulous people. How much would these people pay to get access and how many could resist twice their annual wage in a one-off payment for something that they are very unlikely to get caught doing? Keeping those widely accessed databases secure is nigh on impossible. They'd have to create offline, non-interactive stations with no ports, no CD drives, no access to any kind of device, which is absolutely contrary to the nature of the data, to the intentions of the beast. Even if people could be stopped from exporting data electronically they would be able to store valuable information in their heads to sell on, and do you make them leave their mobile phones at the door? What about errors on these databases? The DNA database contains more than 500,000 false or wrongly recorded names.

Our credit cards can be cloned at the petrol station or restaurant, and me and Mrs Mick suffered the identity theft and associated trauma due to an uncancelled and sloppily handled SIM card. We shred our utility bills and bank statements but many of us would struggle remembering how many SIM cards we've had. Who ever cancels old SIM cards that haven't been stolen? Can SIMs be cloned and if not, how long before they can? Weren't they trialling fingerprint technology for that extra customer security? How long before this becomes standard technology at forecourts and check-outs and how long before computers have built in pads on the keyboards which enable us to access high-security personal areas such as bank accounts? Once these digitally cloned prints saturate the web, can they be secure? Criminals will find a way to clone the identity card – in whatever form it takes – you can rely on that, especially when it'll be accessed through and by so many government databases and end-users.

So in the early twenty-first century, in Britain, the children from 5,000 schools had their fingerprints taken for their library cards, and without the permission of the parents. A few hundred thousand young kids tagged for life. Has this information cross-pollinated, have the records gone to other databases? Is information passed from one database to another? Maybe it isn't but it seems almost inevitable that this information will one day be centralised or that access to all the different databases will be open to so many agencies that it may as well be. Anyway, at some point it simply will, or the info will become so easily manipulated and accessed that it doesn't matter where it's stored.

So what about legal uses? Is it OK for our local authorities to sell the electoral roll? Were you asked? It won't be long before the insurance companies are able to buy information from the NHS database. Governments love easy money and they could hide it on a busy news day. Is it already happening, or maybe about to happen, with no announcement? Is this alright? This consultation with and information given to your GP – or at hospital – is supposed to be confidential. What is the Hippocratic Oath and does it cross over to digital information?

Is the loss of this defence of the patient that has stood for over two thousand years acceptable collateral damage? Let me say now, it's not OK for the government to sell on my personal details. The police can already access your medical records. Who owns that information – they say possession is nine tenths of the law – is it us who own our personal records or is it the government's or council's to sell, share or do with as they will? I bet no one independently monitors this. Where are the lines? So my children may not be able to get life insurance due to the possibility of hereditary cancer that stalks our genes, the insurance companies creaming off the safe bets and increasing the charges according to genetic and social risk. Putting life insurance beyond the means of huge chunks of society whilst the insurance companies get fatter, more bloated and profitable. Foucault insinuated somewhere years ago that this use of classification would have implications for AIDS sufferers like himself, as well as others – he was, he is, he will be right. Once this information is collected, or being collected, we will need to lie. As a smoker, by the time I get any smoking-related illness, I am likely to have paid for the treatment via the tax on cigarettes 600 times. The treatment may well be denied if my records show 'smoker' in favour of a record that states 'non-smoker', even though it is the smokers who pretty much fund the NHS. We may die because our personal entry denies us treatment.

Teachers, doctors, social workers, probation officers, police officers, lawyers carrying sensitive personal information around on memory sticks. ASBOs determining where people can and can't go, electronic tagging doing the same, with added curfews. There's no doubt that many of these people are scallywags or dangerous, but I don't believe that they are all guilty, just easy prey. Mindst you, they'll have been seen wearing a hoody in a built-up area so obviously they're guilty. Let's buzz the little fuckers with mosquitoes if they do what all kids through history have done and hang around in groups. We used to go to youth clubs; doubt there's many of those left. Our justice system was built upon the idea that it was better for guilty people to walk free than an innocent person to be found guilty. We supposedly set the burden of proof high but how confident can we be that this is the case with the ASBOs? Are we sure that these measures will not spread? will they be contained in the lower echelons of the working classes, people with less rights than you and me? After our experience I hate to think how less competent people would cope with the police. It is very possible that some young kid or confused adult would get scared and admit to things that weren't quite true. Does it matter how much access to money you have to defend yourselves? Are you more likely to survive if your name is Jonathan Aitkin or Geoffrey Archer and you are also intelligent?

Is it a central part of a 21C liberal democracy to rule by fear? Scare stories in the media perpetuating fear and paranoia and we pass on this fear, this nurtured apprehension, this dread of our external world to our children. Keep our kids held captive. They don't share the same freedoms of movement and interaction with the new enjoyed by generations of children across history. Create the other and make him wicked. Is it our mentality to intimidate and scare? Scare us with external and internal threats so that we whimper less when our space is invaded. Here is Jerusalem. Wouldn't Mr. Blake be happy? He hated you mother-fuckers anyway, but he likes me, Mrs. Mick and our mates.

On top of the 1,333 authorised bugging warrants from the Home Office in 2006, there were a further 250,000 applications for intercepts and bugging in Britain that didn't go through the Home Office – don't try to tell me that those figures didn't greatly increase in 2007. So if in 2007 this figure only rose to 300,000 – which, with the terrorist attacks, I doubt – and the population is around 57 million, that's considerably more than 1 in 200 people being bugged. At an average Leeds United home game that's well over 150 members of the crowd getting bugged. Yes, I'm aware that some people may get bugged more than once and in more than one place. Today, right now, almost 800 organisations already have the authority to collect information on us such as who you've had phone calls with, where you've sent or received snail mail to or from, who you've texted and which websites you've visited. Can they get transcripts of the texts? With digital memory so cheap, how long will it be before not just our emails but all our phone calls are also stored for access at someone else's will?

I'm stupid enough to go posting online and create a myspace using my real name. My address is easily accessible, as are many personal details. Although most people on myspace use nicknames, Facebook, the social networking site that dominated 2007, stores real names – as does Friends Reunited – and people post personal information. Even if it just stops you from getting that job you were after, are we being smart? Am I being smart? Are we opening ourselves up to unscrupulous people? Maybe I'm simply paranoid.

We pride ourselves on living in a free country and historically we see ourselves as being from a very early modern democracy. We sing Jerusalem with gusto and see Blake's verse as inspirational, but it was aspirational, looking for a liberty that he thought the nation lacked. We've got the biggest citizen DNA database in the world and more CCTV than any other country in the world. In years to come the system will be more unified and contain back-end face-recognition software.

How easy is it to remotely follow someone using satellite technology? What will be the situation in ten years' time? Is Sat Nav one way? We carry around a tracking device in our pockets and I assume that this possibility is less secure in Britain than anywhere else in the world – just that we may not realise it. The more interactive and connected our little electronic box of tricks gets, the more we, in the New Stasi State, will be surveyed and answerable. And in keeping with their Stasi forebears, are they shit at it? Are they such a fucking shambles that – like us – it pretty much comes down to chance whether you get nabbed or not, innocent or guilty? The use of our mobile tracking device may be presented as a way to impose a Green Tax, or simply control the movements of 'undesirables', but rest assured, it won't be long before it breaks out of the original sales pitch. Mobile phones are already tracked through large shopping centres to get a pattern of shopping of the individual; they put up signs but they don't ask permission. It won't be long before our innocent little tracking devices will be used when the police build a case which relies on proving you were there, or simply to ask why you were there. Not having a device could become a cause for authoritarian concern or an incriminating statement in court, similar to not owning a TV or license. Me and Mrs Mick would no doubt now be even more guilty in the eyes of the law were they able to prove some bollocks circumstantial presence in or around the Yorkshire TV building. How long before it raises questions of how often you visit a friend whose husband or wife knocks out a bit of blow, has been convicted for handling stolen goods or has a certain criminal record, no matter how old?

Guilty by association, isolated and compartmentalised. It is already the case that someone with a drugs conviction proved to have called someone else with a drugs conviction can be charged and held on conspiracy to obtain or supply drugs. In certain sections of society, many friends will also handle drugs, or will have done in the past. The suspect may not even be aware of a conviction and, being from that section of society, they are more likely to be caught doing it.

'Wonder Pets, Wonder Pets, Wonder Pets?' Rotating his crunching neck, clicking his knees and stretching out his thigh muscles, Mick looked away from the computer. *This isn't my writing. This is a job for a precise academic, someone who's been studying it for years, knows the background, knows the theory. I can't rant, I can't even get angry. Like my friends? Is it 'like my friends', as in people, or 'my friend's house'?*
Breaking to fix some caffeine in support of his out of control smoking, he determined that he still had to get it out. It may be bollocks but it was messy bollocks cluttering up his head. Wonder Pets*, that's not random, it has to mean something.* He read back through the pages. 'Cold shite, it's cold shite. Oh fuck it.' Stretching out his fingers and flexing his aching hands, he returned to the keyboard.

But anyway, of course we're not censored. Of course we're not controlled or oppressed, led by the nose, cajoled or corralled, but these mechanisms could – over the years – have developed more and more sophisticated cloaks, layering the truth. Leaving exposed pointless freedoms to show, indicate at and quote. Of course we're free. Of course the authorities need to act. Of course they need more powers.

Who knows what our basic freedoms are? Can we protest outside the House of Commons or will we be ushered away to a less obvious place? Can we rise up and spontaneously march? No, we can't, we need to apply to march, bringing ourselves to the attention of the authorities. If we entered into a straight-forward battle of will, would we be allowed to sit across an entrance or would we be carried away? Can a journalist or author guarantee the anonymity of their source? How many D-notices have been slapped on people, and for what reasons? Can we refuse to give our DNA until we are convicted?

Perhaps, when compared with the rest of the world, we are living in an open and free society, but are those freedoms slipping? Maybe the freedoms are gradually waning as the laws get more complex. What's in the fine print of the 'anti-terrorism' laws? Were they designed to allow NatWest employees to be extradited to the US? That's alright, no one likes bankers anyway. The terrorism laws also allowed 82-year-old Walter Wolfgang, after being forcibly ejected from the Labour Party Conference for shouting 'Nonsense', to be denied re-admittance – but yeh, the peace campaigner is your archetypal terrorist. Also, as he'd shouted it twice, he could have been charged under the Protection from Harassment Act which was drawn to deter stalkers. Did you see the hegemon's mask slip? What would have happened had it not been in the full glare of the media?

Some people argue that by introducing 28 days' internment without charge, the Terrorism Law of 2006 slit the throat of Habeas Corpus. Killed the charge-or-release defence of the individual against unlawful imprisonment that came with the Magna Carta (fuck off, Foucault) and was mimicked across the western world. I'm not so sure. I can see that the authorities may need longer to retain people in cases with a new complexity. Although, perhaps, rather than deal with it with urgency, they may just stretch their enquiries to the 28 or 42 days, and there's no doubt that this extended length of time (without even being told what you're accused of) could destroy the life of the individual in question. The setting up of *re-*

education for radicalised Muslims may be useful in the here and now, but that precedence is way open to abuse. I don't give a fuck about local bureaucrats checking people's details to stop them from getting their kids into certain schools, to stop them letting their dog crap in public places or putting the wrong stuff in their bin, but is that why the anti-terrorism laws were drawn and is that where it will stop?

Another thing that sneaked through with the anti-terrorism law fairly anonymously was the retention of innocent people's DNA on the Criminal Database. One eighth of the Criminal Database is made up of people without a conviction. It doesn't matter; it is only a matter of time before the whole nation is on it. In the near future a standard medical record will contain the patient's DNA. I'm sure it will be medically useful but as the chatter between these databases increases – which it inevitably will – the entire population will be on a database easily accessed by the authorities. The existence of the database could almost be denied, or at least the decision to tag the nation will never have to be made or discussed, just silently leach through.

Is Fylingdale, with its motto 'We Are Watching', or Menwith Hill with its two million 'intercepts' per hour, interrogating millions of UK phone calls and emails for keywords – are they simply looking for terrorists and hardened criminals? Are phone calls and emails trawled for keywords? Surely terrorists and hardened criminals are wise to this. If so, what else are they looking for? Who controls these listening stations and who decides their purpose? Is it just for the use of the Americans, GCHQ and MI5? Perhaps these places are innocuous but is this surveillance being carried out elsewhere? Well, yes it is, by the police, who are more precise.

So is there some kind of unwritten social contract between us and them sitting unacknowledged and unagreed? Some pact with at its heart the well being of society – and are the rights and freedoms of the individual necessarily curtailed for the benefit of the society, and do we trust that this is neutral, for the common good? We need to establish what constitutes the common and what constitutes the good. Are the obvious abuses that will occur inevitable bi-products and simply unfortunate but acceptable for the collective safety of the individuals? No, they are neither inevitable nor acceptable, but we will accept them as such. Was and is there a debate? Maybe there is with say the ID card but is there with the slow stalking of related issues of control and surveillance that are deemed less important, like the spread of the retention of innocent peoples DNA, the setting up of biometric passports or the inevitable homogenised databases?

Who decides their importance? What is the accumulative effect of this slow chipping away at the structure of freedom within our society? Is it a slow chipping away at our freedoms? We should worry when who we are, where we are, who we have been in contact with, what we have done, what we have bought, is easily provable, easily trackable. Is it, all of this, the cost of other pay-offs? The capture of criminals, of terrorists, the control of immigration, the control of 'undesirables' born and bred in this country? The central points in all of this – the whole shooting match – are who will have access to what, what level of access, how they are allowed to use it and how transparent it is. What are the checks and balances to stop abuses or incompetent uses of power? There has been a constant stream of proof over the last year that the government, authorities and individuals are not capable of keeping anything secure. No information is secure, none whatsoever. And extraordinary rendition shows that our liberal democracies don't mind breaking the rules. Ship individuals off to 'host' countries to have their testicles sliced with razor blades and then use the unreliable info gained to hold them longer at Guantanamo Bay. There we don't torture them, just waterboard them, deny them sleep and pump the same song into their heads, at full volume, for days on end. I'm not happy if my government was unaware that it was providing information to the US to fuel torture.

Who informs and defines the debates? Where do we get the information, the facts and figures that shape and colour it, and is the information trustworthy? Is information given to simply endorse a preferred point of view and is contradictory evidence suppressed or simply ignored? Just after our arrest I went through all the correct procedures and requested certain information – that is supposedly readily available at the end of your mouse – from the Home Office. Four months ago I received an email stating that the supply of this information had gone outside the acceptable time for me to receive it. At the time of writing it still had not arrived; will it ever arrive, even if I chase it up, which I have and it hasn't? Have the people who should have supplied me with this information checked me out and seen that I was recently arrested under *suspicion of making malicious phone calls*? With me not being a journalist, academic or government official, maybe they phoned the arresting officers to check on the background and sensitivity of the information. Unlikely – or is it? It's certainly possible. Why is the information I want not readily available online? It is the easiest thing in the world to make this kind of information detailed and easily searchable. Although the politicians tell us it is, it is not. Why is that?

Do government agencies take the powers that they decide they need? Should we simply trust them to do so? Is it evolutionary? These agents adapt and change with the developing situation, spawn new roots and powers that creep and embed unchecked into new areas of life and society. What are they and are they necessary? Are the politicians in control of it? The authorities can remotely track where you have been on your computer and when it happens you will not be asked permission, or even informed that it has happened. The kid being put to death in Afghanistan for downloading un-Islamic material – material on the rights of women – from the internet is so anti-democracy, nothing like that could happen here. No one other than paedophiles, terrorists, fraudsters and hackers could be convicted, blackmailed or targeted for the use of their computer in the UK – yeh?

In the UK – and I'm sure around the world – we have huge chunks of the media controlled and funded by the power brokers. Commercial parties and interests already have huge influence in our democracies and the multinationals will insinuate themselves further into positions of increased political power. Why would a government official from the Department of Trade and Industry email senior management at mobile phone companies reassuring them that the UK government would scupper EU plans to reduce extortionate phone charges to customers? Why would the British government represent the interests of phone companies over the interests of the public – of the people they are elected to represent? Nothing to do with the 22.5 billion pounds they received for the 3G networks and any unhealthy relationships that built up around it, obviously.

Could the area between government and commercial power reduce further? It's not like US presidential candidates are funded to the hilt by big business or powerful individuals, is it? They even hedge their bets by funding all the likely candidates, but that's just altruistic indecisiveness, obviously. In the US, Gore Vidal reckons you can watch the lobbyists telling the Congressmen that they funded how to vote. I'm sure in the UK they'll have worked out how to get around the cash-for-questions issue. Will a pharmaceutical company in years to come – if not now – be able to suppress online debate and the exchange of information regarding the safety of new drugs, and could innocent people die as a result? Will petroleum companies be able to target people with outspoken green tendencies? Is it already happening? Or perhaps on their forecourts the CCTV will simple recognise the makes of cars – or the socio-profile, age, race, gender of the occupants – most often involved in doing a runner and deny them petrol.

So, what does your supermarket know about you? But supermarkets are benign and open, aren't they? Liddell proved that. The commercial world is collecting, storing, selling huge amounts of information about me and you. Is it inevitable and how detailed will this information get? Here's a test: go overdrawn by a penny for a day and I guarantee that you'll get a call or letter from another company offering you a *how to deal with bank debts* service or a loan. Is that information private and who supplies it to the second organisation? Is it the bank or is it an Equifax-type company? There's the problem – who is responsible for any of this digital power?

Insurance companies offer lower premiums if you're willing to have a black box in your car to track where you've been and prove your driving habits. It could be that in the next ten years, those insurance companies insist on the black box and proof of car usage. Wouldn't it be useful for government or local authorities to have access to that information to impose congestion charges or start to charge us for certain major roads and in the process open up records to all manner of people about exactly where we have been and when?

I'm not really a conspiracy theorist. I'm sure I'm naïve, but I think more often cock-up rather than subterfuge is at play. But what is certain is that we are creating the perfect control mechanisms for less honourable future authority figures. We cannot afford to believe that the coup that so nearly happened in Britain in the 1970's was just a blip. We are handing some sovereign a multitude of easy ways to stitch us up or simply make us so nervous that we daren't question or stand up for anything.

And what do I do? I sit back, apathetic as a cunt, and watch the changes wash over me or sneak by. As long as I can consume in peace and it doesn't affect me or my family, I don't give a fuck. Our lives fully, wholly commercialised, but at what cost?

Mick sat back from his keyboard and blew out long and hard. 'It's all a bit fucking melodramatic for my liking, a bit conspiracy theory, and I don't like that "apathetic as a cunt" bit. Most of the cunts I've known have been anything but apathetic.' Looking at the digits in the bottom right-hand corner of the screen: 'Bollocks, 5:02?' He pressed 'save' and went to get a coffee. On the way, he laughed to himself as he observed that his writing truly captured and reflected the state of this surveillance world... a jumbled fucking mess. Returning to the computer with his caffeine, he read back through it – 'Fantastic, Mick, just ask loads of questions cos you can't be arsed doing the research' – and sighed like a cunt.

21

Time dragged out at half the speed of that in an airport terminal. The two of them completely obsessed with something that their souls were trying to deny. Fuck, they'd give anything to have him back, and the fact that he was still alive, although a huge comfort, seemed to intensify the urgency. Living a quarter-life of complete contradiction; killing time that seemed so precious. Being completely helpless, living constantly in that dream where something awful happening coincides with the spine-numbing paralysis. A chilling fact that sat in every corner of their thoughts, of their lives. Concentration on anything else being a lost battle – like trying to count to infinity. Along with their minds, their instincts and that innate ability to function around objects had deserted them. Hurting themselves, not just psychologically but dropping things and accidentally burning skin, bumping into door handles and edges – just like Billy did for a period when he was the perfect door-knob height but not experienced enough to dodge them. They could no longer read sentences or people's intentions. They were only able to judge people through some genetic memory. *Ah, that's my mother, she means well.... He's my best friend, probably giving me good advice, although I haven't a clue what the words mean.* People would use a combination of words and all they'd hear was 'Bbblluuhhh'. No concentration or patience, suddenly erupting or mumbling incoherently. Continuously entering rooms with no idea why, and the attempt to drag the reason up from the depths of the brain, only brought memories and worries of Billy, and reason was gone. Someone at work used the expression 'at your wit's end' and all Lesley could do was internally acknowledge her madness and hide her face between her knees.

Everything reminded them of Billy. They tried watching television or listening to the radio but it was nigh on impossible. Even though they'd avoid the places where reports of their predicament were likely, one of the kids would leave a TV on and they'd enter a room to pictures of the police scouring Armley Moor – the same old library of pictures still on that fucking loop – or Billy staring out at them, his image by now simply iconic, a signifier, no longer the heart and soul of their beautiful, immortal son. One of the most remarkable people on the planet had lost meaning, had morphed into the cold, dead image of a situation.

The most ridiculous things brought them back to the horrible truth. Mick watching an advert in which a bloke has an amazing cleaning product that gives him what is perceived by the audience to be magical powers. He can clean at such speed that he can laze around while deceiving his returning wife, who obviously has no knowledge of cleaning products, into thinking that it must have taken him all day. He gives the camera a little wink. It's his and the audience's little secret that he's been watching football all day and that the product is so good that a six-hour job takes minutes. That wink really got to Mick, he had to leave the room, it made him flush, it brought all his frustrations suddenly and violently to the crust, erupting chaos that swept away reason and made him want to burn down a house, any house, his house, your house. He wanted the knowing wink, the astonishing powers; he wanted Lesley to return to witness his magic, his ability to right all his wrongs with the miraculous return of their son. Mick's self-esteem had taken such a battering that even these chavvy, lazy blokes, all bullshit cliché and no soul, were becoming exemplars to him.

The walls were closing in on him. 'Never mind, almost dinnertime.'

While Mick was vaccing the stairs, the words 'it's like *Wonder Pets*' were tumbling through his head just as they had been ever since he'd first heard them, turning upside down and sideways. *What on earth could he mean? It could be anything. What were the things that symbolised the show, the iconic features? If it was simply the plot structure it may only indicate Billy's distress or hopes, perhaps describing his position as he sees it. It couldn't be an animal reference – or could it?* Mick worked again and again through the list of places with a collection of small animals – *Did they need to be small?* Although the animals from the show were young and in reality would be small, the representations on the screen were not small but the standard screen size. *Billy must realise that they are supposed to be baby animals, he must. So this menagerie, unless it is a house, a garden shed or perhaps a flat, would be a public place. People would work there and would be likely to see or hear a small child. Maybe a place with a lot of*

194

space, maybe somewhere where only The Cunt has access – Hare-wood Bird Garden? Nah, anywhere with storage is accessed by more than one person. They have to have time off and cover and it's very unlikely to be a group or couple kidnapping. It's obviously possible for more than one to carry out a kidnap but unlikely that they'd be thrown together through work and share the same workplace. Maybe if they met like-minded nutters online... but then they wouldn't work together – although wasn't that the case with Hindley and Brady? Each thought that circled into nonsense felt like another bit of Billy slipping away, and the barmy thoughts were endless.

Is there some specific storyline that holds a clue? That could be anything. How many episodes are there? Mick had started to watch as many episodes of *Wonder Pets* as he could battle through, constantly fighting to keep his eyes dry so that he could concentrate. The little animal always getting saved, over and over again, different young animals in distress getting saved. It was like penance, like he was trying to cleanse his sins. As he sat there, he'd often slip off into a daydream where Billy could pop up at any time and sit for a second next to him before hurtling off into some other activity. He never did, and Mick would force himself to turn the screw one thread tighter.

'It's like *Wonder Pets*. . . like your friends. . .' He didn't have any friends that kept shitloads of small animals. He didn't have any friends who set off in flying boats to rescue small animals using *teeeeeeam work. Fuck, wait a minute, the boat – is it a boat? Would you describe that as a boat? More importantly would Billy describe it as a boat? Yes, it's a fucking boat.* And Mick did have a friend who lived on a boat. *Has Billy visited? Of course he has, briefly. We couldn't stay long or Billy would have sunk it. Fuck, was Billy telling me he's on a boat? In Leeds? Yes, of course there are boats in Leeds; remember, you fucking visited one with Billy, you dozy tit. Surely Billy isn't smart enough to throw me a clue in a three-sentence conversation. Err-e-er, av' y'heard y'self, y'doylum? Billy not smart enough? Fuck right off, he is. It's not Billy's lack of brain cells that's the problem here.* Mick revelled in the first theory that he couldn't shoot down in a second. He kept it turning in his head. It could be pure chance, complete bollocks, obviously, but the glimmer of hope filled him with the first positive energy that he'd experienced in two weeks. *I've fuck-all to lose. It's worth a try.* His world was insane, spinning on a fucked-up axis. 'I'm doing fuck-all at the moment, really, but it in't 'alf taking a long time – it's gotta be worth a try.'

He talked it over with Lesley, who liked it, with reservations, but she liked it nonetheless. What else was there? She didn't mind if it sounded like the absurd ramblings of a desperate man, she was desperate herself. Any hope, any crackpot theory, would do, no matter how tenuous and logic-defying the assumptions involved were, she'd nail her hope to them with both hands wrapped around the hammer. The whole situation was crazy; from the beginning, it defied logic. It would almost be fitting if Mick's fragile thought process had thrown up a nugget, a life-line. Their world was madness, that was all it was, a big ball of chaotic madness, nothing else; sense would be completely out of place here.

It'd taken ages to get her to agree to keep shtum, to let him do some recces before they mentioned it to the police. Deep down she had no confidence in the filth, so she merely went through the good-girl motions of 'the right thing to do' without actually wanting to do it. He simply didn't trust them and he couldn't run the risk of warning The Cunt, but more than this, although he was struggling admitting it even to himself, he wanted to sort it out his way. He wanted the knowing wink and the magic to be his. It was probably a wild goose chase anyway, but he wanted to be the one to throttle the fucking bird and pull out the feathers one by hopefully painful one.

For this to work, Mick had to lose the press. He couldn't have that fucking circus following him around; he'd stick out like a sore suspect searching for his son being followed conspicuously by the gentlecunts of the press. He'd thought this through. He'd noticed there were times during the night and early morning when the coast was clear, the reporters would disappear off to their hotels or digs or pub. It seemed completely random and there was no way of knowing, without checking, if some of them were encamped further up the lane. He sneaked over the Yorkshire-stone wall right down at the end of the garden and into the paddock.

The paddock. He had no idea why it was called the paddock but it was and had been for years. The old ladies in their empty nests called it the paddock. There was only one old lady left now, the others had been bought out, offered a high price for their tenancy – probably illegally – so that the family homes could be gutted of any character and turned into swanky flats for young professionals. Mick had watched in disbelief as the builders threw six-panelled Georgian doors into their skip. Solid, classic, 200-year-old doors getting replaced by mock-grained, white-painted, MDF shite that would be lucky to last 10 years. *It's the way of the world, we have to consume, even if we're shit at it, we have to consume, the world depends on our consumption.* He'd pulled some fantastic door furniture from the skip; it lay stripped and restored in his cellar. Some of the better handles now sat on the internal doors in their William the Fourth house. Mick had meant to grab the doors and store them in his garage but he didn't get his arse into gear in time.

After he'd seen them ripping out Georgian doors, Mick had involved himself in the planning application for the cottages and, as they were listed, no work should have taken place without permission from the council; but it had, and the council didn't seem to give a fuck. He was determined that they wouldn't ruin these bits of heritage. After all, it was them who'd have to look at the fucking things, not the developer and not the council employees. He got refused enough to make him feel satisfied and most of it was ridiculous anyway – he'd saved the developer a packet. Simple but crucial things, making sure that the replacement windows were in keeping with the character of the cottages and not white UPVC. Stopping them from ripping off the fantastic Yorkshire-stone roof tiles and replacing them with bland, twenty-first-century, grey shite. He'd explained to the developer – who started visiting Mick to negotiate the development – that if he just flipped over the tiles they'd look like new Yorkshire-stone tiles and be fantastic for years; the underside of the tiles would be in near-perfect condition, which, when it came to it, they were.

The paddock lay down an incline from where the old factory used to be. It was quite a big factory by all accounts, although the space left contradicted this, but in its time many of the people from the seven cottages had been employed there. It closed in the 1950's and was pulled down not long after. Stumbling up the incline toward the factory space, his feet skidding on something slippy, Mick cursed the fact that horses grazed there, although it could just be mud, no smell and hard to tell in the dark. Around the corner of the end cottage, Mick didn't even need to be careful, they wouldn't be able to see him from the lane. As he came around the cottage, Mick got a slight buzz from the fact that he'd stopped them from turning the courtyard – that used to be cottage gardens – into a car park and other such criminal and crackpot ideas generated through simple bad planning and economy. He allowed himself a smug smile at the thought that the locale was now a conservation area with the two main points being that no one was now allowed to install UPVC windows or new, grey roof tiles.

The lane and parking spaces were clear, no alien vehicles, just the recognisable cars of tenants. Circling around to his drive, Mick opened his car – it was never locked as the locks were fucked, or maybe his key – and started it up. After driving it around and parking it up on Theaker Lane, he returned to his house over the moor. Black jacket zipped up to the top and hood up, he was invisible. To save time, he climbed back over his garden wall and in through the front door that in his head was the back door, but Lesley was right, it was the front door. The door Mick thought of as the front door was historically the servants' and tradesmen's entrance and therefore the back door.

22

Mick had staked out a couple of marinas. *Fucking marinas! They're fenced-off sections of the canal lined with people living on barges. It's Leeds, not fucking Saint Tropez or Hydra – Fucking marinas.* At some point the press must get wise to his garden manoeuvre; they had to, what with the car being missing a lot of the time and him obviously being at home. He was only surprised that he'd got away with it for the two mornings, and hoped his luck held.

He still couldn't get his head around the best way to do this. If The Cunt worked – which he knew he would – there was no chance of him taking time off work, he would keep his routines steady, not change a thing. He had two other worries, the first of which was that he might spend the time staking out a marina and miss The Cunt when he went to pick up Cal, but Lesley – who was now fully committed to his piss in the dark – was picking Cal up for the week; she was in prep. The second worry was that he may not be around at times that fitted The Cunt's work routines. He felt it possible that The Cunt worked somewhere in the Granada Media organisation but he couldn't ignore the fact that he could be wrong. He couldn't really even make a reasoned guess without asking questions of the filth, and they'd tell him shit-all, so he'd ask them shit all and in doing so keep some important information safe.

His initial urge had been to stake out Yorkshire TV, but how could he without confirming all the suspicions of the police that he was the stalker? *But fuck it, after the waterways, Yorkshire TV is getting staked.* He couldn't work out if his phone being switched off meant that it was disarmed, meant that it was untrackable – was it trackable anyway? He'd kept turning it off and on, just in case, but surely that was pointless – he wasn't moving. Anyway, the Yorkshire TV thing – although he'd little confidence in the police, surely that'd have been the first place they started? Rooting out all the males that fit the description he'd given them. He'd expected them to arrive at the house with a stack of photos but he was still waiting. Perhaps they'd accounted for everybody. The thought that they may not be following that lead really pissed him off – they had to be. Maybe they were being in some way smart, but those mysterious emails confirming the SIM card switch had surely led them to check out the personnel at YTV. Anyway, once he'd finished these recces he'd have less to lose and would be more candid with the cunts.

It was only an informed guess but if The Cunt works in the media he's likely to work weird, unpredictable hours. Might not start until 11 a.m. and not return until seven/eightish, maybe even nine. He could leave his home at seven in the morning and still not return until early evening. His biggest fear was that he worked in Manchester or even London. What then? Everything he was doing would then be pointless. He resolved to come back to this later when he'd covered all the waterways in Leeds.

The doubts and futility in all of this were endless. *What if he goes out for a drink after work? He must be single, must be – if he in't, I'll eat the fucking Corn Exchange. So if he is single, he is more likely to go out for a drink, although if he's got a kid held on his boat, he's more likely to make his excuses. What, and risk changing a routine?* It was all bollocks anyway; he was just killing time, the precious time, the changed time.

Their time had taken on a vibrant urgency. Mick hated to admit it but he felt more alive than he had at any time during his life – how could he not? He resolved that, were they to find and save Billy and get him home, they would battle not to change the time spent with Billy. Not to fawn all over the kid, not to be constantly available. It was going to be a neat trick if they pulled it off, reassuring Billy that he was alright, that they were there for him. Supporting him through the discovery of what had happened to him but maintaining the honest 'bog off' relationship. He didn't want to fuck up the kid anymore than he had to. The thought, the planning of a future with Billy, gave him elemental warmth that radiated from his chest. It was still possible, maybe not likely but certainly possible. Had he passed through to a new stage in the grieving process? A stage in which a fantasy allows the reality to slowly seep into his brain. Was his brain holding out on the most likely scenario, keeping it obscure and replacing it with hope while gradually releasing the truth that he was very unlikely to ever see Billy again?

He'd found it almost impossible to gauge the amount of time that he should spend at each marina, until he realised that he should be counting off the boats and attaching them to people. Halfway through the second recce, at Fallwood Marina, he got a bit bolder. The first one was much smaller but had taken him most of one day and half the next and he needed to be quick. There was an old fella tending a bit of ground in front of his boat.

'Excuse me, sorry to bother you. I'm trying to track down an old mate. All I know is that he lives on a boat somewhere on the canal.'

'What, the whole of the canal?' said the old fella with a twinkle in his eyes.

'No, no, sorry, just the Leeds section - the canal around Leeds or the immediate area.'

'What's his name?' Mick had seen this coming and hoped to be able to blag it.

'Well, that's the thing, I knew him by his nickname, Dosher, but I can't remember his real name. I think it was Rob but I couldn't be sure. He's about 30, 'bout five-foot-ten, short dark hair – well, it was when I last saw him. Is there a single bloke like that on any of these?'

'No, there isn't. Are you police then?'

'What? NO – no, no.' Mick laughed for the first time in what felt like weeks. 'Like a said, just looking for an old mate.'

'Lot of bother y'going t'. Don't you know anyone else who might still be in touch wi' him?'

'No. I just really need to find him. I can't say too much but it's really important that I find him.'

'I can see that, love. Have y'been up to Airedale Quays?'

'Yeh, yeh, I have.'

'Well, Aire Valley Marina is the next one to check. Do you know it?' Mick nodded. 'Give me your number and I'll have an ask around.'

'No, no, you're alright, I err—'

'Don't worry, lad, I'll be discreet. I want you to find the bastard an'get y'little lad back as much as you do.'

'What?'

Mick started to well up. It was like he was trying to block Billy out of his head, like the search was instead of mourning his son, which by now, logically, he should probably be doing. The words dragged him out of his ridiculous mental thriller and back into reality. Back from his hidey-hole and back into the world where his little lad was very possibly dead and it was his fault. Although he'd spoken to Billy a few days before, so why should it have changed? Why would The Cunt suddenly decide to go that extra step? Among all the logic, he harboured a sinking feeling in his gut that he was trying very hard to ignore.

'I knew it was you. I recognised y' – a saw you on the telly just after he'd been snatched. I hope they catch the bastard. A'y' sure he's in Leeds?'

'I'm not sure of anything.'

'Well, don't worry, lad, if he's on the water we'll track him down. Ey, and if you do go to Aire Valley, there's a couple o' boats on there that are only used in the summer.'

Mick passed on his mobile number, was touched by the bloke's concern and a little bit shaken up by the idea of this little personal drama being played out all across the media. Some photo of Billy that started off as a cute child, victim to a nutter, the essence of innocence being shown so many times that it just becomes a signifier for the case. Not a person but an iconic image to be filed in the media files with all the other iconic images – Billy was now more story than person. Maybe they'll help, maybe someone will recognise Billy. Not a fucking chance, he'll be kept well out of sight. Anyway, they'll probably be running stories about the unstable parents by now. The parents that were arrested in mysterious circumstances before the disappearance of the child; reports being given over pictures of the police dragging Armley Moor on their fucking loop. A looped virtual reality hypnotising the audience, making them think they've got a real insight, that they know all the details; that they know the characters and the happenings, when in reality they know fuck-all.

They, the public, don't need to know anything… well, the only things they do need to know are a rough description of The Cunt, the picture of Billy and the contact number of the police should they be suspicious of anything or anybody. But the story has to be kept entertaining to keep it at the top of the news stack. The fat, bloated motherfuckers need to gorge themselves on sick detail and conjecture to con themselves that they feel empathy with the family, rather than facing the fact that they are titillated by all the morbid detail and possibility. Disguising their morose curiosity as concern while deep down knowing they are fascinated by a good story containing the possibility of death and suffering – especially that of a young child – by the excitement of the digital coliseum. Silently chanting for the dead body to be held aloft where they could all get a proper look, but worst of all, not even having the guts to admit it to themselves, let alone each other. Mick felt sick at the media and general fucking public crows collaborating in picking over the carcass of their beautiful son. The maggots nibbling away at his decaying body to ensure that it would compete with all the other soap operas, be worthy of discussion in offices up and down this rancid, monstrous fucking land. This sickness has been normalised by the society, fuck knows how, but it has. He felt the conviction and compulsions of a terrorist. Right in that moment, he wouldn't think twice about planting a bomb in the offices of *The Sun* or the BBC. He'd be happy to do so.

Was the latest media fantasy focussing on the parents? It had to some time as the other irrelevant but obscene details they could trawl through and present as news ran out. At what point would he be the subject of six-page pull-outs with the word *Commemorative* Tipexed out of the template and replaced with *Killer Dad*? The aggressive, road-raging author using foul and abusive language all over the internet, references to hanging his kids by the nipples from his washing-line, jokes and comments taken out of context and surrounded by sinister words and motives. Trawling through all his posts: "'I've burnt the kids' tea,' boasted Mr McCann. 'Fuck 'em, they should learn to cook.' How did our society create such a monster? In his book he revels in violence and boasts about smashing a fellow student's head against a brick wall, a student who was hospitalised." None of the shame, no context, just the creation of a monster. *Mindst you, considering that old fella's response, it can't be that bad, and he seemed genuinely concerned. Perhaps it's just you that's the sick fuck, Mick. Maybe they haven't turned on us... not yet.*

When they do become oppositional, how on earth will they show Lesley as a nutter? Perhaps they'll just paint her as the dateless victim, the mother who had no idea what was going on in her own home. But they can't do that it doesn't fit the story. No, she'll be the vindictive female mastermind, the woman you should never cross, cold calculating and heartless.

Mick craved the safety of home, the certainty of the womb.

23

The press were indeed now wise to his little garden ruse. He looked at his car and from the bumper was hanging a small convoy of cars and a couple of vans – causing untold problems to the flow of traffic on Theaker Lane. Mick got into his car and saw the hand-brakes of seven or eight vehicles being released.

'Fuck, you absolute cunts.'

He felt like he was in an American late-seventies trucker movie and as he released the hand-brake – taking the slack on clutch and accelerator – he couldn't resist it; speaking into his imaginary CB radio: '10-4 Bad-buddies, let's burn some rubber and lose us a couple of journalists.' Trying to ignore the insane and sick buzz of being the centre of all this attention, he watched and waited. The last lot were easy; it was the one immediately to his bumper that was the concern. *Perfect* – a couple of cars drove along the row of vehicles completely filling the remainder of the road. He couldn't resist it again: 'Hold... hold... hold... hold... NOW.' The *Brave Heart* reference made him giggle manically as he slammed down on the accelerator just as the first car was getting close. There was much quite understandable beeping from the car slamming on and screeching. The lead journo had repeated his move and very fucking nearly hit the oncoming innocent car.

'Respect, brother, there was no gap but you took it.... Bollocks.' Mick cursed as he realised that there had been another journalist parked ahead of the car that now entered the hunt, pulling out wildly in front of the one journo that hadn't fallen for his scam. 'Fuck off, you're not coming.' The crossings and lights at the bottom of Branch Road had been no help at all, so Mick had driven steadily, hoping to convince the pack of, by now, four that he was just popping somewhere, no particular hurry, no particular relevance.

Down Canal Road merging seamlessly onto to Viaduct Road. 'Why change the name of a road for the sake of it? No change, same road, takes a bit of a tight kink and suddenly it becomes a road with a new name.' Again, same thing onto Burley Place, same road, different name. Coming around the corner, he saw an opportunity; a couple of cars dawdling ahead towards a green light, the sort of drivers who wouldn't increase from 25 to 30 to try to make the about-to-change lights 200 yards in front. He pulled over to the ahead-or-right-only lane and increased his speed to hit the space just behind the two daydreaming cars. The three cars and one van in his rear-view mirror did the same. 50 yards to go. 'Strap yourselves in, boys, here we go.' He slammed down on the accelerator just as amber announced itself upon the scene. 20 yards to go and the lights were red. Nothing immediate on Kirkstall Road meant that the oncoming traffic was accelerating from a standing start 50 yards away to his blind right – strong red light at ten yards: 'FUUUUCK.' Through the lights and a sharp left, knowing that he was going onto a dual carriageway with a clear view of the outside lane, insane beeping behind with one ear-splitting screech and an almighty crunch.

'YOU FUCKING NUTTER,' Mick screamed.

In his rear-view mirror he could see that one of the journos had followed him and piled slap-bang into the side of a car, around the boot, spinning it up onto a mid-road grassless verge. All the following cars seemed to avoid it – *God knows how*. Mick also saw a car coming around on the inside at speed and flashing and beeping furiously. The car got closer – thank fuck it wasn't one of the journalists. He looked ahead onto Kirkstall Road with his hand in the air, nodding his head in recognition of cuntdom to the manically flashing, beeping car behind.

'I know, I know, I know. I drove like a cunt. I had to.'

This guy wasn't leaving it, he was going to follow him and beep, and flash and beep and flash. Quite rightly, he wanted to rip off Mick's head and ram it up his arse. Mick's adrenaline pumping into a weak quiver, his head spinning at the thought of the urgency of the situation, of the bloke possibly following him to his destination and of having to fight with a righteous defender of the road. He waited for the lights ahead – that are always just turning to red as you get to them – and got out of his car, arms in the air in a 'fair cop' stylee. The red-faced bloke jumped out of his car rather large and menacing.

Mick started the shouting, his voice dripping with the adrenaline and shaking: 'Listen, mate, I'm really sorry.' The bloke wasn't listening.

'I'm going to kill you, y'cunt. I've got my fuckin' kids in the back and you—'

The bloke getting closer, Mick shouted, 'Look, I'm really fucking sorry, I was getting followed, I had to get rid of them. It was red but I knew it'd be clear.'

'You can't jump red fuckin' lights cos yur in a bit of a fuckin' hurry.'

The bloke getting closer and ready to go, Mick recognised that he himself wasn't angry enough, and a vision of Billy popped into his head, scared and confused.

'Look, a just fuckin' told you, I 'ad to get away from those blokes – a know this road. It was wrong but it wasn't fucking dangerous, but let's fucking go if y'want – I wun't if I were you like, because I'll rip your fuckin' head off.'

The bloke was neither convinced nor scared by Mick's routine and was now within striking distance. Mick stepped back slightly to try to disarm the bloke's slowing motion.

'Ey, you're that bloke off telly, art'y?'

'What?'

'The one that's lost his kid? Who w' following y'?'

'A bunch a journalists.... I am, yeh, but I haven't got time for this, mate. I'm really sorry; I've got to get going. Listen if this ever works out, I'll buy you a beer to say sorry for driving like a cunt.'

'No, yur alright, fella. Ey, listen, mate, you get going and I'll bang on mi hazards and sit in that single file bit there – y'see it just ahead?'

'Oh, thanks very much, if you could, that'd be ace. See y'.'

'Yeh, see you later, buddy.'

Just as he stepped back into his car he heard the fella shout, 'Ey, good luck, mate, and I hope you find y'little'un,' and raised the palm of his hand in acknowledgement.

'Ar't people brilliant?'

As he set off, he could see the electric-blue, rhythmical sweeps of emergency vehicles way in the distance and started to worry about the carnage left behind due to his mental driving. His head reprimanded him: *Wait a minute, you weren't driving the car that crashed. Yeh, you jumped a red light, but you did it in a careful and safe manner. OK, so it was illegal, but you've got a lot going on at the moment and it was calculated correctly to not harm anybody and you didn't harm anybody. It was the journalist's decision to jump the red light in pursuit. You couldn't stop and explain that although you'd get through safely he was likely to crash – could you? He needs to take responsibility for his actions not you. Anyway it didn't look that bad – caught him at the rear near the boot. These modern cars, as long as a 4 x 4 isn't involved, give very good protection.* This last thought reared up as Mick pictured the front of the journalist's car which, to be honest, looked a right mess.

Driving down towards Kirkstall, Mick was thinking about the river. *Maybe it's a boat on the River Aire.* He'd have to check that out online when he got home. He turned down past the golf range and the five-a-side outside courts – *Shoot probably more than five-a-side looking at the size of the courts* – over the narrow metal bridge, under a couple of adjacent railway bridges and round past some big electrical sub-plant – much too big to be a sub-station. There was a lovely little spot for him to park up in. The car would be hidden and he could sit in the bottom of a bush invisible both sides while watching the approach road and the car park. He did a quick recce of the perimeter, walking down the outside of the fence, which at the far end had a more than convenient slit that had been used so often that it was an easy through. He looked along the line of barges; very quiet, someone painting the body of a boat further down; there were maybe 20 boats. Very peaceful. A Kingfisher darted by, a flash of blue light. *I thought they only hung around moving water? Obviously not.* He considered walking along the boats and maybe approaching the guy with the paint but decided to sit and suss for a while first.

What was it about today that made the windows steam up? They hadn't yesterday and the temperature must be in the same couple of degrees slot. He switched on the car electrics to lower the window slightly. He could never work out this windows-misting-up thing; has to be explainable through physics but it was well beyond him and seemed to follow no logic. The cold started to snap at the end of his nose and sweat-damp toes so he switched the electrics back on and slid the window back up again. No difference to the windscreen. His bored head wondered why he hadn't slid down the passenger side window and not the one within five inches of his still-cold nose. The misting that really got him confused was only noticeable at the top of Crab Lane. You come up to the junction at such an angle that, realistically, you can only see the left-side oncoming traffic through the passenger-side back window. Sometimes when the car had been running for an hour and was so roasty-toasty that Billy side window would still be misty, he really didn't get that one. After finishing rubbing the windscreen with a mock-leather pad to clear his view, he turned to check if that Crab Lane window was misty now. His heart fell into confusion seeing the little marks of Billy all over the bottom and middle of the window. Marks that for most of the time were invisible were now highlighted by the cold moisture layering the glass. A collage of little finger trails tracking Billy's bored imagined car races and a couple of big hand prints where Billy had banged the window to say 'bye to Cal. A swell of emotion gushed through him, not positive, not negative just pure untainted emotion filling up his chest. The tsunami broken by a simple question – *I wonder if you could extract DNA from that?*

This simple bit of physics had Mick consciously trying to calm his breathing and heart rate but the misty windows at his side felt too close. Although there was a gap in the cool vapour-covered windscreen where he could monitor the road and canal, the rest was obscured. All he could see was directly out front, the rest of the world was a complete mystery. Maybe that was his problem in the real world; he only saw what was in front of his nose. His whole being felt damp as he attempted to clear his mind and focus, but he couldn't focus. He was emotionally imprisoned by frosted glass too close which hid the scary reality that he couldn't even imagine. With brain encased by the haze that surrounded him, he thought about getting out of the car but instead poured himself a coffee from his work flask, lowered the window to his side and lit a fag. *Fuck, I love smoking.* The nicotine kicked in and started to soothe him while the caffeine slowly started to pull him out of his claustrophobic dream.

The mobile started playing its tune by his side – a welcome interruption – bringing him fully out of the maudlin shite – he loved that tune sometimes.

''Ello.'

'Hi, it's me.' Lesley's voice, that little oasis of normality, that link to the real world, reassuring and loved. He immediately wished he could see more of her.

'A'right.'

'I've got news, not big news, don't get your hopes up, but it's good news. You know I told you that I phoned Strangelove and gave her the dates that we were away? '

'Did you?'

'Yes ,I told you.'

'OK.'

'Well, the point was that if any of the dates of the malicious calls coincided with the dates we were on holiday then it wasn't us.'

'I couldn't believe that they didn't ask us about any dates—'

'Yeh, I know, it's scandalous but—'

'Yeh, but we could've still made the calls from Greece.'

'Jesus, Mick, don't you ever listen to me? We had a conversation about this – it'd come through a foreign provider.'

'Ah yes, of course. Sorry, I'm just a bit distracted, I do remember now.'

'Well, there were calls made while we were away and they were made from Leeds. So we're in the clear for the malicious calls. They've cancelled the bail and everything.'

Mick trying to drag up enough enthusiasm to be equivalent or at least appropriate. 'Brilliant. Maybe those tossers will fully concentrate on finding Billy.'

'Yeh, that was the idea. You don't sound very excited.'

'Sorry, no, I am, its brilliant news, I just need to take it in and chew it a while.'

'Well, it makes it less likely to those wankers that you are involved in harming Billy.'

'Yeh, no, that's fantastic, well done. It's nice to have some good news. Did they apologise?'

'Did they fuck. They said that they had to arrest us and that they were a bit embarrassed doing it, but couldn't quite stretch to an apology.'

'Cunts.'

'I know. Listen I've got to get off. Just thought I'd let you know. It's brilliant, isn't it?'

'Yeh, it is, it really is.'

'And I knew we'd have to clear ourselves. They'd no interest in finding out the truth, just in trying to make their crackpot theories incriminate us.'

'Cunts.'

'See y'.'

'Yeh, see y'.'

Although he'd tried to muster up a positive response, Mick couldn't get his head around whether this was relevant at all. Would it have any knock-ons? Would it move them closer to Billy? *Well, as Lesley had said, it would at least clear up one small part of the jigsaw, but what else? Did anything lead from that? Maybe the police would switch their attention fully to looking for Billy, but surely – unless they thought there was a link – they'd dropped the malicious calls enquiry anyway, and would that mean that they'd give extra resources to searching for Billy? No, they'll have a certain amount of people on the case and that won't change, will it? I bet after the initial flurry of activity there'll be fewer officers on it now.* It was all just bollocks anyway. The only thing that mattered was finding Billy, and any other news was just news, not good not bad, just news. Mick acknowledged to himself with a touch of shame that the removal of him as a suspect had dampened his desperate renegade spirit slightly and brought him back within the law, back to being a docile body. The Foucault reference frustrated him more as he lost the battle with the dead fucker and bit on the unequal gaze of the Panopticon CCTV and his role as the obligatory delinquent.

Hopefully, they'll have some CCTV of my mental, pile-up-causing driving and be searching the streets of Leeds for Mad Mick McCann, the renegade detective.... You're such a twat. Fucking think, y'dozy get. He had a couple of ironic snorts at himself while shaking his head. *You've got more in common with Billy fucking Liar than Jesse James, you soft cunt.*

24

That magpie is behaving really strangely – what's it doing? Looking for insects? It's acting like a woodpecker. Isn't it starlings that are the great mimics? They mimic the sounds of things, like other birds or alarm clocks, not their behaviour, y'dick. Static and dark, the surface of the canal looked like wet tarmac, the straight and controlled curve mimicking the layout of a road, or was it the other way round? Stone flags curbed the road, marking the stopping place. The landscape was hard, sharp and barren; the trees looked dead. Ground and grass glistening with cold possibility. Where were the breathing leaves, the buds generating new layers, the signs of life and hope? He knew life was there somewhere, awaiting the alarm of the body clock. He knew life was there, hidden below the temperature and by the lack of light, obscured and tucked away, awaiting its moment. Emerge a day early and die.

Up on the opposite bank, over to the right, he could see clusters of trees alive with ivy to thirty feet, covering the bark, and at its tips stretching up to colonise more of its slow-growing friend. He smiled – 'I told you, Billy, things fill the space' – completely unaware of the possibility of the ivy drawing the moisture from the bark and killing the trees – of the brutality of nature.

Due to an earlier lack of visibility and a glut of cold, he had the engine running, the heater on, and was enjoying a warm panorama. A couple of joggers steamed along the tow path, more steam than that cyclist earlier, but maybe that was because she was going quicker. He was sure Lesley had brought up something during the phone call that did have some significance; he was on the verge of phoning her when he remembered. Now that he'd been cleared of making the mental phone calls to that bint off the telly he was less likely to be on some crazed spree which included harming his son. Mad as it sounded, it was probably true. Surely they knew he wouldn't harm Billy. But as he was less of a suspect, the people making the enquiries may instead look at other leads, make new enquiries – which has to be good.

'Who are you kidding? They are fucking useless, there's not a chance in hell that they'll find Billy. Look at your case; with their resources, you'd have cleared you and Lesley in a morning. No, just as the two of us cleared our names, so the two of us will have to find Billy. Don't rely on those dateless bastards.'

A couple of cars came and went and Mick was very happy with the spot; he could see the drivers' zits – *Perfect* – and as he was tucked back, they didn't seem to notice him: *Even more perfect.* His time-killing, free-falling head was scoffing at the idea of something being more perfect as another car approached. *Different car, but it's him. Is it him? Fuck, that could well be him.* As The Possible Cunt pulled his car round toward the gates, Mick grabbed his holdall, jumped out of the car, ran along the back of the wire fence, under the cover of bushes, to the gap, and eased himself through. He could see the top of the metal gates to the car park slowly inching open, at about halfway. Moving along the boats: 'BILLY, CAN YOU HEAR ME? – BILLY.' He couldn't help but do it in a sing-song voice.

'BILLY – BILLY. . .' Nothing. There was nothing, but he wasn't even halfway along the row of barges. 'Please, Billy.'

The gates were now fully open. The car park was obscured by the curve in the canal and vegetation, but if The Possible Cunt had come through before they were fully open he could come around the curve and along the path at any moment.

'If he's so much as cut Billy's hair I'm going to fuckin' kill him. BILLY. BILLY.'

'Dad. DAD.' Mick's soul sang a late-morning chorus of joy on hearing the muffled little voice from somewhere – but where?

'KEEP SHOUTING, BILLY, THEN I'LL FIND YOU.'

'OK, DAD, I'M HERE.' Fuck, Mick thought he was going to have a seizure. His temples throbbed not with blood but with tap-dancing elephants; his heart was on the point of leaving his chest. The voice so fundamentally good and innocent, a voice of beauty, was coming from the next barge along, close to a big hut.

In a slightly raised but calming tone: 'I'm here, Billy.'

'Let me out, Dad. I don't like—'

'In a minute, Billy. Billy, listen to me. Are you listening?'

Fuck, how was he going to explain this one? He couldn't afford to get Billy out now but having him so close and not cradling him was like trying to remove his nipples with a set of pliers.

'Yes, but I want to come out – I want to see my mum.' Mick chuckled: he did all the day-to-day stuff but when Mum was around it was almost like he was invisible; Mum got all the attention.

'Listen, if you can do this I'll take you straight to see Mum, OK?'

'OK.'

'Listen, you have to be very quiet now, just sit quietly, no more shouting, it's very important. OK?'

Fuck. Mick could see a figure just rounding the curve, and, battling the urge to grab his son and run, jumped behind the hut.

'OK, Billy? It's very important, keep quiet.'

'OK, OK, Dad, Da-a-ad, OK-A-A, Dad, I will, Dad, DA-A-AD.'

Mick raised his voice further. 'Starting now, Billy. No more talking, starting frommmm… NOW.'

Mick went to the far end of the hut and arching his head round the corner he could see The Definite Cunt getting closer, walking slow like he's out for a little ramble around the countryside – *The Cunt.*

'Fuck.' Mick fumbled for his phone. Hands light and shaking, he drew it. He'd planned to fill in the name of the boat but disobedient fingers meant that it was all he could do to get into Draft and press Send. The envelope icon distorted and flew away. His finger hovered over the Off button but he pulled away just in time, memory slapping him with that stupid fucking musical 'off logo' that it played loud and embarrassing in silent situations.

'Please, God, no one phone me in the next two minutes,' he whispered, more air than tone. He knew he had to get this right, not enough time to run but not boat-side of him, and he couldn't risk watching and getting spotted. With a racing heart, Mick just had to judge it. He counted time slowly, pulled up his hood and stepped out looking like he was a bit lost. *Fuck*, he'd got it completely wrong: his anxiety speed meant that the fella had a good start if he wanted to make a run for it, but he was still walking. Mick pulled out his phone and held it to his ear, rocking his foot backwards and forward on a low concrete step. The Daydreaming Cunt kept coming – perfect.

Hood up, Mick stepped forward and shook it down like someone out of *Lord of the Rings*. 'Now then, I wun't mind a bit of a chat wi'you.'

Classic. The Cunt nearly shat himself, but suddenly looked relaxed.

'Fuuucking'ell. I didn't expect you to find me this quickly. I'd a couple of other bits and pieces to do. Never mind, we're here now. He's inside.'

'I know. I've heard him. You don't think I'd have nailed you without Billy do you? – Billy, its Dad again. It's OK now. You did brilliantly, good lad.'

'Dad ,let me out, I want to see you. Da-a-ad, Dad, let me out.'

'In a minute, darling, I've just got something to sort out.'

'Dad, I want to come out now.'

Mick's physiology was screaming at him to see his lad, to get Billy and wrap him in the biggest ball of cotton wool that he could find, but he was safe where he was and he wasn't a distraction, a weakness, or – for Billy's sake – a witness to the impending bloodbath. His physiology was screaming to kill The Cunt here and now, to immediately rip out his heart, but his brain overruled with the logic of the situation. He had to keep calm and do this right. *This is real life, not* Dirty Harry; anyway, his body felt distant and weak, it was all he could do to stand and try to get his breathing back within its lungs.

'In a minute.'

The Cunt interjected. 'Billy, in a red tin under the big chair there's some chocolate, you can have some of that now if you like. I hope you don't mind, it'll keep him quiet. You've trained him well, he's a very obedient child – if a bit stroppy at times.'

'Billy, don't have the chocolate.'

'But Da-a-ad.'

'Billy, don't touch that chocolate. I'm telling you, Billy, leave the chocolate or you won't have any more for a month.' As a young child's universal urge for instant gratification invaded the space that should have been concentrated on the matter at hand, he re-engaged with The Cunt, breath returning.

'Don't you ever tell my lad what to fuckin' do again. And he's four, f' God's sake, he gets tired, so don't you even think about judging him, or I'll rip out y'spleen and feed it to the fuckin' crows.'

'I'm sure that's your immediate urge, but you need to let me tell you a couple of important things first.'

'Yeh, like did you feel a cunt hiding in bushes watching ar 'ouse?'

'There was no need for that. Just watched a couple of times online and printed out a satellite image...'

'Fucking knew it. So why did y'do this?' Mick shrugged quizzically, palms showing. 'You do know that I'm going to kill you?'

'It's what I'd expect, knowing you as I do.'

'You don't fucking know me.' Mick was breathing deeply, trying to get his violent impulses under control without losing them altogether.

'Listen, Mick, before this gets nasty, there's stuff you need to know. But I'll come to that. I do know you. I've read loads of your posts. And Lesley: I've met her a couple of times and had a good root through her emails – very interesting stuff.'

'Fuck off, how would you do that?'

'Easy, I've got access to everything I need to get into her emails and, as I say, very revealing. There's stuff in there that I'm sure you'd like to know about.'

'Ohh, fuck off, there's bog-standard emails to mates and colleagues, so don't try that one. There's always the possibility, but don't try and cause more trouble – you're in enough shit as it is.'

'OK, OK, forget I said anything. There isn't owt like that anyway.'

'Yeh, I know there isn't. I know her inside out, so don't you pretend you know either of us, because you don't.'

'I know you alright. I've even chatted to you a few times.'

'What? Have y'fuck.'

'I have, on OMJ. *The White Crow*. We've exchanged words a couple of times. Anyway, I've been studying you; I've got to know you intimately.'

'Bollocks, you know an online persona.'

'Oh, I know you alright. I've read the book as well, y'know – very good I—'

'Fuck off, you don't. You know a part or maybe parts of me embellished, not the rounded individual.'

'Oh, I know you alright. I—'

'Bollocks you don't. You can't, not from online posts—'

'Yeh, but you can get—'

216

'No that's not the real me, it's got parts of me exaggerated and bits of me that rarely come out. Everyone does it to some extent. If you've been given a persona by people's responses, or part-developed one without realising it, you just slip into it.'

'Da-a-ad, I want to come out.'

'IN A MINUTE, DARLING – WE'RE NEARLY DONE. Anyway, look at us chatting away like we've got all the time in the world.'

'We have, haven't we?'

'I have… but not you, y'cunt; your time is very fucking limited.'

Mick sees The Cunt getting a bit twitchy and is aware of the importance of the first move, but craves answers, some sense from all this chaos.

'So come on, why did you do this?'

'Oh, you know, infamy. To leave a marker on the world, be famous – to be renowned as a brilliant Twenty-First Century criminal. To fill the Red-Tops and sicko TV channels for years. I know at first there'll be a huge surge of interest in me and that it'll die down. But whenever there's a crime against children – one using a phone, a boat ,or involving identity theft, hacking or a writer – I'll be mentioned. It's a bit like the search terms in the title of y'book. I'll be talked about on the news, in documentaries, in fiction, in gossip columns – I really will be immortal.' The Cunt fixed Mick with a stare. 'I'll be known as the smart one. You'll just be the witness to my brilliance, and the victim. Just imagine how much material there will be about me on the web already, before the situation has reached a conclusion to speculate on. You see, we're very similar in that regard, Mick – craving the attention.'

'We're not alike in any fucking way. I didn't publish the book as some desperate attempt to become famous. I wrote it on the off-chance of being able to buy mi kids a better pair of trainers and, well, sounds shit, but I felt compelled.'

'Snap. I understand the compulsion. But come on, you're always on OMJ banging on about—'

'Well yeh, I go online, but I forget it's a public board. If someone brings it up, I'll do my flogging routine, but that's into parody now and everyone knows it but you. I published my book because, once written, I'd have felt it was yet another creative thing that I'd failed at if I didn't get it out, get it into the real world – it wasn't about being famous.'

The Cunt straining and stuttering to get his words in. 'Come on, you love the attention, being popular on—'

'Bollocks, there's plenty of people think I'm a cunt on there. More than anything, it was like buying a ticket to the lottery but with slightly better odds – debatable – but there was always that chance, that small possibility, that I could sell boatloads. Maybe get it taken up by a production company, make shitloads of money and remove shitloads of stress from our lives – live a more happy and fulfilled life. It's only people with money who pretend that it doesn't bring happiness, and maybe it doesn't, but I'll tell you something, not having money or living just beyond your money definitely brings stress and tension. If we had money, we'd be fucking happy, a tell y'that for nowt.'

Billy had started up shouting again. This was dragging out, and Mick didn't want anyone turning up before he'd had chance to nail The Cunt. No witnesses meant self-defence.

'In a minute, darlin'.' Mick felt a warm glow as Billy started counting to 60. 'Maybe two or three, Billy.'

'Oh, come off it, you're a right show-off, always going on about how good it is.'

'Fuckin'ell, a' y'stupid? I've got no idea what it's like. I—'

'It's really fucking good and you know it. That's why you're always boasting about it, that's why I chose you to—'

'Really – a' you stupid? That's just part of the persona. You say you've read the book? I bring a bit of that teenage cockiness from the book to the boards. But yes, sometimes I'm proud of it and you do hope people enjoy it. I know it's not everyone's bag and I have no idea really how good or bad it is. It was also a way of hiding from the real world, of throwing my passions at something.' Mick tried to rein in this distraction, 'Wait a minute – good ploy, get me talking about that fucking book and anyway, what the fuck d'y' mean "why you chose" me?'

'You really don't get it, do you, Mick? I'm a fan, a real fan, not a mate – a fan. I fucking loved your book. It made me laugh and think. It was so spontaneous. It wasn't just recognising the places and accents and, in a way, a lot of the characters, but I loved your voice, you felt like a mate. And some of the prose bits were fucking inspired. You moved me – you almost changed mi life.'

Mick couldn't resist it. 'I've got a gift, an't a, mate?'

'You have, you really have. That's why I chose y'.'

'Whaaaat? You mean you liked mi book so much that you decided to try and wreck mi life.'

'No, no, no, I chose you because… well, it kinda fell into mi lap, a gift from God. I already had the SIM card. I saw your book at reception at Yorkshire telly, bought one, asked around to find out how it got there and was told it was by Lesley Jackson's husband. I couldn't believe it, the same Lesley Jackson whose SIM I had. Anyway I saw Charlotte introduce you on *Calendar* – shit, those crap puns really pissed me off, and I knew they'd piss you off as well – and it all clicked. I had a Eureka moment and the more I thought about it the better and more interesting the plot became. I mean, f'fuck's sake, Mick your surname, McCann, y'know like Maddie. How could I resist?'

'Plot?'

'Yeh, plot – anyway why should it always be vacuous fucking air-head women that get stalked? Fucking celebrities who've achieved nothing, been born to someone famous or appeared on some dumb reality TV show. A mean some of them, their only fucking talent is being able to get dressed, put make-up on and go fucking clubbing. Another thing is, it's so predictable for the plot – some fucking bimbette soap actress or local TV presenter. So I decided I could use Charlotte as the foil, as the smokescreen, and have the gritty writer as the real quarry.'

'You need fucking help, mate – what the fuck are you talking about, plot? This is real fucking life, this isn't a film or a TV drama.'

'No, Mick, it isn't. It could be but it isn't… but I'll tell you what it is, it's your next book.'

'WHAT? My next fuckin' book?'

'Yeh, think about it – how could you resist writing this up? You couldn't, don't you see? It's perfect. You'll do a fantastic job of it as well, Mick. You are fucking perfect for it. You know the story inside out and anyway, the story will be out there by the morning, Mick, but—'

'F'fuck's sake.' Mick was stumped.

'You've lived it, you've been it, you can write what you know, and with all this publicity, I've broken you, got you into the big time. You'll sell fucking millions. How many has *Coming Out* sold since all this happened? You know as well as I do that you'd never have made it. You'd have stayed an obscure, underrated, Northern writer—'

'Neither of us know that – fuckin'ell, I don't believe this.'

'You deserve more than that, you're better than that; better than those air-head, C-list celebs. Think of the books you wouldn't be writing if you had to work nine to five. You should feel honoured that I chose you. You should thank me – I know it'll be hard to see right now but I've made you, mate.'

'You're off y'fucking trough. No fuckin' way am I going to write this. No fuckin' way. I'm not a performing chimp. I'm not going to let you control everything, read me like a fuckin' book – dictate what a do.'

'Oh, but you will. You won't be able to resist it; might do it straight away, may take you 20 years, but you'll have to write it up. And I'm not trying to control you. It's more like I'm hiring you without payment but, well, there will be a fucking huge payment for you and I won't try to claim royalties or anything.'

'Ohh, cheers.'

'Anyway, I didn't have a choice really. If I'd have come to you with the plot you'd have said it was too unbelievable – you'd have thought I was a nutter.'

'Aye – I'd a'bin fuckin' right.'

The Cunt smiled, there was a moment of silence – almost calm – and the two broke eye contact. In the stillness Mick's gut started bubbling anger up into his chest - *Time to make a move.*

'Ey, Mick.'

'What?'

'I'll tell y' what might interest y'.'

'Yeh?'

'I've removed your records from the Criminal Database.'

'Whaaat?'

'Yeh, yours and Lesley's. Well, I wiped yours clean off but—'

'Fuck off.'

'A did, but I didn't remove Lesley's – I changed all her details. If Lesley ever gets arrested again and they check her DNA or fingerprints, it'll come up as Elizabeth Regina and bring up a photo of the Queen.' The Cunt looked really pleased with himself while Mick couldn't make his mind up whether it was good or bad – if he should be grateful, if he should be laughing. His face reflected this, which increased The Cunt's smug satisfaction.

'Lesley should go out, smash a window and leave some blood. Don't think they'd go to Buckingham Palace but I'd love to see their faces when they open their database to bag a wrong 'un.' The Cunt was actually fucking chuckling and, to intensify Mick's frustration, he was struggling to keep a straight face himself. The thought of Lesley going on a crime spree and nailing the Queen was class.

'Yeh, I thought it was going to be a bit of a challenge, which, to a certain extent, it was, but once I'd sussed it, it was an absolute doddle. I just had to find the paths and override a couple of things. Took me a couple of days, like, but it wasn't that difficult. They should be able to suss that I've been there but I doubt they'll be able to work out what I've altered – too many smokescreens.'

'The Criminal Database? Bollocks. You couldn't just hack the Criminal Database.'

'Check it. There's always a way in, always someone who... anyway, they'll deny it, of course, but ask them to show you your records or Lesley's. Also, with you two being high-profile and just in case they've backed it up and reinstated you both, I've put in further proof that they'll be too stupid to spot.'

'What?'

'You need to listen to this one and be careful—'

'No, sorry mate, you really are deluded.'

'Listen, this is your proof and you must be really careful with it. Don't blow it, don't mention it unless you can verify it and have witnesses.'

'Yeh, right. How am I going to get access to the criminal database? It's not the fucking NHS.'

'Go to the press. I think you'd be surprised what access you'll get with the press clambering for controlled admission – with the public screaming, "If it's secure let them check it." They simply won't have the balls to hold out against that, they're *Catch-22*ed –

how cool is that? We could bring the government to its knees, my friend, and certainly get the ID shit stopped.'

'I'm not your fuckin' friend – you need to remember that. Once we've finished all this fuckin' flirting I'm going to rip your heart out... know that.'

'Yeh, yeh, whatever, but think of it. It's also fantastic for the plot and sales, adds a bit of resonance and humour at a tense point. It brings the real world and questions of freedom, security and the police state slap-bang into the middle of it; which, let's be honest, is the backbone of our plot – you can drop down and then do a rebuild on the tension.'

'Our plot? Our fuckin' plot? What fuckin' plot? This is real; I am not going to write this, y'cunt.' Mick was starting to get very angry – which he liked.

'Mmm... can you see it? You're an author and I've dropped an exceptional plot in your lap. Couldn't write it myself. *The Perfect 2008 Crime in Leeds, Yorkshire, England.* Anyway, whether you write it or not, this whole thing will be one of the defining stories of the early twenty-first century. It's got everything – we're creating history.'

'Fuck, you're delusional—'

'Whatever. Now listen, this is the one you've got to keep secret, don't tell anyone until you can safely prove it—'

'I won't be in a position to prove shit.'

'You're wrong. Now listen, the Criminal Database. I've inserted Tony Blair and Gordon Brown, although I've spelt Tony with an 'i', he should be there really anyway, so I've put him in. All his details present and correct. I've put his convictions as deception, fraud, perjury and – you'll like this, Mick – mass murder—'

The Cunt was so excited that he looked like he was about to shit himself. Mick was a mess; he was fighting the fact that – within his anger – he was developing a creeping admiration for the bloke – if it was true.

'Oh yeh, and I've added John Sessions as a child molester. Like you, I never liked that smarmy cunt.'

'Bollocks. I just don't believe that you'd be able to access any of that.'

'Yeh, like there's no precedent, like in the real world there isn't a kid somewhere in Britain that the Americans want to extradite.

Want to bang up for the rest of his life for fucking their most sensitive databases – for fucking with NASA. Anyway, it doesn't matter if you believe me or not, just get it checked. Isn't it brilliant? It just gets bigger and bigger.'

'Oh yeh, fuckin' fantastic – well done. You've probably destroyed my marriage, you've definitely traumatised my whole family – you've kidnapped my fucking son, f'fuck's sake.'

'Oh come on, Mick, it's hardly *The Count of Monte Christo*. If you're smart, which you are, I've made your family secure for fucking centuries. You'll make shitloads a money out a this. I've been good to Billy. As far as he's concerned, he's just had a little holiday with his Uncle Stuart. I haven't hurt or harmed him in any way.'

'You better fuckin' not a done.'

'I haven't. I've looked after him and I've made sure he's had stuff to do. He's OK. Oh, and diddums, you and Mrs Mick have been a bit worried! Get a fuckin' grip. Think what people have to endure around this horrible fucking world; women being forced to hang their babies from trees by the neck. Nine-year-old kids made to shoot their family, mothers holding their dying babies in their arms that could be saved for the price of a family day out – you know the stuff. Awww... I've put you under a bit of emotional pressure – poor you. It's not like I've forced you and Mrs Mick to walk around Basra in a fuckin' miniskirt.'

Fuck... what a line – why hadn't Mick thought of that line? Finding this increasingly uncomfortable, Mick was starting to like The Cunt – found him fascinating – almost wished he'd gone out for a beer with him. The empathy was short-lived as he reminded himself of just what The Cunt had done.

'Anyway, listen to us chatting away like we're on a fucking date. Why the fuck am I still talking to you, y'cunt? You're not a real person.'

'You know I am, Mick. One thing that you have got is a bit of understanding; you know that there'll have been a series of things brought me here. Not enough attention as a kid, or maybe too much. Getting screwed over by women; we don't all have your way with them you know. You've written it, f' God's sake – "a death at the wrong time, the wrong age".'

'I've been screwed over by women lots of times, y'dozy get, and I haven't got a way with them.'

Slowly winding up, Mick was still reminding himself that all this bollocks, all this heartache, was down to him. Who knows what deep-sitting damage this had done to the family, the extended family, never mind Billy – but he'd be alright. *Billy's a strong little bugger.* All down to him, this almost likeable fella stood in front. *LIKEABLE? For fuck's sake, Mick, he kidnapped y'fucking kid!*

The Cunt could see a shift in Mick's body language, a tightening of the lips, widening eyes. 'Mick, much as you'd love to kick my head in, I'd have a quick look in at Billy first, you might find he's looking a bit drowsy. If he's had some of that chocolate, I'd say you've got about 10 minutes left, tops, to get him to hospital and maybe save his life – then again, maybe not.'

'CUNT.' Mick shouted out, 'Billy have you had any of the chocolate?'

'No,Dad, I haven't. You said I shouldn't have any and I didn't. Can I have some now?'

'No, Billy, don't have any. It'll make you very poorly.'

'Awwwe, but Da-a-ad, I want some.'

'No Billy, you can't. Now Billy, listen, this is very important, if you've had some you have to tell me. It's very important. I won't be cross if you have – I promise. Have you eaten any of the chocolate, Billy?' All through this, Mick didn't take his eyes off The Cunt. It felt like a perfect set-up, perfect distraction to mask some happening. The Cunt didn't move.

'No, Dad, I haven't.'

The Cunt raised his eyebrows. 'Do you believe him? Do you trust that he hasn't even had a nibble? He's four, Mick, just mastering the art of lying.'

'Don't look so fuckin' smug, cunt. I'm going to fuckin' kill you – painfully.'

As planned, Mick was torn between getting Billy straight out and dealing with The Cunt first. Maybe Stuart had made a mis-calculation because Mick decided that only the latter would work. He fixed eyes with The Cunt. 'Yes I do trust him he'd tell me. Do you actually *want* me to kill you? Is that part of your plot? Anyway, y'sick fuck, you do understand that I can't risk losing this fight, don't you? I'd chin you anyway, I've got more at stake than you, but I can't risk it.'

Mick yanked the holdall around from his shoulder and pulled out a nail-gun.

The Cunt stepped back and laughed. 'What the fuck is that? It's hardly *Dirty Harry*, is it Mick? A bit *James Bond*, like, but hardly *Dirty Harry*.'

Mick had lost this little battle in the psychological warfare and felt a bit of a tit. The thing was that he couldn't risk getting a gun, not with the police round all the time and the fucking press camping out. A nail-gun in the back of his car was explainable and very tidy.

'No, this is real life. I've adapted mine so don't worry, y'cunt, it'll do the job.'

The Cunt appeared to make a move towards his pocket so Mick squeezed the trigger. He'd developed a technique to control the kickback by aiming it well below the target. A second's gap and The Cunt doubled up from the waist with a yelp that could've found the *101 Dalmatians*.

Mick got a huge gush of weird pleasure. 'Fucking bull's eye, incant. Y'laughing now?' Mick quickly stepped towards him. 'Ar' y' – ey – incant? Laughing? Y'still laughing?' Mick was up to him now. The Cunt tried to straighten up quick but howled. Mick stepped back and then quick in, smashing the gas cylinder end of the charging gun down on the top of the bloke's head. A sweet crack.

'Where's y'sense of humour gone now, y'snidey cunt?' A thudding kick to the bloke's head, blood, saliva and mucus erupting from the face. 'You think it's alright to traumatise my kids, my family?'

Pulling up the whimpering head by the hair, he took a full swing and hurled his fist into The Cunt's face, which flew away from him, thudding and cracking on the paving slabs. The gibbering stopped.

'All this, all this fucking nightmare down to you.' He launched a quick-fire series of kicks into the still torso and straightened up, pulling in breath. 'I fucking warned you – cunt.'

'Da-a-ad, Dad, I want to come out.'

'I'm coming, darlin.' Mick bent over and checked The Cunt's pockets – nothing unexpected – and stepped over onto the barge, carefully picking his way down the slippery-looking steps.

'I'm coming, Billy – keep away from the doors.'

Mick tried the door: locked. 'Why didn't I bring his fucking keys?' Knowing that Billy was further along the boat, he kicked it with the bottom of his foot and it flew open. Unable to suppress a *Starsky and Hutch*-inspired smile, Mick shouted, 'Billy, you OK?'

'Yeh, Dad. I want to come out now. I didn't have any of the chocolate, Dad.'

'Good lad.'

The immediate reference sounded slightly suspicious and Mick scrambled quickly across the narrow space to the door in the corner. No locks, just a latch, and there he fucking was – he looked bigger. Mick flew across the space and flung his arms around him, being careful not to squeeze the life out. He loved his smell – although it was now slightly contaminated with a thin whiff of piss. He broke off quickly to check Billy, who was looking a little woozy.

'Are you OK, Billy? Billy, how do you feel?'

Tears started to well up in the little lad's eyes. 'I'm tired, Dad.'

An obviously melted and reconstituted lump of chocolate lay on a small table; a few crumbs and finger-marks, but it looked unbitten and unlicked. Mick wrapped it up in a tissue from his pocket and dropped it in.

'Billy, listen to me, you mustn't go to sleep.'

'But I am tired, Dad.'

'I know darling, but you mustn't go to sleep, not just yet.'

'Awww, but Dad, I'm tired.'

Mick raised his voice and added a severe tone. 'I don't care if you're tired, Billy, you must *not* go to sleep.'

'But Da-a-ad,' was all that Billy could muster. Mick, seeing that he was on the verge of uncontrollable and, crucially, uncommunicative sobbing, gentled his tone. 'Listen, Billy, you've been such a brave boy, such a big lad. Now y'have to listen.' Billy's face starting to twitch and crumble. 'You can't cry now – it's very important. Did you have any of the chocolate?'

'No, Dad, I didn't, I didn't have—'

'Not even a little bit? You can tell me, I just need to know, I won't be cross. Don't cry, don't cry, Billy.'

Billy battling the tears. 'I'm a bit tired, Dad, but I didn't, I didn't have any.'

'Good lad. Now listen, what else have you had just now? Not your breakfast, just since you heard me talking outside – what else have you had?'

'Nothing, Dad, I haven't had anything.' The tears beaten, Billy was starting to drift.

'You can't go to sleep, Billy. Have you had a drink?'

'Where's Uncle Stuart?'

'Don't worry about that. Have you had a drink?'

'I've had some apple juice, but I didn't like it. I want to see my mum. Da-a-ad, I want to see my mum.'

As tears were re-entering his eyes, Billy was starting the pre-crying tension and slight facial shake. Now was as good a time as any. Mick pulled some tissues out of his pocket and moved Billy sideways on. 'Billy, open y'mouth – good lad – a bit wider if you can.'

Mick pushed two fingers down Billy's throat and Billy started to retch. Nothing came out so Mick shoved them in again and held them their briefly. Just as he moved them out, Billy threw up all over his arm – nothing solid, just fluid and mucus with brown stringing.

'Good lad, Billy,' Mick wiped the sick from the shaking boy's mouth with the tissue and wiped his arm on the carpet. 'Shit... Sorry, Billy, I had to do that.'

'I want my mum.' Billy wept with eyes full of injustice.

'Oh, we will see Mum, and soon, don't worry, but only if you stay awake. If not, I'll put you straight to bed. Where's the juice? Where's the apple juice, Billy?'

'Aw, but Da-a-ad, I'm tired – I want to see my mum.'

Mick was scanning the room all the time, looking for the glass or container. 'You will, Billy, but only if you stay awake.' He saw the end of a blue plastic container sticking out from under a blanket on the couch.

'Was this it, Billy?' Mick holding a half-full blue-and-yellow, football-themed children's drinks bottle in front of Billy. 'Was this your apple juice?'

Billy's head, starting to slip towards comfort, nodded sleepily.

'Right, that's it, you are not seeing Mum,' Mick said in a raised chastising voice, Billy's head jolting up at the injustice of the words.

'I wasn't asleep, I wasn't – I want to see my mum.'

'Well, you can't. Are you hurting anywhere, Billy?'

Tears started to well up in Billy's eyes. 'But I want to see my mum.'

'Billy, you need to tell me if you are hurting anywhere.'

'I've been scratching a bit, Dad – not too much but a bit. It was really itchy, Dad, but I didn't scratch it too much, just a bit.'

'OK, darling, let's have a look.' His legs were red-raw with seeping scratch marks, as was his torso, bum and inner arms at the elbow. 'Does that hurt, Billy? It's not too bad, we'll soon sort that out.'

Mick grabbed the bottle and scooped up the sobbing child. His gut turning somersaults and landing on its back, he headed for the door.

'I told you you had to stay awake and you didn't, so we're not seeing Mum.'

Billy's sobbing hitting new peaks of intensity. 'Aww, Dad—'

'Look, Billy, listen, Billy, listen. Stay awake and I *might* change my mind.' Mick, leaving the barge, saw The Cunt still lying on the ground in a pool of blood. He arranged Billy on his chest so that his head pointed the other way just so that Billy didn't witness the mess – just in case he'd developed Stockholm syndrome. The damp lump was a sudden reminder that he should call the police. 'Fuck 'em – what have they ever done for me, the cunts?'

'Billy, if you go to sleep I'll leave you asleep and you won't see Mum until tomorrow. Are you listening, Billy?' Arching his head away from his chest, Mick could see Billy starting to drift. Rright, you can walk now.' Mick dropped Billy suddenly to his feet. Billy wobbled but Mick supported him from the side. 'And we need to get a move on.' Billy stumbled forward but Mick caught him. 'Come on, stop messing about, Billy, and get a move on.'

Mick reached into his pocket and pulled out his mobile, quickly hitting 999. 'Thank fuck.' He'd never been sure if 999 would work on a mobile and knew he should have checked it before now.

'Come on, Billy, let's get moving.' Billy lurching along, battling to get one foot in front of the other, torso jerking with the big breath-inhaling of the oppressed.

'Yes, it's Mick McCann. I'm bringing my lad ... Yes, the one that's been missing ... I'm taking him to the LGI. He's very sleepy – come on, Billy, get moving – I think he's been poisoned ... Yes, The Cunt told me he'd poisoned some chocolate that he'd given to Billy and he keeps drifting in and out of consciousness ... Yes, but I'm not sure if it's that, it could've been in his juice ... I've got the container. I don't know that it's right but it's the only one I could see ...Yes, I made him throw up as soon as I got suspicious ... Well I think this is it but it might be worth – be careful, Billy – searching the place ... It's a barge on Aire Valley Marina ... I don't know, but there's an unconscious man lying just outside it ... FUCK HIM, get them to search it. I'm almost at my car now ... About ten minutes ... Yeh, please ... I *am* trying to keep him afuckingwake. 'Bye.'

Mick thumbed his mobile again while nudging Billy along with his knee. 'Keep going, Billy – Oh, what a surprise. Yeh, yeh ... Lesley, it's me. I've got him. I've got Billy. We're on our way to the LGI, A & E – give me a call.' Mick flicked his phone shut and looking at the gate to the compound remembered the way it lumbered open.

'Right, Billy, keep walking. You've got to see if you can get through the big gate before it shuts again.' Mick sprinted to the big red button at the side of the gate and gave it a jab. There was a reassuring buzz and click and the gate unlatched and started to slowly clank open.

'Come on, Billy, keep coming. We're racing the gate.' Billy was shuffling in the right direction, feet hardly leaving the ground. Mick ran back to him and scooped him up, one forearm under his bum, the other around his back, hand cupping his head. He ran a few yards and dropped Billy to the ground. Billy too long and heavy to be carried like that at speed. Turning his back to him Mick said, 'Jump on, Billy, come on.'

Billy clambered on to his back and Mick raced towards and through the gates, trying to exaggerate the bumps and shouting, 'Yee-haaa.'

At the car, Mick dropped Billy to the ground in one movement, guiding him down his back with his arms and hands. He pulled open the rear, Billy-side, door and started to unclip the child seat. 'FUCK OFF.' It was locked into position by the seat-belt and clip that wasn't loosening. 'Thank fuck.' The clip gave way. He yanked the child seat out – 'Come on, Billy' – threw it in the front passenger seat and hoisted Billy around into the seat. 'Sit up straight, Billy.'

'I'm not strapped in, Dad.'

'Ahh, so what?' Slamming the door, he skidded around to the driver's side and dived in.

'Da-a-ad, I'm not strapped in.'

'You'll be alright.' Mick started the engine.

'Strap me in, Dad. Da-a-ad.' The more Billy protested, the more awake he became.

'You'll be alright.' He motioned to strap himself in.

'BUT DAAAAAD.'

Mick leaned over and strapped Billy in. 'OK, Billy, I'll strap you in if you stay awake but if you're falling asleep I'm unstrapping you again.'

'OK, Dad.'

'I love you, Billy.'

'I love you too, Dad.' The wheel-spin had already happened and the car was flying towards the electrical plant, the acceleration resonating around their chests like a bass-bin at a Motörhead gig and bringing Billy to life.

'Whoa Dad, this is like *Top Gear,* isn't it, Dad, like *Top Gear*?'

Mick laughing hysterically, it was so right having Billy by his side; he felt like he'd been reborn, like he'd found the eternal. 'It is Billy, except I'm faster than *The Stig*… obviously.'

The back-end slid a bit as Mick threw the car around the corner next to the electrical plant.

'We skidded, Dad, didn't we? Didn't we skid, Dad?'

'We did.'

'I didn't know you could drive fast, Dad.'

'I can though, Billy, can't I?' Mick could hear a siren that didn't sound too far off.

'Yes, Dad, you can go really fast.'

The brief burst of excitement was waning as Billy became less animated. Head angled towards the window and suspiciously low.

'Ey you, I can see y'.' Mick prodded Billy, who yelped. 'Messing about and going to sleep.' Mick prodded him again.

'Aaaaye,' protested Billy as Mick prodded him again.

'Messing about. I'll show you,' said Mick in a more playful tone, trying to get him fully awake. With each prod, Mick added, 'Wake up,' in a teasing tone and Billy, after a few more protestations, started to giggle at the repetitive jabs.

Coming onto the straight, Mick could see the spinning blue lights of a squad car hurtling toward the bridge, the police car's right of way. The two cars entered the single-track bridge at the same time, Mick hammering his horn and flashing his light furiously. 'BACK UP, Y'CUNT, BACK UP.' The squad car was smoking from the tyres and suddenly moving the other way with the young lad's head facing the boot of the car.

'Good lad.' Mick flew by the bemused-looking officers, gesturing toward Mick.

'Fuck orfffff.' Mick accelerated towards Kirkstall Road.

'Billy, wake up, you can't go to sleep.' Mick shook Billy's leg. 'You won't see Mum and I'll unstrap you.'

'But Da-a-ad, I'm tired.'

'It's up to you, Billy.'

Coming towards Kirkstall Road, Mick was worrying about merging; it could take ages from there and would be very dangerous to just fly out onto. He slowed his speed slightly as the junction reared up before them. To his amazement there were traffic cops both sides, blocking both lanes.

'Aw, fuck it.' Mick flew out, any fear of the police – of the repercussions – secondary to the fear of Billy dying because his Dad was a spineless cunt.

Across both lanes, Mick hung a right onto Kirkstall Road, townbound.

'Look, Billy, look how fast we're going – BILLY, LOOK.'

Billy's head lifted slightly and gazed towards the window. Mick could see one of the traffic cops hot on his bumper, sirens screaming and lights flashing.

'CUNTS. Look, Billy, a new Renault. Is that a new Renault? Look, there. Billy, don't go to sleep.' Mick shoved Billy hard in the ribs but his head was starting to droop.

At the top of his voice Mick screamed, 'BILLY, WAKE – UP.'

A slight jolt of the head but not enough. Mick struck him hard on his thigh. 'BILLY, WAKE UP.'

A small sleepy yelp but nothing else, other than his phone starting to ring in his pocket. 'F'FUCK'S SAKE, Y'REALLY WANT ME TO ANSWER THE FUCKIN' PHONE WITH THE TRAFFIC CUNTS ON MI TAIL AND MI SON DYING NEXT TO ME – CUUUUNTS.'

Mick shook Billy again; nothing but half-movement. He squeezed his fingers onto his little lad's thigh and nipped and twisted as hard as he could while moving his car across the two lanes to make sure that the traffic cops didn't get in front to stop him.

'AAAAAYE, Dad – that hurt.' Billy started to cry. 'That really hurt, Dad, you shouldn't hurt me like that, you shouldn't.'

'You've got to stay awake, Billy. Look how fast we're going – look, Billy, faster than *The Stig*.' Billy seemed to have perked up and was gazing out of the window, chest jerking with the cruelty of it all. The phone still playing. 'Fuck 'em.' Mick pulled it out of his pocket. ''Ello.'

'Mr McCann, let us get past you – we'll take you in.'

'What?' Mick snorted and shook uncontrollably. *Y'dopey twat, they were there on purpose, they were there to help, y'stupid wanker.*

'We'll get you to the LGI much faster and maybe without crashing if you let us in front.'

'Ahhh... OK, sorry. I thought you were trying to get me to pull over and I'm in a bit of a rush. Get by – but you'd better not be bullshitting me.'

'No, Mr McCann, I'm not, but it might be quicker if you pull over and get in with us.'

'Fuck that.'

'Fine, your choice, just try and stay with us.'

Glancing over, Billy was drifting again. 'No, wait a minute, I will, but whatever you want with me, we'll sort out after we've got him to hospital, yeh?'

232

'Of course, whatever.'

Mick pulled up sharply just beyond the viaduct, unclipping Billy as he jumped out and pulled him through the driver-side door. Billy was looking really peaky, heavy eyes still open, the cool blast of air waking his inquisitiveness.

'Da-a-ad, have we run out of petrol? Have we, Dad?'

'No, darling, we're going in that really cool police car, look.' Mick gestured over to the police car behind. One officer was standing in the middle of the road holding the creeping traffic at bay while looking towards Mick. The rear door of the police car open. The traffic cop pointed at the two front cars and held the palm of his hand up while pushing it towards them and back-tracking towards the car.

'Dad, it's a Volvo, isn't Dad, a Volvo?'

'It certainly is, Billy. Can you see what sort of Volvo it is?' As he ran towards the police car, Mick noticed that Billy was burning up, the back of his head layered with sodden hair.

'A'you alright, Billy?'

Tears started to well up in the corner of Billy's eyes – 'I'm just very tired, Dad, and I want to see my mum' – and he started to cry.

'Billy, you're doing brilliantly – it won't be long now.' Mick was filled with new hope. The switch to the police car meant that Mick could pay all his attention to keeping Billy awake, which he'd found nigh on impossible whilst driving. 'And you've done so well that you'll definitely see Mum.'

'And will you strap me in, Dad?'

Mick laughed tears. 'Of course I will.'

Jumping into the back of the car, Mick pulled the strap right across him and Billy, with Billy sitting on his knee.

'Do you think it might be safer, Mick, if you strap him in by your side?' asked the younger-than-expected driver.

'Just fuckin' drive.'

'Yeh, yeh, alright I was just...'

The car pulled away and Mick chatted excitedly to Billy, making huge whooping sounds as they went round corners at speed and jumped red lights for fun.

'Look, Billy a red light, shall we stop? Shall we? Naaaah, keep going, Mr Policeman. Get out the way, get out the way, we're coming through. Look, Billy, everyone's getting out of the way for us –fantastic. He can't half drive, can't he, Billy? Faster than *The Stig,* I bet'

At Accident and Emergency, Mick dived out of the car clutching Billy to his chest. 'Cheers, lads.' Billy still beating the urge to drift – only just.

'Nearly there. Stay awake, Billy.'

At the door, someone was waiting with a wheelchair.

'Drop him in here, mate…. Hold on, little fella, I can go really fast with this.'

Through to an examination room with a gaggle of white coats waiting.

'Hello. Are you Billy?' asked one of the women while shining a light and looking intensely into Billy's eyes. 'Look at your dad…. No, without moving your head. Try to keep your head still and look at your dad – yes, good.' Billy's top lifted, she moved on to listening to his chest.

'This might prick a bit,' said another while pushing a needle into Billy's arm. Billy recoiled a bit.

'Don't worry about that,' said Mick, 'Billy's a right little trooper, he's really brave.'

Billy turned to his dad. 'I am, Dad, aren't I? I'm really brave, aren't I, Dad?'

Mick could hold it in no longer and tears started to stream down his face as he pushed out the broken stuttering words. 'You are, Billy, you are *really* brave.'

'I love you, Dad.'

'I love you too, Billy,' said Mick, blubbering like a girl.

'I love you more than you love me.'

'Don't think so, Billy, I love you to infinity.'

Blood pressure taken, the examination continued.

'Shit. I've brought these.' Mick pulled the chocolate wrapped in tissue from his pocket and passed it over with the drinks bottle.

'There's still quite a bit left in that. You know the details of the case, yes?'

'Yes, we know all about it. So these are the things that you are suspicious were used to administer any possible substance.'

'I can't be sure but they're the most likely culprits.'

'Do you know how long ago he had it?'

234

'I don't, no... I'd say at least half an hour ago.'

'He's certainly looking drowsy but I'd have thought anything very serious would be showing more definite symptoms by now. He's not looking much more than a bit sleepy at the moment but you never can tell. The tests shouldn't take long.' she gazed down at the dopey kid, smitten. 'It could be anything, so let's just hold fire until we know more – it's impossible to be certain at this stage. Keep him awake. Come on, Billy, shall I show you some pictures? Maybe you'd like to do some colouring?'

About fifteen minutes passed with Billy sleepy but kept awake by the excitement of the new environment and buzz of people. The doctor entered what Mick thought was the family room.

'Mr McCann, we've had some results back from the juice and the chocolate.'

Billy chipped in. 'Hi, have you seen this car? Look, I've put a booster on it and a biiiiiiiig spoiler.'

'Wow that's a cool car, Billy. How are you feeling?'

'OK.' Billy killed the conversation and returned to his picture.

'Yes, it's good news. We've found trace, off-the-shelf, sleeping tablets in both items but at a fairly low concentration. Looks like whoever put it together was extremely cautious – which is good. Now these drugs aren't meant for children, but at this dosage there's no danger there. We do have some more results to come in but, all being well, we should be able to get Billy settled in the children's ward within an hour or so.'

'Can't we just take him home?'

'Well, yes, of course you can, and it's completely understandable that you'd want to, but I'd err on the side of caution. We'd like to monitor him – we're only thinking of an overnight stay. But if there's something that we haven't spotted we'd like him here so that we can respond to it immediately. Honestly, there are so many things that we could have missed, I strongly advice that he stays in overnight. You can stay as well, obviously.'

'Yeh, I'm sure you're right. Could you stay with him in here for a few minutes while I go and phone my wife and get a sneaky fag?'

'I'll send someone in.'

'Thanks.'

Within minutes, a nurse entered the room and started talking to Billy. Mick thanked him and left the room. Heading for the entrance, coming through to Accident and Emergency, he was greeted by a cluster of police officers. Strangelove stepped forward.

'Michael, could we have a little word with you?'

'Oh, fuck off. Listen, we've got all the time in the world now – there really isn't a rush. I'll talk to you later. I'm off outside to phone Lesley and have a fag, and don't try to fucking stop me.'

Dragging nicotine deep into his chest and fumbling for his phone, Mick laughed as he saw Lesley abandon her car in an ambulance bay. He was completely disinterested in the bright and flashing lights, the reporters right in his face, shouting questions as he simply meditated on the loud chant of: 'FUCK OFF, FUCK OFF, FUCK OFF, FUCK OFF, FUCK OFF.